A Brush with Murder

A Brush with Murder

The Shepherd Sisters Mysteries

Tracy Gardner

TULE
PUBLISHING

Dedication

For Joe

Believe me, my young friend, there is nothing—
absolutely nothing—
half so much worth doing as simply messing about in boats.
—Kenneth Grahame, The Wind in the Willows

Carson, Michigan

Chapter One

LAKE MICHIGAN STRETCHED west along the horizon as far as Savanna Shepherd's eye could see. She tipped her face toward the sun dropping low in the pink sky. Red telltale ribbons near the top of the mainsail were drawn straight back, a reflection of their northwest course up Michigan's coast. The gentle rolling waves beneath the bow of the luxurious sailboat lulled her almost to sleep. The fifty-five-foot X-Yacht belonged to her father's friend Sebastian Alexander, a reclusive, once-famous local artist. The summer had flown by—the last two years had flown by. Her former life in Chicago on the other side of this vast lake was now a distant memory—a decade away from her family, honing her art authenticator's skill with sixty-hour workweeks and spending very little time actually living. Two years ago, she was sure she'd lost everything when her engagement and career ended at once, as she'd worked at the renowned Kenilworth Museum, owned by her fiancé's family. But sometimes a worst-case scenario turned out to be exactly what was needed. She'd landed back home in Carson, embraced by her family, just in time to snag the elementary art teacher job—a path she'd never meant to take but loved instantly.

Since then, her older sister had made their parents grandparents a second time, her free-spirited younger sister was engaged and so was Savanna, and she'd learned she'd never really been in love before she met Aidan Gallager.

"You awake up there, Savanna?" Harlan Shepherd called.

"Just barely." She yawned and stretched, getting to her feet to make her way along the side deck toward her father and the rest of the group in the cockpit. "The sunset and waves nearly knocked me out."

"Dangerous to fall asleep on the bow; you'll slide right off into the water," Sebastian said from the mahogany helm at the back of the cockpit.

Remnants of pale greens and grays clung to a few fingers and the side of one hand as he gripped the large chrome wheel, a giveaway of his work in oil paints. In their town, the man was an eccentric, independently wealthy sailor with hermit tendencies. But to the world, Sebastian Alexander was a brilliant postimpressionist artist who'd launched a stunning collection of work in Paris twenty years ago, garnering instant fame as his paintings sold for seven figures, and then disappeared as quickly as he'd arrived. No one knew what prompted his retreat into anonymity—not even Harlan. Savanna had asked and gotten nowhere.

"Then we'll have to turn around and fish you out of the lake. Unless you think you can swim to shore from here," her dad joked.

She laughed. "Just leave me to float. It's such a beautiful evening."

Sebastian's wife, Winnie, spoke. "It's supposed to be gorgeous sailing weather tomorrow morning too."

"As long as that storm system holds off. Radar has it hitting late afternoon tomorrow; it'd be nice if missed us completely," Sebastian replied.

"I saw that too," Savanna said. "Aidan's new partner is covering the practice tomorrow, so we're planning a sail after the regatta boats leave. We'll tail the procession for a bit. Mollie's excited."

"You and Aidan have turned that girl into a tiny sailor," her dad, Harlan, said.

"We all love it." Savanna's cardiologist fiancé had stunned her by buying a gorgeous Catalina sailboat this past spring despite his own phobia of water. He got around her protests over the extravagant gift by putting both their names on the title. *I didn't buy you a boat*, he'd said. *I bought it for us.*

"Have you thought about entering next year's regatta?" Sebastian asked her.

She stared at her dad's longtime friend, at fifty-nine, a year older than Harlan and starkly opposite in appearance. Where her father was deeply tanned and broad shouldered, long legs stretched across the cockpit, Sebastian was pink skinned and compact, his frame mostly covered with lightweight sun-protective clothing, captain's hat and bushy red beard obscuring half his face.

"I'd be out of my league," she said.

"You've been on sailboats your whole life," Harlan said. "The Catalina more than meets the requirements. Why don't you give us some competition next year?"

"No competition. This is my last race," Sebastian said.

"What? Why?" Savanna asked, noting her dad shaking his head. "You've been doing it forever. Ever since I can remember. This must be your fifteenth or sixteenth year, isn't it?"

"Thirteenth."

"Won't you miss it? Just seeing the video is thrilling, sailing along with hundreds of other boats all the way up the coast to the top of the mitten. I'd think it'd be tough to retire from."

"It's time I hang up my captain's hat. I'll lend you my first mate, if you'd like. He's decent help as long as there's plenty of food on board." Sebastian's eyes crinkled at the corners with a smile she couldn't see. He set the wheel lock and stepped out onto the side deck. "We need to check out why that keeps happening—the jib sheet is caught on something."

The sailor's dog woke from his slumber the moment Sebastian left the cockpit. The dog bounded easily after him toward the bow, wavy black curls poking out around the bright yellow life vest. Ringo, a Bouvier des Flandres, was a gentle giant Sebastian had adopted earlier this year from a rescue shelter after his owner had passed away.

"He's really quitting?" Savanna asked her dad and Winnie.

Today's sail was a short outing, a final test run before tomorrow's regatta. They were five in the spacious cockpit not counting Ringo. Harlan and Sebastian had been friends forever. Winnie and Charlotte had spotted Savanna at the marina this afternoon and waved her over, inviting her out for a quick sail.

Harlan sighed, moving to the wheel. "He's always been superstitious. He thought about skipping this year altogether. His thirteenth Lake Michigan regatta with his thirteenth boat falling on September 13 is throwing him for a loop."

"He's ridiculous," Winnie said. "He poo-poos anything I mention about Mars being in retrograde causing energy shifts or the spats he and Griffin have being because they're both fire signs, but he's spooked by the number thirteen. I'm sure he'll be in years of sailing regattas after this." She glanced up at her husband as he returned.

"If you say so." He took a seat beside his wife, leaving Harlan at the wheel.

"We see Griffin in town from time to time; he's always so sweet. He looks so much like you, Sebastian," Charlotte said. She looked from Winnie to Savanna. "Weren't you and he in school together, honey?"

"I graduated a year after he did. He's an artist, too, isn't he? I saw something on social media about his art show coming up." She knew the little gallery in neighboring Grand Pier; maybe she'd go check out Griffin's exhibit. Sebastian's son was a barista at Carson's only coffee shop, but from his socials it was clear art was his passion.

The cloud that crossed her father's friend's features told her the topic was a sore one. A quick look at her mom did nothing to enlighten her—Charlotte shrugged, eyebrows raised.

"He considers himself an artist," Sebastian said, his tone

nonplussed.

"He's still figuring things out—" Winnie began but Sebastian cut her off.

"Let's not spoil the sail. I've dealt with that kid enough for one day."

Savanna changed the subject. "I am so excited to get into your collection, Sebastian. You've no idea how well received this exhibit will be. Lansing's liaison, Britt, is helping coordinate marketing, and they've gained a lot of early interest from potential sponsors. How many new paintings do you expect to add?"

"There are nine completed new pieces, you'll find them near the south wall of my studio, separate from the handful of older pieces I couldn't bring myself to part with. Sentimentality," he said. "I was too attached to my own ego back then."

"It's nice you held on to a few. There's nothing wrong with that."

"Well, they'll make a nice addition to the exhibit, and no hoops to jump through trying to get them for the museum on loan from elsewhere. That's a plus. My valet, Mr. Bishop, will send you the lock code so you may come and go at your convenience."

"He did. Thank you. I should have most of your certificates ready by the time you get home from the regatta." She'd received a detailed text message this morning from Kyle Bishop. She had her work cut out for her. Sebastian had hired her to catalogue his collection, which meant she'd create provenances—certificates of a piece's authenticity and history—for his new work and verify the legitimacy of the existing provenances for his older work that would be included in the exhibit. Her longtime colleague and friend Britt had been instrumental in coordinating three additional pieces of Sebastian's to arrive in Lansing soon, loaned from private collectors. The exhibit would go live a little over two weeks from now, a tight but totally doable deadline.

"I've been telling him for years to do this," Winnie said. "The art world misses his talent. Now is the right time. You feel that too, Bas, or you wouldn't have picked up your paintbrush again last year. Wait'll you see his new canvases, Savanna. They're breathtaking."

Sebastian raised an eyebrow at his wife, not cracking a smile. "We'll see. The art world may decide I'm no longer relevant."

"That's impossible," Savanna said. How surprising that someone of Sebastian's caliber possessed an ounce of self-doubt. "Britt's fielding insane offers. The first three days are already sold out. Dealers and private collectors are paying close attention, waiting for you to decide the outcome of each piece. You'll be able to name your price, if you choose to. Your namesake gallery in Paris has already reached out."

"That's not going to happen," Sebastian said. There was a hard edge to his tone that Savanna hadn't heard before. She didn't push.

"We don't have to decide anything now," Winnie said, giving her husband's knee a squeeze.

"Sun'll be setting soon. We've got an early start tomorrow; let's head back. I'll take the wheel," Sebastian said, trading spots with Harlan.

Her dad crossed the cockpit to one of the two jib winches, a large metal handle and spool assembly around which the jib sheet—rope—was wrapped. The winches controlled the ropes attached to the jib sail, the forwardmost sail at the tip of the bow. With the big yacht set to change direction, Harlan would wait until Sebastian turned slightly off course, taking some of the wind out of the large mainsail overhead. That was his cue to release the winch to unspool the lines on the right or starboard side, while quickly pulling in the attached rope from the opposite—port—side to rein in the jib and capture the wind.

"Char, Savanna," Harlan directed, "move over to starboard side here with Winnie. Prepare to come about!"

Sebastian turned the wheel incrementally. The big ship began to turn, sails suddenly rustling with slack as their direction and wind changed. Overhead, the boom—the horizontal arm attached to the tall mast holding the mainsail—faltered, the ropes attached to it no longer taut.

"Coming about. Lee ho!" Sebastian called, loud and clear, and the boom swung with all the force of the wind now trapped in the mainsail, arcing widely above their heads and snapping to a halt on the opposite side of the yacht. The mainsail expanded and went taut with air just as the jib sail did, her father quickly tightening and securing the lines, propelling them forward the way they'd come and bringing the hull of the sailboat into a tipping keel, the four of them perched on the high starboard side. The bench seat where she'd been a minute ago was now inches from the choppy waves crashing against the side, water splashing onto the side rigging and seat. Even after all her hours aboard boats, Savanna's heartbeat thrilled rapidly through the momentary rush of a good tack—changing direction into the wind without losing a bit of momentum.

"Nice work." Sebastian nodded to Harlan.

Her dad grinned. "It's what we do."

"Smooth," Savanna said. When she was a kid, she'd been sure the boat would tip over when the hull was angled at ten or fifteen degrees like this. Now she understood that heeling was just part of sailing and not typically dangerous. "It's definitely an art. You two make a good pair."

"I see another first-place trophy in your future," Winnie added.

Charlotte laughed. "I have a feeling they'd be out here just as often even without a trophy on the line."

"Griffin missed a good sail," Sebastian said.

The group in the cockpit fell silent. If Griffin was supposed to come tonight but hadn't, was he also dropping out of the regatta? A 198-nautical-mile race to Mackinac City at the top of the state shaped like a mitten, the complete round trip typically lasting from Saturday morning through Monday night, the voyage could be exhausting with only two people aboard. Her dad and Sebastian had done it before, but they typically had either Griffin or another willing deckhand along to help.

She stopped her mother in the marina parking lot once they were back on land. "What's going on with Sebastian's son? Was he set to go tomorrow—is he still going?"

"I'm not sure," Charlotte replied, frowning. She tucked a smooth strand of chestnut-brown, shoulder-length hair behind one ear, leaving her hand at her collarbone. She pursed her lips, quiet for a beat, relaying her concern without saying a word. "Winnie says Griffin and Sebastian haven't been seeing eye to eye lately. She seems to be a sort of buffer, but with him being her stepson, she tries not to overstep, you know?"

"I thought they all got along. I just ran into Winnie helping out at Chelsea's shop the other day; they seem really friendly."

"Oh, I think the family is pretty close in general," Charlotte said. "It'll all get ironed out. I'm sure your father would've mentioned it to me if Griffin had dropped out of the regatta."

Chapter Two

SATURDAY MORNING, SAVANNA rushed from her kitchen to the big picture window to make sure Aidan and Mollie hadn't arrived yet. She was in the clear. She finished packing up the two dozen mini sandwiches she'd made for her dad, Sebastian, and Griffin, fitting the container into a cooler bag on top of another that held fresh grapes and sliced watermelon.

Her little Boston terrier reminded her he was at her feet, waiting patiently, with a whine and a paw on her bare leg. She'd dressed for the regatta today in white shorts and a nautical blue and white top, complementing the last of her summer tan. She'd tied her long brown wavy hair into a high ponytail; it was warm out already, with an unseasonable ninety-degree heat wave predicted to start today, Michigan's final warm-weather hurrah before autumn set in. Her dog whined again but kept his paws on the floor.

"Here you go, Fonzie. Your mandatory dog tax payment. Sit." She held out half a slice of turkey, and he delicately took it from her fingertips. "Ready?"

She was clipping on his leash when a knock at the door prompted a burst of whines and wiggles from the little dog. Savanna opened the door for Mollie, Aidan coming up the steps behind her. His eight-year-old daughter dropped immediately to her knees, giggling and hugging the dog as his compact black and white frame nearly vibrated with excitement. "Fonzie gets to come too?"

"Sure! Fonzie loves seeing all the boats."

Mollie stood and stuck a hand into the pocket of her sundress. "We made this for you, Miss Savanna." She handed her a blue and white braided bracelet with a painted sailboat charm on it. "See? Just like mine."

"And mine." Aidan spoke from her doorway.

His normally deep blue eyes were a shade lighter today, picking up the color of his short-sleeved blue henley, the thin fabric stretched across his firm chest. He took the bracelet from her fingertips and tied it around her wrist. She studied the matching bracelet on his wrist, her cheeks flushed at his closeness.

When he'd finished, he slid one hand up her bare arm and pulled her into a brief embrace. "I missed you," he murmured before he kissed her.

"I *knew* there was gonna be kissing!" Mollie clutched at her throat and stuck her tongue out, making a face at Fonzie. "Ew!"

Savanna laughed, trying to regain her composure despite Aidan's kiss turning her legs into spaghetti noodles. She took a deep breath, focusing on the faint few freckles on Aidan's cheeks beneath black lashes, the curve of his smile, that unruly black colic at his left temple, silky under her fingertips as she brushed it back reflexively before realizing she'd done so.

She met his gaze. "You just saw me yesterday."

"And?"

They'd been dating—off and on due to work and parenting obstacles—for nearly two years. She still had no control over her response to him after nearly two years. All the butterflies he stirred up in her chest might eventually settle down, but for now, she basked in the feeling. "I missed you too," she admitted. "Thank you for the bracelet; I love it. I really love it," she said, turning her attention to Mollie.

"I painted the boat myself," the girl said.

"You did a lovely job. Very artistic," she said, turning the bracelet on her wrist and examining it. "The kissing part is over for the moment. Are we ready? We have a whole bunch of loud cheerleading to do. We'd better get going."

When Aidan and Mollie had proposed together to her on their new Catalina, Savanna had immediately said yes. In retelling the story to her sisters the next day, it struck her even more what a precious gift this was—finding Aidan plus gaining as a daughter the sweetest little girl she'd ever met. Today's sailboat bracelet was a generous extension of an insider love language between Mollie and her father. Aidan had shared with Savanna that after they'd lost Mollie's mother four years ago to cancer, Mollie had begun choosing and then eventually creating matching little accessories each morning for her and dad to wear, a way to keep her father close. Savanna felt her heart swell, knowing Mollie was now including her in that custom.

Their little trio made their way through crowds of cheering family and friends along the Carson Marina boardwalk, half the town, loads of visitors, and nearly two hundred sailboats in various stages of prepping and heading toward the starting area on the still-blue lake. Sweetwater Boats had really pulled out all the stops for the event. The rental and catchall shop that served Carson Marina had added a large tent in the adjacent parking lot, complete with a shaved ice station, hot dog stand, and a few vendors offering services boaters were sure to need—sail repair, mechanical help, and the like.

As they passed by Sweetwater Boats, the gruff but kind old sailor Gus, who ran the place, raised a hand in greeting. Augustus Connelly looked every bit of his seventy-five years, with freckled leathery skin and deep crow's feet around pale blue eyes and sun-bleached eyebrows. She'd known him since she'd started coming to Carson Marina with her dad as a kid at least twenty years ago.

"Hey there, Gus." She waved back.

"Safe sailing to ya," he called.

She was about to say she wasn't in the regatta today, but his attention was already occupied. A customer in wire-rimmed glasses and baseball cap at the checkout glanced over his shoulder at her, as if to see what was distracting the proprietor. He shoved some papers across the counter and tapped them, his body language impatient and irritated to match his tone. She couldn't hear the exchange, but she felt bad for Gus.

"He must really love this job to put up with people like that," Aidan murmured beside her.

"For real," she agreed. She'd be sure to pass on Gus's

wishes to her dad and Sebastian.

Huge fluffy white clouds dotted the sky. Sebastian's yacht was still in the slip, the two men making adjustments to the rigging. On the boat slip's dock, Charlotte and Winnie were chatting with another woman who looked vaguely familiar, and at the end of the dock on a phone call, Savanna recognized Sebastian's daughter, Chelsea, from Main Street Sweets, the chocolate-themed bakery down the street from Sydney's dog salon.

Uncle Max and Uncle Freddie were in the viewing area and gestured wildly for Savanna to join them. She waved back, motioning she'd be right there. Her uncles had moved to Carson last year to be closer to their daughter, who was now a sophomore at the university. They'd snagged a great spot in the bleachers; viewers would be able to see the boats for at least the first mile or two of the race. Savanna left Aidan and Mollie at the bleachers with her uncles and wove her way to the yacht.

She handed the package of food over to Harlan. "Just some extra provisions in case you get hungry—and to keep you both hydrated," she said.

Harlan grinned. "These'll be gone before the starting shot."

"Wait! Hold on, don't leave yet," Sydney Shepherd called, rushing toward them in a rustle of multicolored sheer caftan over bright pink tank and torn jean shorts. She nimbly climbed aboard, stepping easily over the deck railing. She fastened a small gold-toned horseshoe to the metal stern pulpit supporting the wheel where Sebastian stood, the horseshoe's open area facing upward like a U. "There; for luck. Love you, Daddy." She hugged him and then Sebastian. "You guys be careful, and make sure to hydrate like Savvy said!"

Savanna held out a hand, helping her younger sister back onto the dock. "That was sweet."

"Mom said Sebastian is nervous, which isn't like him. Maybe that thing will help. A client gave it to me for the shop, but I think it fits better here. Ugh, it's so hot already." She swept her long red locks back, impatiently wrangling them out of her face and up into a wildly unruly top knot.

"Skylar's going to miss them leaving," Savanna worried. "Is she still coming?"

At thirty-two, middle sister Savanna was two years older than Sydney, and two years younger than the eldest, Skylar. Syd's gourmet dog salon was kitty-corner across Main Street from Skylar's law office, which typically meant her sisters kept tabs on each other without even meaning to.

"We were supposed to come together. But when I texted her, she just said she's tied up and to give Dad her love."

Charlotte turned, inviting her two daughters into the little circle on the dock. "Maeve, these are my daughters Savanna and Sydney. Girls, meet Maeve Davis, a friend of Sebastian's."

Savanna held out a hand, stunned. Now she knew where she'd recognized her from. Maeve Davis was only the most prolific, gifted, boundary-pushing, mixed-media artist of their time. Her style was timeless. She wore black jeans and a black-and-white-striped boat neck top that slid slightly off one toned shoulder, shiny silver hair falling just to her chin. She'd graced the cover of *Art Aesthetic* magazine last year for their trendsetter series. At sixty, Davis had been an art world icon for over half her life and was known for her contemporary pieces created as honest, compelling commentary on the state of the world as she saw it.

"An art authenticator in Chicago at the Kenilworth Museum," Charlotte was saying. "She's keeping her skills sharp helping out Sebastian, but now she's the art teacher at the elementary school. And Sydney owns Fancy Tails & Treats, a gourmet treat and grooming salon for nearly every four-legged creature in Carson."

"I was just there! I stopped in for some biscuits for Ringo. He devoured them—they were little cookies decorated like hamburgers. Your shop is darling, Sydney," Maeve said.

"Those are Ringo's favorite; Willow must've helped you. She somehow keeps track of every dog's favorites. It's nice to meet you. Savvy, stop staring." Sydney pinched Savanna's arm.

Why were baby sisters the best at embarrassing their siblings? "I wasn't—I'm sorry, I didn't mean to stare. Ms. Davis, I love your work. I did my BFA program senior project on your *21st Century Woman* exhibit. You've changed the creative landscape for women in art with your controversial pieces. I'm honored to meet you."

The artist tipped her head, bringing one shoulder up in half a shrug. "Thank you, but don't be. I'm just here to wish these sailors fair winds and following seas, the same as you. Sebastian told me you'll be validating his work for his

Lansing show. I may have a little work for you in the future too, if you've the time."

"Absolutely," Savanna said. There were some job offers you just accepted immediately, no questions asked.

At the end of the dock, Chelsea's voice rose above their conversation, aggravation oozing from her tone. "No. *You* need to talk to him. Grow the hell up, Grif. Leave me out of it." She jabbed a finger at the phone screen then drew her arm back as if to hurl the thing into the blue water. "Ugh!" She shoved it into her purse instead and spun, joining their little group gathered by the yacht.

"Oh no," Winnie said. She shook her head, staring at her stepdaughter. "Tell me that's not what it sounded like."

"He's not coming. He knows they need a third, but he's being a baby. How are they supposed to find a replacement deckhand twenty minutes before the starting gun?"

Sebastian spoke from behind them on the boat. "We're good, no worries. I could've predicted last night that Griffin would drop out. It's not a tragedy."

"It's a fifty-four-hour round trip, and that's if all goes according to plan and you don't stop to sleep," Charlotte said. "It doesn't sound safe."

Harlan had finished with the halyard he was working on and came to stand with Sebastian. "We've done it before. It'll be fine."

"Years ago! No offense," Winnie said, "but you aren't as young these days, Bas. It may be too much. Besides...you weren't keen on going anyway, what with the thirteens. Maybe they really are bad omens." Winnie's eyes were big and filled with concern.

Her words seemed to have an activating effect on her husband. "That's a bunch of bull pucky. I don't care about the thirteens. It was just pre-sail jitters. We're going. We'll trade off sleep. It's fine," Sebastian echoed Harlan.

Harlan said something under his breath to Sebastian and then climbed out onto the dock. He drew Charlotte a little away from the group, a light hand on her elbow. "I don't want you to worry. We'll be perfectly safe."

Savanna exchanged glances with Sydney; neither spoke, both wanting to eavesdrop.

Their mother looked up at him, brow furrowed. "Do you really think so? I can make a call and try to push my next consult out a few days; if I can't, Savanna might be able to come, she'd probably be more help than I would."

"No. You've been preparing for Monday's consult for weeks, and the girls have lives and jobs too," he said. "Nobody is missing work to be our deckhand."

"Harlen. I won't ask you to withdraw from the race, but think about it for a moment, honey, please. You have two grandbabies, all three of your girls back home, your brilliant wife who's sort of attached to you being around..." She didn't smile; she was focused on her appeal to her husband. "A sailboat race isn't worth risking everything for."

Harlan slid one large hand over his wife's cheek and loosely cupped the back of her neck, not breaking eye contact. "This isn't that. I'm just going for a sail with a friend. If we get tired, we'll sleep, I promise. No risk. But I'll call it off if you want me to, Char, no complaints. Up to you, my love."

Charlotte was quiet, unmoving. Finally, she placed a hand wide open on his chest and crumpled his shirt into her fist. "Go. Be safe." She stood on tiptoe to kiss him. Whatever their dad whispered into their mother's ear before they separated was lost to Savanna and Sydney, meant only for her.

When he stopped for a quick hug from his daughters, he left them each with a promise he'd return, disguised as mundane little nothings.

"I'll see you at dinner Friday," he said to Sydney, "after Finn, Aidan, and I finish our tuxedo fitting appointment.

"Don't forget to pick out your tile sample," he told Savanna. "I'll be over to lay the flooring this weekend. That bare plywood is a hazard, be careful," he added, stepping back onto the *Serendipity* with Sebastian.

Chapter Three

F ROM THE CARSON Marina stands, the cheers began with the shot from the starting gun and didn't die down until the last sailboat left line of sight going around the curve of the Lake Michigan coast, halfway between Carson and Grand Pier. The boats shrank into tiny white triangles on the blue water, sunlight reflecting off sails.

Savanna tried to convince Sydney to come out on the Catalina with them, but Syd had a wedding cake tasting scheduled with Finn.

"At least we know which florist we'll be using," her sister said, slipping a hand through Uncle Max's elbow. "I'm so glad you're doing the flowers for us."

Max was dressed in linen trousers, a pale yellow button-down, and a navy blue waistcoat with tiny white anchors; Savanna imagined his closet must be filled with vests like these of varying colors and patterns. Max Watson and Charlotte's younger brother, Freddie Quinn, had met overseas in London. They'd eventually married and called Manhattan home until last year, when they'd moved to Carson to be closer to their daughter, Ellie, at a nearby university. Uncle Freddie worked as an architect for a Fortune 500 company, and botanist Uncle Max was now the proud proprietor of In Bloom, the flower shop across the street from Sydney's Fancy Tails & Treats. He'd bought the shop after Sydney's good friend Libby, the former owner, was tragically murdered several months ago. Max had retained Libby's staff and kept most everything the same, except the name.

Uncle Max smiled at Syd. "Wait'll you see your bouquet and the arrangements, love. It's going to be such a beautiful event."

"Our dining room table has disappeared under dozens of trial bouquets," Uncle Freddie added, a hand on Max's shoulder. Freddie's confident demeanor made him impossible not to like. Deeply tanned from his love of golf, with an easy smile and thick, prematurely silver hair, her uncle collected second glances the way some folks collected coins. "He's turning our house into a botanical garden experimenting with different designs."

"Guilty as charged." Max tossed a grin over his shoulder at his husband.

Uncle Freddie leaned down, speaking more quietly. "Do you mind if we make a stop on our way home? I thought we'd keep Charlotte company for a bit. She seems out of sorts, but I'm not sure why."

"She's just worried about Dad—they ended up being a man short for the trip," Savanna said. "They've done it before; I'm sure it'll all go smoothly."

"I'm sure it will," Uncle Freddie said.

"Of course it will," Uncle Max said. "We'll pick up Lady Bella on the way. Bella and Daisy will be a good distraction for your mother."

"Great idea," she said.

Daisy on her own was already a distraction. The golden retriever mixed breed puppy had been a gift from Sydney to their parents at the beginning of the summer. Daisy was an energetic whirlwind their parents had fallen instantly in love with despite protesting they didn't want a dog.

Savanna, Aidan, and Mollie were out on Lake Michigan less than an hour after the race began. In his bright orange life vest, Fonzie's wide-legged stance and rapidly wagging curly Q of a tail had Mollie giggling beside him as they maneuvered out of the channel and followed the regatta's northward course.

"We're catching a lot of wind," Aidan observed after a while.

"Too much, do you think?" Savanna tipped her head, waiting for him to decide. It was his call. After a summer of lessons from her, helping him not only learn to sail but overcome a weighty childhood trauma he and his brother had undergone related to boats, he'd been slowly gaining confidence. She and her sisters had grown up around their father's boats and those of friends. Savanna had her own small craft when she'd lived in Chicago and was a skilled sailor, but Aidan still needed encouragement toward independence. This beautiful Catalina was, after all, their joint venture, not just hers.

The small muscle in his jaw pulsed, his gaze taking in the telltale ribbons, the taut jib sail at the bow, the navigation screen. "We're heeling more than I'd like. Do you mind if we head west? It'll be a calmer sail. Unless you're hoping to catch them?" Aidan glanced to the north, where the last of the sails were still visible in the distance.

She smiled. "Not at all. I think changing tacks is a good call; you're right."

In some ways, he was such a contradiction. Put him in a busy, chaotic ER handling heart attacks and accident victims and he was cool and unfazed but drop him into a sturdy sailboat on a relatively calm lake and it was the only time she'd seen his self-assuredness falter.

"Prepare to come about," Aidan said, using the jargon she'd taught him.

With Mollie and Fonzie now below deck in the cabin, Savanna released the starboard jib line, nodding to Aidan. He changed course, both sails gently filling with wind on the opposite side of the Catalina, slowing the boat and settling the hull more evenly on the water.

She cast a last look north as they turned, scattered points of sails receding in the distance. She closed her eyes for the briefest moment, sending her version of *fair winds and following seas*—a blessing for safe voyage—through the air and sky to her dad and Sebastian on the *Serendipity*. They'd be in Mackinac by tomorrow.

SUNDAY MORNING, SAVANNA tapped her brakes, slowing as her GPS indicated she'd need to turn right soon, though the dense forest of tall pines gave nothing away but layers upon layers of green. The text from Sebastian's personal assistant had included the keyless entry code along with instructions to watch for a sailboat-shaped mailbox as her landmark to turn. Despite her father's longstanding friendship with Sebastian, this was Savanna's first time here.

The artist's home was a well-kept secret around Carson. Nothing she had ever read revealed what prompted Sebastian Alexander's abrupt retreat into anonymity shortly after he stunned the art world with his raw and emotional postimpressionist art debut in Paris. Reports of his whereabouts claimed sightings of the artist now and then, usually in an exotic location, when some collector sold a piece and interest was momentarily piqued again.

A half mile after she'd turned, the gently winding trek through the trees opened on a clearing and the artist's gorgeous home. Beyond it was nothing but blue. Sebastian and Winnie's house sat atop the bluffs at the southern end of the sand dunes overlooking Lake Michigan. She parked in the circle driveway and climbed the wide steps of the stone and cedar lap house to the front door. Ten of her house would fit inside this one. She tipped her head back, taking in the three stories of floor-to-ceiling windows, an elegant chandelier and catwalk high over the foyer visible from where she stood.

She was about to type in the code when movement caught her eye; how awkward if she were to just walk in when someone was home. She rang the bell instead.

A man who looked to be in his early forties wearing a crisp white button-down and black trousers opened the door. "Ms. Shepherd?"

"Yes, hello. Savanna," she offered. "I hope this isn't too early?" Nine a.m. didn't seem early to her and had been fine with Sebastian, but the house was so silent and quiet; maybe she should have waited until later.

"Not at all, come in. I'm Kyle. I'll show you to the studio." He took the heavy black case she carried, lightening her load. She hadn't brought her full set of authenticating tools, but the basics were still bulky, packed into their protective case. "Right this way."

"Thank you." Something about him was so familiar. She covertly studied his profile. They must've crossed paths in town at some point. "Do you have kids?" she blurted.

He tipped his head at her curiously. "No, I don't."

"Sorry. I'm a teacher. I just wondered if I've seen you at school. You look familiar."

He shrugged. "It's a small town. Maybe we've accidentally grocery shopped together."

"That's probably it," she said, smiling. "The Alexanders have the perfect setting. It's so beautiful here."

"It is," he agreed. "Sebastian spent some time among the Carson artists' colony in the 1990s as an unknown. He always planned to return. Mrs. Alexander found the house before we even left Europe."

"You've worked for him since Paris, then?"

"Yes. We worked so well together, it just made sense for me to stay with him for the move back."

"That's some serious dedication," she said. "He's fortunate to have you."

"I'd say we're both fortunate. I have no complaints."

"I've followed his career since I learned about him in my sophomore year of college. His work is just incredible," she said.

Kyle provided a running narration as she followed him across the stone-tiled foyer. He led her up a wide, curving stairway and across the catwalk, drawing her attention to the lighthouse on South Haven point through the second-floor windows, and pointing out a serious-looking library with deep reds and leather seating, a brightly lit parlor done in pastels, a wing that held a few of the large home's bedrooms, ending at a set of imposing double doors.

He pulled a key ring from his pocket, and for the first time she noticed his left hand was injured; a large flesh-colored bandage stretched from his thumb to the back of his hand. He unlocked the doors, throwing them wide open, and handed her a single gold key. "Sebastian asks that you lock his studio upon leaving, even if only to retrieve supplies or get a snack from the kitchen." He deposited her tool case on a long desk against the wall.

She stared at the key, trying to arrange her features into some sort of nonchalant poker face, but knew she'd failed by Kyle's reaction.

He removed his wire-rimmed glasses and cleaned the lenses with a white handkerchief from his pocket, nodding toward the multiple works of art on easels and lining the walls in the vast room. "Sebastian is...exceedingly cautious. It's a proactive measure to protect his work and to avoid any unnecessary...conflict." He met her eyes. "Make sense?"

She nodded quickly. "Yes, absolutely. I understand. I

promise I'll keep it locked." It did make sense. Sebastian was a smart entrepreneur. With a house this size, there was bound to be staff—maintenance workers, housekeepers, landscapers, various people with access to the property. Guarding the assets that had earned him such a grand home in the first place was logical. The cliché of the absent-minded creative, the bohemian soul dealing only in abstracts, was overplayed in pop culture; she'd learned in school that some of the world's greatest artists were also fantastic mathematicians and shrewd businessmen, just as others were probably the reason that cliché existed.

Alone in the studio with artwork she'd only ever seen in textbooks, Savanna set her purse and oversize tote on the desk. Her friend Jack called the tote her brains and he wasn't wrong; the tote was a catchall for everything she might need on any given day, including the laptop and charger she pulled out now. Aidan had bought the laptop for her this summer for her work at the Lansing Museum of Fine Art after watching her deposit three different bags plus a mini portfolio with some sketches on his back seat, file folders spilling out from under one arm. Between her day job, moonlighting painting the massive murals at the Carson Theatre, and her authenticating work with good friend Britt Nash at the museum, she'd begun to get overwhelmed, keeping track of everything. Aidan had presented her with the gorgeous and ridiculously large red leather tote and oversize planner, perfect to corral her stuff—and organize her work. He had a knack for fixing things before anyone even realized they needed fixing. She supposed it was why he was such a good doctor.

She surveyed the impressive space around her. As long as her father and Sebastian had been friends and as starstruck as she felt when crossing paths with the artist in the past two years since being back home, she'd never dissolved into giddy, hero-worshipping, effusive praise. He was brilliant, but he was just a person. He'd retreated into anonymity for a reason. But when Harlan mentioned that the artist was thinking about a comeback, she'd seized the chance to offer her expertise, and it was working out better than she'd dreamed, especially now with Britt at the helm of acquisitions and marketing for the highly anticipated upcoming exhibit. She slowly strolled around the large studio, taking in years of unseen canvases.

One of the most well-known postimpressionists of his time, Sebastian Alexander's paintings were evocative and emotional, often compared to van Gogh's body of work. With a wide-ranging palette, some pieces striking in their rich jewel tones while others were more subtle in soft, muted shades, the canvases were characterized by bold brushstrokes and a focus on eliciting feeling through the use of perceived colors and tricks of light rather than starkly realistic portrayals. Each bore a figure or figures, some so abstract they afforded but a glimpse of the subject, others with concrete and painfully breathtaking details. A few landscapes were in the mix, though they were in the minority. She was taken by the differences in mood between paintings. When she was in her third year of the fine arts program in Chicago, a favorite professor had referenced Sebastian's work to illustrate a hallmark of Postimpressionism—the ways in which artists' moods seemed to influence the end result. She drew in a hitching, stunned breath; how lucky was she to be in this room?

She crossed to the window, trying to shake off the sense of the surreal. At this early hour, there wasn't a single boat out yet on the blue water. A flashy candy-apple-red power boat waited on one side of the dock, two jet ski watercrafts on the other. Once she'd opened her laptop and removed her handheld Firefly microscope from its case, she was finally able to get her mind into work mode. She'd begin at the beginning, with the artist's earliest works here in this room. Once she'd examined each of those and created provenances—certificates of authenticity and ownership including the origin and locations where the works were kept—she'd move forward toward the more recent pieces.

The wireless Firefly, a powerful high magnification video camera with bright LEDs, was her most portable tool. It was used by authenticators and appraisers to validate art and valuables. This one was an upgrade from the one she'd started out using in her career at Kenilworth. Having transitioned from authenticating art to teaching it, she'd missed using her finely honed skills. But since Britt had tapped her this summer to consult at the Lansing Museum of Fine Art, she now enjoyed the best of both worlds—sharing her love and knowledge of art with the young minds at Carson Elementary while keeping her keen authenticator's eye sharp at the museum a few times a month.

Savanna was halfway through completing the provenance

for the third piece, a large canvas with bold, disjointed images of a couple done in rich rose and deep brown shades, when she was startled from her focus by a loud shout. Halted with Firefly in midair, she listened intently. Silence. She hadn't imagined it. She moved to peer out the window. At first, she saw only the dunes and blue water and sky. But then a figure came into view, emerging from the covered deck, head bent over the phone in her hand. The woman turned, and Savanna was surprised to recognize Maeve Davis. She barely had time to wonder what was going on when another bellow pierced the still studio from the main floor below.

She left her work and went through the double doors of the studio, remembering to lock up even though she was coming right back; she had no intention of breaking Sebastian's rule. She followed the hallways toward the front entrance, stopping on the catwalk over the foyer. Below, Sebastian's family was gathered in a chaotic mess of sobbing and angry yelling.

A disheveled Chelsea cried into Winnie's pink-silk-clad shoulder, long blond strands of hair sticking to her wet cheeks. Griffin, fists balled at his sides and red-faced above his beige Holy Grounds Coffee logo T-shirt, was inches away from Kyle Bishop, so close their noses nearly touched.

"And what? You just dropped the ball? I'll never know why he trusts you," Griffin shouted.

Sebastian's assistant was pale, eyes wide. He put a hand up between himself and Sebastian's son, appeasing. "I'm sorry. I didn't realize—I assumed he'd spoken with Mrs.

Alexander," Kyle said, speaking calmly, slowly, but unable to keep the quaver from his voice.

"You assumed," Griffin said, his tone dripping disdain. "Isn't it your actual job to know what's going on with him? You never thought to check in with him last night?"

"I—I'm his—I didn't think—" Kyle stammered, gaze moving to Winnie.

"It's not his fault, Griffin," Winnie said, her voice barely audible. She sniffled and swiped at her cheeks. "Your father is always so self-sufficient. I didn't give it a second thought last night when he hadn't checked in."

"She's right. Leave him alone, Grif," Chelsea said, her volume rising. "If you'd been with him, none of this would be happening!"

"Like I could have gone," Griffin spat the words. "You think he'd have actually let me on the boat? He hated me. This is his own fault."

The whooshing in Savanna's ears that had begun upon seeing Chelsea crying faded. A gripping wave of dread washed over her as the scene began to make sense. Her mother. She had to call her mom. She patted her pockets for her phone, her mind's eye seeing it zipped into her purse on the desk in Sebastian's studio. She'd set it to vibrate to avoid distractions. As she turned to race back and fetch it, Maeve Davis appeared in the doorway from the deck, phone still in hand.

"Hey." One word drew every eye to her, the foyer suddenly quiet.

Savanna stopped, heart in her throat.

"Race authorities confirm the *Serendipity* never made it to Mackinaw," Maeve said. "The last boat checked in hours ago. They've dispatched the coast guard."

Chapter Four

S AVANNA'S PHONE SCREEN flashed seventeen missed calls and countless text messages. In a panic, she frantically called her mother. Her dad had to be okay. He was fine. There was no other option.

"Savanna? For God's sake, where the hell are you?" Skylar's voice on her mother's phone startled her.

"I'm working—I was working. I'm at the Alexanders' house. I—What's going on? Have you talked to Dad?" It was just a miscommunication—Harlan must have been in touch, and both men were fine and had maybe had some type of technical issue with the boat. She clung to this hope even as her older sister huffed out an impatient breath.

"No. Dad's missing. There's been no word since last night."

A stab of pain jolted her—she hadn't realized she was biting her lip until she tasted blood. "He never called this morning? He always calls, morning and night and at every port, every trip. But maybe it's still too early—"

"It's almost three, Savvy," Skylar said, her tone softening. "He and Sebastian should've checked in hours ago. What does Winnie know? Have they given her any updates? They won't tell us anything."

Savanna drifted in a daze out of the studio, phone to her ear. Skylar was still talking but none of the words made sense. She descended the curving staircase to the foyer.

"Savanna, are you all right, hon? Who's that on the phone?" Winnie asked.

"Is it your dad?" Chelsea asked, rushing to her side.

She stared wide-eyed at the woman who sold her chocolate donuts every Friday. "No." This had to be some kind of mistake. She'd just hugged her dad goodbye yesterday. He'd smelled of aftershave and those tiny cigars he smoked but tried to keep secret from their mother. "It's Skylar." She tapped her phone screen. "I'm with Sebastian's family. You're on speaker."

"Has your dad called at all since they left yesterday morning?" Chelsea asked.

Kyle joined the little circle gathered now around Savanna. "What have they told you? Do they know where the boat was last seen?"

"There'd be no way to know that," Griffin chimed in. "Not if they went off course after dark."

His words startled Savanna—the yacht veering off in the wrong direction would be manageable, her dad and Sebastian should be easy to find. It seemed like a much better possibility than them being in the water or hurt, the first things that had popped into her mind.

"How do you know they went off course? Or when?" Skylar's tone was sharp, clipped, through the phone. "Did the race authorities tell you that?"

"No, but then where are they?"

Charlotte's voice came through the phone. "I talked with Harlan last night around seven. They were doing fine and planning on sailing through. That was the last time I've been able to reach him."

"What about the tracking system? Race authorities would have access to the *Serendipity*'s GPS tracker, right?" Savanna asked.

"They didn't share any of that with me," Maeve spoke up. "I asked. But it may just be because I'm not next of kin."

The foyer was abruptly silent with her words—next of kin. In Savanna's field of vision, the light grew dim, haziness creeping in around the edges, a sensation she'd only felt once before—after discovering the dead body of her friend John last year. She was about to faint. An abrupt wave of nausea hit her. She stumbled through the open front door and threw up on the bushes beside the wide porch steps. "I'll be right there," she said into her phone. "Mom, I'm leaving now. I'll be there soon. I have to go," she said, straightening up and facing Winnie in the doorway. Her head felt clearer.

Sebastian's wife looked pained, her eyes red and puffy. "Of course. Should someone drive you?"

She shook her head quickly. "No. I'm okay." She glanced down and noticed she had none of her things. "My keys—"

"I'll get your purse," Kyle said from behind Winnie. He disappeared up the stairway.

"I'm so sorry about that," she told Winnie, glancing at the bushes, her cheeks burning now. Tears spilled over without warning.

"Don't be, it's okay. It'll wash off, no worries."

Her words echoed in Savanna's ears. "No worries" was the most ridiculous thing anyone could say right now. She had so many worries. Winnie looked as shell-shocked as Savanna felt. They all did.

SAVANNA DIDN'T REMEMBER the drive to her parents' house, but she felt every single step toward the side door as if there were hundred-pound weights on each foot. She wasn't sure she wanted to go inside, to know whatever the rest of her family might now know.

In the bright kitchen, bathed in afternoon sunshine, Charlotte pulled Savanna into a tight hug without a word. Her mother felt smaller, slighter than Savanna had ever noticed before.

Gathered around the kitchen island were her sisters, uncles Max and Freddie, and Finn. Skylar's husband, Travis, must be with the kids; her older sister was smart not to allow five-year-old Nolan or baby Hannah to be here for this.

A knock at the front door made Savanna jump and hurry to open it—it must be Aidan. Finn must have told him. She hated knowing her family had probably been assembled here for a while before they could reach her.

Detective Nick Jordan greeted her instead. She was relieved he was here; he was great at his job, and he'd become a good friend. Jordan always played things close to the chest, maintaining an impenetrable poker face. So, the sympathy in his tone and expression now, meant to be comforting, just made this feel even scarier. "Savanna. Can I come in?"

"He's fine," she told him, her volume louder than she'd meant, full of bravado she did not feel. "I know he's okay. My dad is the strongest person I know. We have to find him."

"We will."

Finn stopped her on her way back to the kitchen. "Hey," he spoke in hushed tones, "I just wanted to let you know I called my brother. He's tied up in surgery."

Her eyes welled up, whether because Aidan couldn't be here or because she was grateful for Finn looking out for her, she wasn't sure. "Thank you."

Aidan Gallager's younger brother, Finn, had arrived in town a little over a year ago via the helicopter he piloted as a dual-licensed medevac paramedic, complete with aviators, swagger, and a swoon-inducing grin. Her sister Sydney hadn't stood a chance. He was exactly her type, except for the fact that he was temporary—Finn never stayed in one place long, taking short-term travel assignments all over the country. So, when he'd come up with a creative way to stay in town permanently while still exercising his Air Med flight muscles and then proposed after just a handful of dates, he'd stunned them all.

"The circulating nurse said to let you know he plans to come straight here the moment he's finished. I'm sure it'll be soon."

She nodded. "I really appreciate that, Finn. It's okay."

The presence of Detective Jordan in her parents' kitchen was oddly soothing while also making the situation suddenly very real. "Let's all sit." He gestured to the dining room table.

He must have sensed that none of the Shepherd family was thinking clearly enough to know what was next or what to do.

Uncle Max offered to make coffee and Jordan nodded. With everyone else now seated, he focused on Charlotte. "I understand this is hard. I want you to know the coast guard is out looking at the last tracked coordinates, and we've got state police on alert for anyone matching the description of Harlan or the yacht's captain."

"Last tracked coordinates? They have their cell phones. Can't you see their location that way?" Savanna asked.

"They'd have lost cell service well before the yacht's nav system GPS failed. We aren't sure their phones are functional at this point. Can you tell me again exactly what time you last spoke with your husband?"

"He called around seven p.m. last night," Charlotte said. "They'd made it halfway up the coast by then and planned to sail through the night, as most of the boats do."

"Did he call from his cell phone or land? Or using the VHF radio?"

"I only hear from him on his cell when he's in port. He called from the marine radio."

Jordan made a note on his yellow legal pad. "Did you get the impression that all was well? Did anything strike you as off or out of the ordinary?"

"What do you mean?" Skylar interjected.

She sat at the head of the table and was typing notes into

her iPad, a variation on Nick Jordan's old school system. Skylar and Jordan had plenty of amicable experience working in the same courtroom. The eldest Shepherd sister and an excellent attorney, Skylar was making sure to capture everything discussed just as Jordan was.

"Anything different in his tone or what he spoke about."

Charlotte was quiet, considering. "I really don't think so. Nothing seemed off. Harlan sounded a little tired. He said they were about to dive into the cold fried chicken I sent, and then Sebastian was going to take the first shift while he got a couple hours of sleep."

"When they've done this in the past," Sydney added, "they do three-hour blocks, trading off turns manning the yacht or down in the cabin."

Jordan flipped a page in his notebook, consulting something he'd written. "There was supposed to be a third—a deckhand—on the trip, but that fell through, is that right?"

"Griffin," Savanna supplied. "Sebastian's son. He called and told his sister he wasn't coming right before the regatta began."

"Do we know why?"

"No… I don't think so," she said.

"Maybe," Charlotte spoke. "Winnie—Sebastian's wife—told me they were having some trouble. Sebastian gave Griffin an ultimatum a couple weeks ago, something about wanting him to get back in school or find a way to support himself. I don't remember the details. But I don't think they saw eye to eye."

Savanna nodded. "I got that impression too. It was a sore

subject for sure. But I'm not sure Sebastian really even planned on him going. Chelsea's angry with Griffin for not being on the boat with their dad, but Sebastian wasn't surprised when he backed out of the trip."

Uncle Freddie interrupted. "Apologies, Detective, as I don't want to seem impertinent. What does this have to do with the boat going missing?"

"We have to consider every possibility," Jordan replied. "Did Harlan have any kind of conflict with anyone? Disgruntled workers, maybe? Anyone around lately that you all don't know?"

"*Pffft,*" Sydney scoffed. "No. Do you even know my dad, Nick? Because I really thought you did." She leaned on her elbows across the table toward the detective. They'd dated briefly a few years ago… Sydney had dated quite a few of the town's first responders throughout her twenties. She had a type. Jordan was now happily married, the past relationship just a blip in their history. Syd was the only one in this room who could call him by his first name without it sounding disrespectful.

"I do know your dad, Sydney," Jordan said dryly. "Again, we have to consider everything. So, forgive the next question, please," he said, turning back to Charlotte. "Does your husband have any, er, bad habits? Substances…gambling…other, uh, women? Now isn't the time to hold back; any little detail helps." The detective had the grace to look uncomfortable, but he didn't break eye contact.

"No." Charlotte placed a hand flat on the table between them. "I understand why you have to ask. My husband's greatest quality—and fault—is his integrity. It makes him unpopular at times, but never to the point of causing a grudge against him. At least not that I'm aware of. He has a beer on Friday nights, he smokes the occasional cigarillo, and he's the best man I know. No gambling, no drugs, no affairs."

"I'll back that up, Detective," Uncle Freddie said. "I've known Harlan nearly as long as my sister has. We'll continue to supply any information you need to get him back home. Everything's on the table; you won't find any skeletons in these closets. Maybe your time would be best spent looking into the Alexanders."

Savanna exchanged a wide-eyed glance with her sisters. Goodness. She could have high-fived Uncle Freddie for cutting through Jordan's insinuating question in defense of their dad.

"We're doing exactly that, I promise," Jordan said, unfazed. "We're almost done here. I'll try to wrap it up. Can you remember exactly what he was wearing yesterday morning? Anything helps, type of clothing, color, if he had a coat with him he might have worn last night?"

Between them, they were able to provide the detective with an in-depth description of their dad's attire, including his tan boat shoes and black and yellow windbreaker.

"Last question," Jordan said. He cleared his throat. "Does he have any unique identifying marks? Tattoos, birthmarks, scars, that kind of thing."

Their mother's composure cracked. Her sharp, hitching breath intake jabbed at Savanna's heart. She wrapped her arms around her mom, saying nothing. From within her embrace, Charlotte nodded. "On his forearm. A tattoo from his time in the Marines. It's the globe with the eagle atop it and the words SEMPER FI underneath."

Detective Jordan quickly jotted the note and stood. "Thank you. I appreciate your candor, all of you. Every piece of information you've given me helps. What questions do you have before I go?"

"What can we do?" The question came from Finn, the soon-to-be newest member of their little family. "There must be something we can do on our end."

Charlotte reached across the table and grabbed Finn's hand and squeezed it, her tears spilling over.

Savanna expected Jordan to issue some platitude—*stay calm, try not to worry, let us do our jobs.* He didn't.

"Think hard. Think about the days leading up to the regatta, the night before, the morning of. Any recent communication you might have had with Sebastian or his family. The phone calls from Harlan yesterday. Search your memories for anything that strikes you as odd or off-kilter, even if you can't say why, and let me know. Any other questions?"

There were too many, all too terrifying to ask. How cold was Lake Michigan this time of year? How long could a person survive in that water? How could an entire yacht just drop out of sight? And exactly what skeletons were hidden in Sebastian Alexander's closets—had he done something to put her dad's life in danger?

Savanna walked the detective out to his car, hoping but failing to summon the nerve to ask any or all of the questions swirling in her mind. She watched Jordan's unmarked car turn the corner and then started to head inside when Aidan's SUV pulled into the driveway.

Savanna met him halfway up the walk and he wrapped her in his arms, stubbly jaw brushing her forehead. She tucked her head into his neck, catching the scent of surgical soap, sweat, and beneath that, the slightly spicy, masculine scent of his shampoo. He pulled her closer, arms tightening around her. She'd needed him an hour ago, but he was here now.

Chapter Five

"I CAN'T JUST sit here." Charlotte spoke first. She sniffled and Uncle Max handed her a tissue. They were all still gathered around the table, quiet since Detective Jordan had left.

Sydney spoke. "I know. I feel like there must be something we could be doing. How are we supposed to just do nothing and wait for news?"

Skylar ran a hand over her hair, smoothing it. She tapped the screen on her iPad, typing something on the detachable keyboard. She turned a map of the west coast of Michigan and the blue Great Lake that sat between Michigan and Chicago. "I'm wondering if we should also be out looking somehow. Dad and Sebastian left from Carson Marina here." She tapped the screen, placing a check mark on the map at their town. Then she drew a wide circle on the lake, halfway up the mitten. "Jordan said the GPS signal failed around here, somewhere between Ludington and Manistee. Varying lake depth is shown here, but we have no way to know if they were closer to Michigan's coast or out farther, toward Wisconsin so—"

Savanna pulled the iPad away from Skylar and put it to sleep, the screen going black. "I'm all for us finding a way to look, but this isn't helping."

"I'm just saying, it'd be nice if we knew the water temperature where they—"

"No! It wouldn't be nice. It's irrelevant. They didn't end up in the water. We're not entertaining that," Savanna said, bugging her eyes out at her older sister and tipping her head toward their mom.

Skylar had know-it-all tendencies but, good God, for a smart person, she could be dumb sometimes.

Charlotte's gaze was fixed on Skylar; she'd gone even paler, if that was possible. "I assumed they got lost," she murmured. "That lake is like an ocean in spots. It'd be easy for anyone to lose their way, especially if the navigation system failed. The coast guard will find them...unless...you're thinking the boat capsized, Skylar?" Her tone was eerily calm and even.

Skylar shrank in her chair. She folded her hands on the table. "No, not really. I don't think that's likely. I wasn't thinking."

"Is that even possible with a yacht that size? Doesn't seem like it," Uncle Max said, trying to help. "Not with clear weather and two skilled sailors aboard. I think you're right about what happened, Char."

"The simplest explanation is usually the truest," Uncle Freddie added. "There are a dozen ways they could've gone off course. Skylar, turn that thing back on," he said, pushing the tablet across to her.

When she did, Freddie swiped on the map, zooming out. "Look. If they veered even a little westward without knowing it, they could be anywhere around Sturgeon Bay or one of these other inlets off the Wisconsin coast, or even north toward the Upper Peninsula by now. As you said, it's a big lake."

"The US Coast Guard doesn't just use boats for a search and rescue," Finn offered tentatively. "They'll have helicopters out looking too. They'll be able to cover a wide area."

"And I'm sure it won't be necessary, but all local hospitals and urgent care facilities along the coast near their last known location get notified of the EMA, so they're aware too," Aidan said. "Just in case. That means a whole lot of people in addition to law enforcement are keeping an eye out for your dad." He squeezed Savanna's shoulder, and she leaned into him.

"What's an EMA?" Charlotte asked.

"Oh. It's, um." He exchanged a glance with Finn that didn't escape her, but she let it go for the moment. "It's like an all points alert for a missing person."

Charlotte sighed. "I didn't realize that; that's good to know. I—" Her phone rang, and she jumped, grabbing it and peering at the screen. Hope surged through the room and then plummeted as her face fell. "It's just work. I have to take this." She left the room, but part of her end of the conversation was impossible not to hear. "Now is fine. Send me the client's contact info and I'll reach out."

Savanna shook her head. She stood, pacing. It felt better than sitting still and doing nothing. "Listen, can we come up with a schedule for each of us to be here with her until Dad's home? She's not okay." She kept her voice low.

"Absolutely," Uncle Freddie said. "Let us go first. Max can go pack a bag and get Lady Bella and we'll stay here tonight."

Uncle Max nodded, spurred into action, keys already in hand. "Good idea. I'm free all day tomorrow too. I'll get Annie to cover the shop, or we'll just leave it closed for the day."

Skylar spoke. "The kids and I will come spend the night tomorrow—*if* he's not home by then."

"I think he will be," Sydney replied. "He has to be. If he isn't, I'll take Tuesday."

Before Charlotte returned, the family had the next several days covered—if necessary.

"I've got some work calls to make before my flight tomorrow morning," she said from the doorway. "I'll be upstairs if anyone needs me." She was gone again before anyone could speak.

Their mother was a management consultant, which involved a good deal of virtual conferencing and frequent short business trips to be on-site wherever her current clients were located.

"Yeah, she's very much not okay," Sydney whispered.

"She's not thinking clearly. She's not flying anywhere tomorrow; work will have to wait," Skylar added.

Savanna found her mother in the master bedroom, sitting on the edge of the bed near Harlan's nightstand, cell phone and laptop forgotten beside her. She stared down at Harlan's watch in the palm of her hand. "He never wears it on sail trips. He worries it'll get wet. It was his father's watch."

She joined her mom on the bed. "I remember."

"Your grandpa would have wanted him to have it with him right now. Grandpa always thought it brought him luck. I wish he'd have worn it yesterday."

Savanna took the watch, turning it over in her hand. "It would have made him nervous. It's better that he left it here, so it'll be in fine shape to wear when he comes home. Right?"

Charlotte nodded, not answering. She put a hand on her laptop. "I have so much work to do. Deadlines I can't ignore. But I can't think of anything but your dad."

"I'll help you cancel your flight, Mom. We'll figure the rest out after that."

Skylar and Sydney stood quietly in the bedroom doorway. The chatter from downstairs had dissipated, and they heard car doors closing outside.

"I can't work," Charlotte said, sounding surprised at the realization.

"No," Skylar agreed. "Your clients will understand, Mom, I promise."

Sydney scooted onto the bed, wrapping their mother in a tight hug. "He'll be okay, Mom. I can feel it. I'm positive. We have to believe he is all right, and he'll be home soon."

Skylar joined them, Charlotte in the middle of a four-way hug. Savanna didn't know how long they all sat like that, surrounding their crying mother, their kind but tough, soft but strong, pragmatic, self-contained, independent role model, the ruling force in the family, while Harlan was the sturdy, dependable foundation. Together, they'd always been relationship goals to anyone who knew them. Savanna couldn't imagine her mother without her dad. She shook off the thought as quickly as it had come.

Savanna found Aidan outside, sitting beside the Shepherds' big orange tabby cat on the porch swing. She squeezed in beside him, not wanting to disturb Pumpkin. "Mom's sleeping. Thank you for staying."

"You don't need to thank me. Thank Finn, next time you see him. He called in a favor—he'll be another set of eyes in the sky in a couple hours. He's heading up there in the Air Med copter."

"Oh my God. That's amazing." Relief lightened the worry weighing her down; they were so lucky to have Finn pitching in.

"Finn can be amazing sometimes," he agreed.

"Aidan, what does EMA really mean—what does it stand for? And don't fluff your answer, Google will tell me the truth if you don't."

"It's a missing persons protocol. It means Endangered Missing Advisory."

"Oh. Endangered." She looked down at her hands. "Like an Amber Alert for adults?"

"Kind of. At the hospital, we get notified of those when the person who's missing is…when police have reason to believe there's something suspicious about the disappearance, or if the person is believed to be in danger. Detective Jordan issuing the EMA is a good thing. It means much wider public awareness of the fact that authorities are searching for your dad," he added. "It just helps in the efforts to get him home."

"So…it means Jordan thinks they may not have just gone off course." She was grateful for his caution. She trusted him to find her dad. But now the queasy feeling in her stomach made her wish she hadn't asked about the acronym.

"It could just mean he's using every resource at his disposal," Aidan offered.

"I keep thinking about what Uncle Max said. About there being no chance of the boat capsizing because Sebastian and my dad are skilled sailors. But what if it really is something else? Maybe the yacht didn't capsize but maybe they aren't lost. What if someone did something…like an attack?"

Aidan stretched an arm along the back of the swing behind her. "I don't know. Why would someone do that?"

"I don't know. Maybe—this might sound crazy—but would someone do something like that to steal Sebastian's yacht? I looked it up. Those X-Yachts go for a lot. Over a million, especially that size."

"Maybe? But it doesn't seem likely. I do think your dad will make it home safe. We'll hear something very soon." He stroked her shoulder, keeping his arm loosely around her.

"I hate feeling helpless. Ugh—Jordan better look at every possibility."

"I'm sure he will. Your uncle said the police are asking Sebastian's family all the same things they asked you."

"That's the other thing," she said, turning to look at him. "That whole scene over there today was so strange, the more I think about it. Something seemed off, like Jordan said, but I have nothing concrete to tell him. Chelsea and Winnie were so upset, understandably, but it was awful how

Chelsea blamed Griffin—I'm not sure it's even his fault that he ended up not going. Sebastian seems very tough on him. I need to talk to them."

"To the family?"

"To Chelsea and Griffin. But not at the same time. Jeez, there was so much animosity today in that house. Griffin even lashed out at Sebastian's personal assistant. I can catch Chelsea tomorrow morning after the morning rush at her bakery, and then maybe I can find out how to reach Griffin. I think he only works part-time at Holy Grounds." She could feel herself rambling, trying to keep up with her speeding thoughts; she would get further than Jordan probably could, and then she could update him on anything odd that she picked up on.

"Savanna." Aidan traced a slow pattern on her shoulder with his thumb. "I know how important it is for you to help find your dad. I fully believe you could find something Jordan might miss—I've seen you do it before. But I've also nearly lost you before when you've gotten tangled up in dangerous investigations."

He wasn't wrong. But—"I have to do something. I have to. If something happened to me, my dad wouldn't rest until he'd done every last thing he could to save me. I owe him the same."

He sighed. "Of course. I get it. Then you need to let me help. We have no idea what we're getting into."

"I promise. For real," she stressed. "I won't do anything without making sure you know about it first."

MONDAY MORNING, INSTEAD of setting up the *Very Hungry Caterpillar* project she'd planned for her students this week, Savanna waited at a small table near the back of Main Street Sweets for there to be a lull in the morning rush. Chelsea Alexander handled a steady stream of patrons stopping in to satisfy their pastry or chocolate cravings, offering samples and boxing up items before sending the customer to the end of the display cases to the young man at the register.

Savanna had taken a chance on Chelsea working today. Savanna's favorite substitute teacher was filling in for her. There was no way she'd have been any good with the roughly 120 students rotating through her art classroom; she'd barely been able to pick out an outfit this morning, and she'd left home in her slippers and had to turn around and go back for her shoes. There'd been no word at all from Detective Jordan last night or this morning.

She got in line as the last two people stepped up the counter. Chelsea finished boxing up an order for the elderly woman in front of her, throwing hopeful glances at Savanna.

"Have you heard something? I haven't had time to check my phone. Did they find them?"

"No," Savanna said. "I'm sorry. I didn't mean for you to think I had news. We've heard nothing so far. I wondered if you have a few minutes to chat?"

"Sure. Oh, would you like something?" Chelsea looked down at the rows of croissants and muffins in the case between them.

"Always," she replied automatically. Normally, she always wanted some kind of sweet from Chelsea's shop. She hadn't been able to eat much since yesterday. Still, she had to get something; it'd be rude not to. She pointed. "How about two of the chocolate croissants."

"Good choice. These are fresh as of an hour ago. I almost didn't open up today," she shared. "But baking all of this is my stress reliever."

"Eating all of this is my stress reliever," Savanna said, eliciting a small smile from Chelsea.

Seated across from Sebastian's daughter, she felt compelled to at least nibble on the delicious croissant; she placed it between them and tore off a small piece. "I thought since our dads are missing together, maybe it makes sense for us to work together as much as possible, too, to get them back home," she began.

It wasn't entirely true but close enough. So much secrecy surrounded Sebastian Alexander's life and early career, it'd be naïve to assume they were on the same side. For all she knew, the artist had enemies. Financially, he made more sense than Harlan as a target.

Or they'd just gotten lost, she reminded herself. Or they'd had technical problems—what if there was an issue with the sails or the onboard motor or any other number of possibilities? The artist had been an aspirational figure to her for so long; there was no reason to place blame on him for whatever had happened. But she needed to be smart about this.

"I agree, we should keep each other updated on any

news," Chelsea said. "Detective Taylor was with us for a while yesterday, going through every little detail. Lots of questions, but no answers."

"We had Detective Jordan at our parents' house," Savanna said. George Taylor was Nick Jordan's longtime partner at the sheriff's department. "And same. He asked a lot of questions." She paused. "My mom fell apart when he asked about identifying marks like scars or tattoos. I can't even think about it coming to that. How's your stepmom doing? How's everyone else?" She remembered Chelsea and her husband had two daughters but was blanking on their names.

"Not great. My girls took it hard—they're ten and twelve. Their other grandfather just passed away last year, so this is really tough on them."

The words struck Savanna; she spoke as if their fathers were gone for good. "They're not—" Savanna began, before Chelsea interrupted.

"No, no, of course not—I mean, it's just hard with them recently losing one grandpa. They're so afraid of losing my dad too. We showed them on a map where the boat was last, and they know everything possible is being done to find Dad and Harlan."

"I'm sure this is awful for them... It definitely is for all of us. We're all taking turns staying with my mom. My uncles are with her today. You and Griffin are probably trading off checking on Winnie, too, huh?"

"Not really. Her younger brother, Daniel, lives in Lake Haven. Maybe he'll come stay at the house with her for a few days. She said she'd call him. She and Sebastian helped move him to Michigan after they did, they had no other family in Paris. I hope he'll step up for her. I've got the shop, and Griffin went home last night before I did. He's still focused on his art opening," she said, putting air quotes around the words. Her tone was laced with disdain. "He's in his own world. But Dad's assistant, Kyle, lives on the property. He's amazing. He moved with us from Paris; he's very dedicated. He'll look out for my stepmom if she needs anything."

"I'm sure that's helpful for your dad and Winnie." It answered the question of whether Griffin still lived at home. She was working her way around to what the deal was between Chelsea's dad and brother, unsure how to broach it.

Chelsea took it out of her hands. "I'm sorry. I don't mean to sound like a jerk about my brother. I'm just so mad at him for dropping out of the regatta. Maybe if he'd been on the boat, this wouldn't be happening."

"I should have gone." Savanna winced as she said the words—saying them aloud made her feel even worse than she'd felt since yesterday. It might have been enough. If she'd been there, her dad and Sebastian might already be sailing back home right now, part of the regatta.

"Why didn't you?"

She sucked in her breath, eyes widening at Chelsea's question. "I tried—my dad convinced us they'd be all right on their own."

"Sorry," Chelsea said. "I didn't mean that the way it sounded. Or maybe I did. I don't know. They never should've gone without a third. You sail, right?"

"I do," she said. "I should have gone. I could have taken time off work. I don't...I don't know why I didn't see how risky it'd be for them." Her stomach flipped over nauseatingly.

Chelsea sighed, shoulders slumping. "You didn't go for the same reason I didn't. He taught me to sail years ago. I'm rusty but I still could have stepped up."

"Why didn't you?" she echoed the question.

She shrugged. "Because I always assume Dad will be fine. He won't ever let us help him with anything." She tipped her head, studying Savanna. "Your dad seems the same, stubborn, tough, independent. I think we all took for granted that they'd be fine."

"You're right," Savanna admitted. "My dad's a good sailor, and I know yours is, too, but I shouldn't have assumed anything. I should have insisted on going the minute you told them Griffin wasn't going," she added.

"Honestly, I think my dad was relieved that Griffin dropped out. They have...issues."

"I picked up on some of that when we were out on your dad's boat last week. Has it always been that way between them?"

"It's gotten worse lately. Grif is so focused on his art he cut back on his hours at Holy Grounds. He keeps thinking he's about to get his big break, the way Dad did. But even back then in Paris, Dad was working two jobs to support our family and painting at night when he could find the time. It wasn't until he'd split up our family and nearly lost our house financing his early shows that he finally woke up.

Maeve Davis put him on the map, you know."

"Wow," Savanna said, trying to process all of that. "It sounds traumatic, especially for you two as kids. I'm so sorry."

Chelsea shrugged. "I'm over it. Plenty of kids go through worse. He was fighting his own demons. It's not like he purposely tried to hurt us."

She marveled at the woman's sensibility. Chelsea had obviously worked through her childhood issues, but perhaps Griffin hadn't taken the same approach. She circled back to the bigger question mark Sebastian's daughter had just triggered. "What do you mean, Maeve Davis made him famous? They were both up and coming artists back then; how could she have impacted his career?" Nothing she'd ever read about either artist referred to whatever Chelsea was talking about.

"Maeve introduced him to her agent. His stuff took off shortly after that, bypassing Maeve's gallery showings for a while. He put us through a lot during that time. Griffin was old enough to know at least some of what was going on. He knows everything Dad achieved came at a cost, but he's glamorizing it in his head, and Dad's about fed up with supporting him. I mean, he's thirty-three. He needs to grow up." She sat back, glancing over her shoulder as if remembering they were sitting in public, but the shop was now mostly empty, her cashier in the back. "I'm sorry. You came here to talk about our dads and what to do, and I'm just crabbing about my little brother."

Savanna shook her head. "Don't apologize, seriously. It's

okay. Every family has their baggage, you know? That whole situation sounds pretty stressful. Who knows? Maybe it's for the best that Griffin didn't go on the trip. It might have made things harder for your dad."

"Maybe. I don't know." The bell rang over the door with a trio of women entering the shop, spurring Chelsea to her feet. She pulled her phone from the pocket of the small apron tied around her waist. "Give me your number. That way we can keep each other updated on any news."

She did, and her phone dinged a moment later.

"There, now you have mine. I'm glad you stopped by, Savanna. I'm hoping for the best, but trying to brace myself for the worst, y'know?"

Savanna nodded, not meaning it. She was not in that mindset. On no level was she striving to be ready for terrible news from Detective Jordan. "Oh—" She stopped on her way toward the door, while the three ladies were still studying the delectables in the display cases. "I almost forgot to ask—Maeve Davis isn't still in town, is she? I've followed her work forever. I had no idea she and your dad were close. I'd love to invite her to speak to my art students or even give a demo, if she'd like to."

"She only came in for the regatta," Chelsea said. "She drove in Saturday morning from Chicago and left last night. If you'd like, I can pass on your number and ask her to call you."

"That'd be amazing," Savanna said sincerely. "I'll let you get back to work." Outside Main Street Sweets, she turned left and strolled slowly past the front of Holy Grounds, peering inside through the enormous front window. Past a smattering of patrons were two baristas behind the counter, neither of them Griffin. Only in a small town would a sister and brother work right next door to each other while carrying on what seemed like a love-hate relationship.

Savanna continued on to her sister's Fancy Tails & Treats two doors down. She stopped with one hand on the door. Diagonally, across the street in front of the law office, Skylar sat in her car sobbing.

Chapter Six

S KYLAR DIDN'T KNOW how much more she could take.
Her husband's voice came through the vehicle's
Bluetooth speaker. "I don't care. You're blowing the whole
thing out of proportion. It doesn't have to be such a big deal.
I'm just...I'm done."

"Travis." She rested one hand on the steering wheel, closing her eyes. Inhale, count one-two-three-four-five. Exhale,
count one-two-three-four-five. She repeated the cycle again
before responding to him. It worked in court to help her
maintain her calm, but it wasn't doing a thing to stop her
infuriating tears right now. She only cried when she was
really, really mad. "You're *done*? What does that even mean?"

"This isn't working. We should talk when your dad's
back and you can think more clearly," Travis said.

"Do you hear how condescending you sound?"

"All I hear right now is that you think I'm the bad guy.
You're acting like this was meant to hurt you. Everything I
say is getting twisted around. You're not being rational. I'm
giving you some space."

Condescension *and* gaslighting. Who was this man?
"Can't you even see how ironic this is? While you're telling
me everything will be fine? This is really what you want?" she

asked, hating the quiver in her voice. Keeping her emotions in check came naturally in her work life, but she'd rarely had occasion to test that in her marriage. She and Travis never fought. Until now.

He laughed, a harsh sound devoid of any mirth. "This is the furthest thing from what I want, Sky."

"I can't keep doing this," she said. "I can't keep going in circles with you while nothing changes."

"Fine. Don't." He ended the call. He really hung up on her.

She broke down, a sob escaping her lips. She swiped under her eyes angrily, fumbling around in her purse for a tissue. She drew in a hitching breath, letting out an aggravated growl—this wasn't her. She didn't sit in her car crying helplessly because she had a fight with her husband. To be fair, it wasn't just a fight. It was the same fight, over and over, too many times in a row, and she was exhausted. They were at a crossroads, a fundamental disagreement over how to move forward if their marriage was to survive. At least that was how this felt to her. She wasn't sure Travis saw things that way. Or if he even cared to move forward.

She flipped the visor mirror down and smoothed the flyaway strands of hair around her face, starting her car now and blasting the AC to help alleviate her flushed skin before heading into her office. She hoped with all her heart that her paralegal, Kara, wasn't here yet; Skylar wasn't about to answer a bunch of questions from Kara about why she'd been crying.

Someone rapped on her car window and Skylar jumped,

letting out a little shriek before turning to find Savanna staring in at her. Her sister raised one hand in a hello, face painted with concern.

She rolled down the window. "What're you doing in town—did you call off work today?" Of course her sister would find her like this. *This is why you should never fall apart in broad daylight on Main Street*, she thought.

"Is there news? Is it Dad—what happened?" Savanna's pitch rose in panic.

"No. No, I haven't heard anything. I'm—"

Savanna was already moving around the car to the passenger side. She climbed into the front passenger seat and tucked a leg underneath her, facing Skylar. "Are you okay?"

Skylar turned down the air-conditioning. It was almost too loud to speak over. "I'm fine. Sorry. I didn't mean to scare you."

Savanna reached over and hugged her. "We're going to find him." She sat back, leaving a hand on Skylar's arm. "I mean...God, I just feel so useless here, waiting and hoping. I wish there was something we could do. This whole thing feels like a bad dream. Dad will be back home soon. He has to be. The coast guard will find them and bring them home safe."

"You're probably right," Skylar said, trying to sound hopeful. God, she felt selfish throwing so much energy into trying to fix things with Travis when none of them even knew whether their dad was alive. The thought brought new tears to the surface, and she tipped her face upward, blinking. "Ugh. I'm sorry."

"Why? We're all upset, don't say sorry." She continued to stare at her. "Sky, really, did you...did Jordan or someone call you about them?"

"No." She met her sister's gaze. Crap. She'd never lied to her sisters. She didn't want to start now. "Nobody called me. I'm just dealing with something else on top of Dad missing," Skylar finished, knowing how vague that sounded.

"Oh." Savanna was quiet for a moment. When she spoke again, her voice was small. "What is it?"

She hated how worried Savanna looked, watching her with those wide eyes. *This.* This was exactly why it was so much easier to keep her emotions in check. If she'd just held it together instead of crying like a baby because of Travis, her sister wouldn't be staring at her like this right now, clearly riddled with concern.

"Is it Nolan? Little Hannah? Sky, are you *okay*? Is someone sick? You can tell me. I can help. Whatever it is, it'll be better if you can let me help, I promise."

"I'm fine. Nobody's sick, Savvy, don't worry. It's just...marriage stuff. I don't want to get into it right now. I'm already late for work." She couldn't afford to fall apart again.

"I'm so sorry," Savanna said. "I didn't know. You always seem...you two always seem so solid."

Skylar's phone rang, still connected to the car's Bluetooth. It was her receptionist. She cringed. Zach could probably see her sitting in the car right out front. She hit the green button on the screen. "Hi, Zach. I'll be right in. Would you let Dave know I had an unavoidable delay?"

Dave was Dave Sydowski, a senior partner at Black, Jones, and Sydowski, Michigan's largest law firm. While Jillian Black worked here, out of the Carson office, Pete Jones manned the Lansing and Detroit offices, and Dave had driven in from Grand Rapids this morning. She'd kept him waiting a full ten minutes now, completely unlike her.

"Of course. Would you like me to reschedule with him?"

"We can't," she replied, putting one finger up to Savanna and mouthing *Sorry.* "I need his input for the Andrews deposition this afternoon. I'll be there in two minutes." She ended the call and grabbed her purse from the console, quickly covering her blotchy pink skin with light makeup and reapplying her lipstick.

"Hey. You don't always have to be *fine.*" Savanna squeezed Skylar's arm. "You have partners for a reason. I'm sure they'll understand if your real-life stuff has to take priority over work right now."

Her sister's words sent prickles up the back of Skylar's neck. "What the hell does that mean? My job is part of my real life, Savanna."

Savanna sat back, brows raised in surprise. "I just meant—I should've said your family life."

"My family always comes first. You know that. I can't—I have to go." She shouldn't expect either of her sisters to understand. Maybe Savanna meant well, but beneath the benign words was scrutiny and judgment, she could feel it.

"Skylar, you always say how great your partners here are. Don't kill yourself trying to make everyone happy. You're entitled to a personal day now and then too. I can barely focus today, and I know now that I'm not even half as stressed as you are. I love you. I'm just trying to help."

She softened. "I know you are. I can't get into any of this right now. I really do have to go."

"Later, then. Anytime. I'll supply the wine and listen, I promise," Savanna said.

She smoothed a hand over her sleek blond bob. "Okay. I'll take you up on that." *I probably won't take you up on that*, she thought.

"Promise."

"Sure." She got out, grabbed her briefcase from the back seat, and was heading toward her office when Savanna nearly tackled her with another hug.

"I mean it. You don't have to go through whatever's happening on your own. Let me know when and I'll grab Syd and come over. Whenever you want."

She shook her head. "No. Not Sydney. Not right now. Her wedding's two weeks away, I'm not doing that." Syd was practically glowing lately; she was so happy and in love. She didn't need to hear about anyone's marital problems, not right now.

"But—" Savanna's expression spoke volumes.

"Not a word," Skylar commanded, her tone nonnegotiable. "I don't want her worrying about me."

"Okay. I don't agree with you, though," she said, defeated.

"Call me if you hear anything about Dad. Love you." She blew a halfhearted kiss toward her sister as she headed inside. She could count on one hand the number of times they'd said *I love you* to each other as adults. But since their dad's disappearance, her emotions were like an exposed nerve. Everything was dialed up to ten. The tension between her and Travis had escalated too. Was she overreacting? Her younger sisters confided in her anytime they needed to vent or work through something, but she'd always been more comfortable dealing with difficulties on her own. She'd figure this out. She didn't want to burden Syd right now, but more than that, she didn't want to talk about it at all. Talking about it would make it all real.

Zach met her as she moved through the lobby, placing folders and a stack of papers in her arms. "He's in conference room three." He scrutinized her. "I'll bring coffee." Zach was a godsend.

After work, Skylar stopped at home to pack up the kids' overnight bags and relieve the babysitter. An early childhood education major who was amazing with Nolan and Hannah, Carly informed her that Travis had popped in and packed a bag of his own, saying he'd fill Skylar in later.

She did her best not to react but heard the waver in her own voice. "He took an overnight bag with him? Did he say what—never mind, maybe something came up at work." *What the* hell, *Trav.*

Carly shrugged. "He was in a rush. There was someone waiting for him in the car outside."

"Right." The young woman's words bounced around in Skylar's chest. She nodded like it was the most normal thing in the world for her husband to be gone overnight without telling her. "No worries." She jammed a handful of diapers and Hannah's Winnie the Pooh sleeper into the diaper bag. Grabbing blindly from the dresser, she added what she hoped was an outfit and pajamas for Nolan and scooped up the baby in her carrier as she headed toward the front door.

"I can help—" Carly said, but Skylar's nerves had kicked her motions into high speed; she had their bags and her own assembled by the front door in minutes and then headed into the family room where Nolan was watching his favorite cartoon. She turned off the TV and was hit by an ear-piercing shriek from her five-year-old.

"Mama, no! I have to see what happens to Wally!" He reached for the remote.

"No, you don't," she snapped. "You've had enough television today." She held out a hand for him. "Come on, Grandma and the uncles are expecting us."

Her son's face scrunched even more into a fierce scowl. He nevertheless scooted off the couch. He stomped his little feet over to her and then skirted widely around her, going to stand behind the sitter by the front door.

Skylar was met with a wide-eyed Carly watching her silently, Nolan hugging her around her waist while Hannah now fussed in the girl's arms. "I'll help you out to the car," she said softly, slinging the diaper bag over one shoulder.

In the driveway, both kids buckled into their respective car seats and bags and sundries thrown into the trunk, Skylar stopped before climbing behind the wheel. "I'm sorry."

Carly shook her head. "Don't be. I'm sure it's been an awful day. There's no news yet? Can I do anything?"

"No. I mean, you already have. Thank you." She gave

the girl's arm a light squeeze and got behind the wheel.

The sitter leaned down, keeping her voice a whisper so it wouldn't be picked up by the back seat. "We only turned on *Wally Walrus* a few minutes before you got home. That was his first TV time today. I really hope they find your dad soon. I just know he's gonna be okay; my family's praying."

"Thank you so much." She heaved a sigh. "Thank you for taking such great care of the kids. Let me send your payment." She picked up her phone, but the girl stopped her.

"Travis already paid me. See you Wednesday, then?"

She nodded. "Yes, Wednesday." She'd decided a few months ago not to return to a full-time work schedule yet and now worked three days a week, and the time it allowed her with the kids was invaluable. Nolan was still talking about their trip to the zoo last week. Kindergarten was only half days, so she was trying to soak up as much kid time as she could now. Her off days were spent ignoring housework and errands and calls from the office as much as possible while she spent time with Nolan and Hannah, even though it meant late nights catching up on everything else. She knew her mom was right. Charlotte had reminded her after Hannah was born, *Laundry waits. Our kiddos don't.*

She glanced in the rearview mirror on the short drive to her parents' house. "Nolan." He met her eyes in the mirror, his bottom lip still sticking out. "Baby, I'm sorry I turned off Wally. I was in a crabby-pants mood. We'll watch it at Grandma's, okay?" Thankfully, he was oblivious to the fact his grandfather was missing, and she planned to keep it that way.

He rewarded her with a smile, white-blond hair even lighter than hers falling in his eyes with his excited nod. "Uncle Max loves Wally, he can watch too." She mentally added getting her kid a haircut to the running to-do list in her head.

As she pulled into her parents' driveway, her heart leaped. Savanna was on the way in with Aidan close behind. He carried a literal black bag, still in his lab coat and hospital badge. Her dad was home—and he was here at the house, safe and sound, with Aidan checking on him. That had to be a good sign. If it was bad, he'd be in the hospital.

She scrambled getting Hannah and Nolan released from their car seats and hurried up the front steps. Why had no one called her? Fumbling getting her phone from the outside pocket of the diaper bag, Skylar felt her heart plummet as quickly as it'd leaped. There were no missed calls. Her notifications showed one text message from Travis, nothing else. She dropped it back into the pocket. She couldn't bear to read it. Not yet. It'd likely be a stupid, meaningless apology, and things would continue as they'd been and nothing would change.

In her parents' living room, her mother reclined on the couch, feet up on a pillow, while Aidan checked her blood pressure. What in the world?

Uncle Freddie cleared up her confusion, Nolan already perched on his forearm. "She was having a bad bout of dizziness. I wanted to take her in to be checked but she wouldn't listen to a word we said. So, Max called for back-up."

"And I'm not sorry," Uncle Max said pointedly, frowning at Charlotte.

"So," Aidan said, straightening up, "your blood pressure is pretty low. What have you had today to eat and drink?"

"Nothing," Uncle Freddie answered for his sister.

"Oh stop. That's not true," Charlotte protested.

"Really?" her brother challenged her. "Enlighten us."

"I had—Max made eggs for breakfast."

"That you didn't eat," Freddie said.

She ignored him. "I had some crackers. And coffee."

Savanna appeared from the kitchen and handed Charlotte a tall glass of water. "Here. Remember when I passed out after finding the councilman last year? My blood pressure was low. They made me drink a bunch of water."

Charlotte slowly sat up. She took the glass and drank the entire thing, rolling her eyes at the cluster of people gathered around her. "There. Happy? I'm fine."

Aidan took a seat beside her on the couch. "You're probably a little dehydrated. Let's just give this some time and I'll recheck your blood pressure. How about a bite to eat, and maybe another glass… Do you have any juice or pop in the house?" He glanced up at Savanna.

Skylar sat on the other side of Charlotte while her sister disappeared again into the kitchen. "Mom, you have to take care of yourself. Dad will be home soon. I'm positive," she lied. She wasn't sure of anything at all lately.

"This will sting a bit," Aidan said, taking Charlotte's hand. "Your blood sugar might also be low." He'd opened a small black kit on his knee.

He was quick. He poked the pad of her finger and touched the spot of blood that appeared to the tiny strip sticking out of the machine. It beeped, the screen displaying a flashing fifty-eight.

Savanna was back, placing a glass of orange juice in her mother's hand. She held a plate with the fastest sandwich ever made. "Is fifty-eight low?"

"It is. It'll come right up with the juice, don't worry. The sandwich will help stop it from dropping again too fast." Aidan covered Charlotte's fingertip with a round spot bandage. "Skylar's right, Charlotte. You need to take care of yourself. You've got plenty of support here, but they can't help if you don't let them."

She met Aidan's eyes and nodded. "Okay. I know. I'll be fine. Can we all stop focusing on me now?"

Her mom's words hit Skylar square in the chest. She sounded just like her. "No," she said sharply. "The focus is on you for a reason. You aren't fine, Mom. Stop pretending you are."

"Sky," Savanna said. "She gets it. Don't yell at her."

Charlotte put a hand up. "No fighting, no biting," she said, a phrase from one of their children's books that she'd used their whole entire life to get them to settle. "You're right. I am far from fine. I was about to call Detective—" She cut herself off abruptly, gaze resting on Nolan.

"And we were about to take Fonzie and his pals for a walk," Uncle Max said to Nolan. "Ready, young sir? The poor dogs have been waiting all day for you to get here!"

Nolan giggled, hopping down from Freddie's arms and sprinting into the kitchen, all three dogs following him. Once the screen door out into the yard had clapped closed, Charlotte finished her thought.

"I've not heard a single word from the police since last night. No updates. Neither has Winnie. Sitting here doing nothing while he's out there somewhere, maybe hurt, maybe...worse...is killing me." Her voice was even and calm, her posture unnaturally still.

Skylar shifted Hannah and hugged Charlotte around the shoulders. Walking in and seeing her mom lying flat on the couch was, in itself, a scary feeling. Charlotte didn't lie down on the couch. She didn't nap. She almost never got sick, and if she did, she'd put herself to bed early and wake up all better. But this eerie, unmoving calm, an exaggerated version of her usual composure, unnerved Skylar. She felt as if her mom might break into a hundred pieces if she hugged her too tightly. Like she was holding herself together with sheer will alone.

It was exactly how Skylar felt lately. "Let's call Detective Jordan."

Chapter Seven

SAVANNA WAS GOING to throttle Nick Jordan in her parents' sunny kitchen if he didn't start to show some shred of humanity. He'd stopped by as promised quickly enough following Uncle Freddie's call. He had nothing to share, no updates, no sightings of Sebastian's yacht or the two men aboard. She understood that was beyond his control. But she'd asked him twice now for details on the search and his nonanswers were maddening.

"I can't give any specifics. It's a coast guard open investigation."

"Have they widened the search area? What if they went off course farther north, closer to Traverse City than Manistee?" Savanna asked.

"I'm not privy to that information. I'm sure they're following protocol."

Skylar spoke. "Jordan. We're struggling here. Give us something or give us a better contact with the coast guard. The number your partner gave me this morning goes straight to a general voicemail."

His lips were pressed thin, new frown lines between his eyes Savanna had never noticed before. "Listen, I want to put your minds at ease. I do. But—" He sighed, pulling at his tie to loosen it and leaving it askew. "I'm almost as far out of the loop as you are. What I do know is the coast guard's Ninth District Response Division is handling the investigation. The Lake Michigan and Sault Sainte Marie sectors are coordinating efforts since the last sighting of the *Serendipity* was near the Michigan–Wisconsin line around twenty-five miles west of Glen Arbor."

"Wisconsin? What do you mean?" Savanna asked at the same time her mother spoke.

"Glen Arbor is north of Manistee, nearly past Traverse City, right?" Charlotte asked. "So that means they were spotted a long while after race officials lost track of them?"

Uncle Freddie spoke. "You told us their nav system failed between Ludington and Manistee. Who spotted them all the way up there? And *when*?"

Jordan opened his hands, palms down, shaking his head. "You're right. It is new information. One of the other boats confirmed seeing them—or what they thought was the *Serendipity*—early Sunday morning, around two a.m. I didn't mention it because we're not sure it's a good lead. The vessel that was sighted was much farther westward than the rest of the boats sailing through the night."

"You seem to be very much in the loop," Skylar said, her tone quiet. "Keeping us in the dark is only going to make the situation here worse." Her gaze went to her mom, who looked even paler now.

"I understand. The lead investigator isn't confident the sighting is legit. It was dark and at a great distance. The last thing I want to do is give you false hope."

Charlotte spoke. "Thank you for sharing, Detective. Any kind of hope is still hope."

He nodded. "I can't imagine how difficult this is for all of you. Before Fred called tonight, I'd planned on coming by on my way home anyway. The coast guard teams running this are seasoned and thorough, I promise you. All medical centers along the west coast of the state have an eye out. Sebastian Alexander's yacht is substantial; fifty-five feet is well over the minimum craft size for the Great Lakes. There's truly no reason to doubt they'll be found safe."

Jordan left them with the name and direct contact number for the lead investigator, Admiral Sam Moore, and promised to check back in the morning with any new updates. The uncles plied Savanna with comfort food, Max's ultra-rich baked mac and cheese, while Aidan headed back to the clinic. Despite Jordan's assurances, dinner was somber and quiet, Nolan lending the only chatter to their normally boisterous family meal. The sense of dread that had arrived yesterday was now settled heavily around Savanna's shoulders, making her simultaneously restless and exhausted.

Alone on her deck that night, Savanna stared out over the black water of Lake Michigan, moon hidden behind clouds. She'd never have bought this house last year if not for her dad. Set back on the sandy bluffs, it was a major fixer-upper, the only reason she could afford it on a teacher's salary. Harlan and a few of his trusted subcontractors had basically taken the little cottage down to bare bones and then renovated it with Savanna lending her artistic flair, room by room. The end result was a lovingly crafted home infused with a joyful mix of her and her dad's creativity. She'd loved it every day since, until right now. Would she ever be able to look out over that water without thinking of what it took from her?

But it hadn't. They didn't know that. *Yet*, her mind added against her will. She shoved it away. Her dad and Sebastian were too skilled, too strong, the X-Yacht itself too enormous and sturdy a boat, for anything awful to have happened. Her dad would be home soon. He'd be home soon. She repeated it like a mantra as she dialed Sam Moore from the sticky note Detective Jordan gave her. Her heart sank when the call went straight to voicemail. Maybe she shouldn't have called the investigator this late at night? She couldn't bring herself to care. She left a voicemail, repeating her name and phone number three times. She'd call him again in the morning.

Before she fell asleep, Fonzie abandoning his usual spot by her feet and instead snuggling up against her side, she tried for the thousandth time to call her dad. His phone was probably dead by now, even if he'd somehow had a signal. His voicemail was too full of messages from her family to let her leave a message. She double-checked again to make sure the ringtone volume was all the way up and set the phone by her pillow. Fonzie nosed his way under her arm, cuddling closer. Sometimes animals just knew when they were needed.

Her phone woke her early the next morning, an unknown number on the screen. She fumbled it, and it clattered behind her headboard, and she dove after it. "Hello?" She got to her feet, breathless and wide awake.

"Hello, this is Savanna Shepherd."

"Ma'am, Admiral Moore here with the ninth district. I've got no new updates," he quickly added, practiced in sharing the most important bit of information first. "I'm returning your call."

"Thank you. I—" Now that she had the lead investigator on the phone, her mind was blank for what to ask.

"I understand from Detective Jordan he's providing your family with periodic updates. Is there anything specific I can help with?"

"I think we're all confused about the location—possible location—of Sebastian's boat the last time it was seen. They do the regatta every year. The fleet of sailboats always stays within ten miles or so of the west coast as they sail north toward Mackinac. How is it that the yacht may now be close to the Michigan–Wisconsin line? Wouldn't that put them really far west of where they should be?"

"You're right. We are not certain the early Sunday morning sighting is valid. The craft that reported seeing your father's boat was a few miles west of Glen Arbor. Visibility that far out at night is questionable. But we take every possible lead seriously. We've expanded the search perimeter significantly with both CGPD vessels and drones, which sometimes capture missing crafts not easily seen from the water."

"Good. That sounds good, thank you." She felt panicky at the thought of the call ending with no more information than they already had. "What can we do? We all feel helpless. My mom isn't doing well, as you can imagine. There has to be something we can do."

"I understand. This process can be incredibly frustrating," Moore said, his tone sincere, sympathetic. "The only thing you can do is keep communication open. Keep your phones on. Think back to race day and the days leading up to it; was anything out of the ordinary? Anything that struck you as odd or incongruous? If you know the Alexander family well, I'd advise staying in touch. Sometimes the smallest thing will trigger a memory of something that could be important in our investigation."

She voiced her fear. "So, you're thinking something deliberate happened to them?"

"Not at all; just routine factors to take into account."

Savanna felt no better after talking with the admiral. She forced herself into routine, even though she was well ahead of schedule to get to work. It wasn't until she'd showered, dressed, packed her lunch, and grabbed her keys that she realized her red leather tote bag was gone. She stared at the spot where it typically hung, next to her windbreaker. She and Jack Carson called the bag her brains for good reason. It held her planner, laptop, grocery lists, duplicate lesson plan schedule, outgoing mail, her tote Chapstick, and whatever else got thrown in there on any given day. A moment of panic struck her and then she remembered where she'd left it—right beside her laptop on the desk in Sebastian Alexander's studio.

She fought the urge to call in sick again. She needed her tote, but then what to do with another entire day besides worry about her dad? She'd stop by after work to get it.

In Carson Elementary's teachers' lounge, Savanna joined Jack Carson and his girlfriend, Elaina, a third-grade teacher, steaming cup of coffee in one hand. Jack was town matriarch Caroline Carson's grandson and the first person to be kind to her in her new job here two years ago.

He frowned at her. "You could've taken another day off, you know. Any word about your dad yet?"

She shook her head. "Not really. I didn't want to be alone with my thoughts all day; being here helps. There was an iffy sighting of them; the coast guard investigator doesn't trust it, but they expanded the search area just in case."

Elaina pressed a hand on Savanna's arm. "I'm so sorry this is happening. The worry must be overwhelming. Is there anything we can do?"

"There isn't really anything any of us can do, except wait."

"My great-uncle worked on a commercial fishing boat that went missing from Lake Michigan back in the nineties." Savanna turned around to find the school's gym teacher, Andy, staring at her. "I read somewhere that Lake Michigan is the Great Lake with the most shipwrecks."

"No, it's not. That's Lake Erie," the fourth-grade teacher to his left argued.

"That doesn't make any sense. Erie's smaller and shallower. Lake Michigan's maximum depth is nine-hundred-something feet. That plus higher wind speed is why we get those crazy high swells now and then, way more dangerous than Erie," Andy said.

Stephen pulled out his phone and typed something,

turning the screen toward Andy. "Dude. See? This says Erie has more shipwrecks than the Bermuda Triangle. Lake Michigan has the most drownings—that's probably what you heard. It's the deadliest Great Lake."

"Guys!" Elaina said sharply, glaring at the two men. "I'm sure your dad is fine, Savanna. He knows what he's doing; didn't you say he's been on boats forever? Come on, first bell's about to ring, we should get going." She gathered her things and made some racket in the sink with her coffee cup and plate.

"I just meant—" Andy, the gym teacher, started. "My uncle disappeared decades ago. I doubt that kind of thing happens anymore, not with all the technology we have now."

"I think a lot of the drownings are tourists," Stephen added. He looked down at his phone. "Over 60 percent are swimmers, not boaters."

Rosa Taylor smacked Stephen's shoulder with the back of her hand. "It's not trivia night, doofus. Read the room." Rosa was married to Detective Jordan's partner, George. She had been less than friendly to Savanna in her first year at Carson Elementary but was slowly—incrementally— warming.

Savanna had been to trivia night with this bunch; she wasn't offended. Andy had no filter, ever, and Stephen couldn't help himself—he was a walking encyclopedia. But she really could've done without all the statistics before her second cup of coffee.

After the longest day of school in her life, Savanna found Rosa out front manning the pickup lane. Waiting for a lull in the steadily moving flow of cars, Savanna finally spoke. "Hey, thank you for that this morning. Stephen was getting to me."

Rosa shrugged. "No problem. Are you doing okay?"

"I guess so, under the circumstances. I just wish we'd get some good news."

Rosa nodded. "I'm praying for your father's safe return. And Sebastian's too," she added. "Although, I'm sure Winnie is enjoying the extra few days without that man underfoot."

Savanna's eyes widened. "You know Winnie? Did she say something to you?"

"We have a yoga class together. She's always complaining about him. She could do so much better than a hermit artist twenty years older than her."

"I didn't know there was that big an age gap. They seem happy, at least when I've been around them."

Rosa shrugged. "Who knows. He scooped her up off the runway during fashion week in Paris after his first wife left him, while he was at the peak of his fame and living like a rock star. At least that's how Winnie remembers it."

So that was what Chelsea had meant. Savanna had had a feeling, but didn't want to ask. It sounded much messier than she'd ever imagined as a fine arts student learning about her contemporary artist heroes.

"Anyway. I guess he cleaned up his act and got sober and decided the spotlight wasn't for him. They ended up back here, where he'd started. But Winnie never planned on spending her life locked away in the woods. She's so excited he's finally making a comeback; she's been pushing him for years to get back out there."

"Ah. I wondered what prompted Sebastian to finally take an interest in doing another exhibit after all this time. I'm glad he finally listened to his wife. I'm sure he won't regret it; the art world hasn't forgotten him."

"I don't know much about art. I'll take your word for it. Hey! Keep it moving!" Rosa blew her whistle and motioned for a dawdling minivan at the front of the line to hurry up. "It's called the kiss-and-go lane for a reason, y'know? It's always the repeat offenders holding up the line," she grumbled.

Savanna laughed. Rosa was right—and any parent would be crazy to tangle with the tough veteran teacher.

KYLE BISHOP BROUGHT her things outside onto the elegant stone front porch when she rang the bell. He carried the tote bag and laptop and set her authenticating tool case beside him.

"Hi there," she said. "I didn't expect you to have to gather all my things for me."

"It's no bother. Let me help get everything to your car." He started down the steps, laden with her tote—her brains—plus her laptop under one arm and the tool case in the other hand.

She eyed the heavy case. The Firefly was temperature sensitive. She really didn't want to lug the whole thing back into her house and then back here again as soon as her dad and Sebastian were home. Because they would be home. Soon. And then she'd be sorely behind in getting all the work done on the provenances before Sebastian's exhibit. She'd lost so much time already, not working since the awful news Sunday morning. "Kyle—can I leave my authenticating tools, please? They're a pain to tote around, and I know I'll be back to work here in a day or two as soon as Sebastian and my dad are home safe. Is that all right?"

The personal assistant hesitated a beat, not moving, and then seemed to recover. "Uh. Yes, of course. You won't need them for anything else at the moment? I'd hate for you to have to drive all the way out here again, if you have another appraising job before Mr. Alexander returns."

"Oh, I'm not appraising. I'm creating certificates of authenticity—" She stopped herself. She so automatically launched into clarifying the difference between appraising for monetary value versus her authenticating role, but it didn't matter right now. "I've kept my schedule open to work on Sebastian's collection. I won't need the case for anything else."

He nodded, turning and opening the front door. "No problem, then. I'll go put your case back in the studio."

"Thank you—sorry for the trouble."

"Oh," he said, turning to glance back at her.

Whatever he said next was lost to the abrupt noise in her brain—she knew why he looked so familiar; not now, but the first time she'd met him, Sunday morning, right here. That déjà vu response suddenly made perfect sense. She hadn't seen him at the grocery store or anywhere else in town—he'd been at Sweetwater Boats the morning of the regatta, arguing with Gus Connelly. She blinked, staring at him. That was it. She was certain.

"Do you boat?" she blurted. Good God, she really needed to work on her filter. Sydney was rubbing off on her.

"Do I boat?" he asked, turning to face her from the doorway. He frowned, staring at her like she was an annoying bug on his windshield. "No, unless I'm a passenger. I suppose you could say I'm a skilled boat passenger." He cracked a brief smile, and it looked odd on his normally serious face. "Why do you ask?"

He was throwing her off. She was positive it was him; the glasses and mildly irritated expression were the same as that rude customer talking to Gus. But Kyle had no reason to lie to her. Maybe he wasn't renting a boat at Sweetwater; maybe he'd just talked with Gus about something the morning of the regatta. Her gaze dropped to Kyle's hand, where there had been a large flesh-colored bandage a few days ago. It was gone; a red abrasion now visible. He followed her line of sight down to his hand.

He opened and closed his fingers, holding it up. "Rope burn. Sebastian needed help with the yacht lines Saturday morning; he sent me for a new set. He probably should've gotten your dad or someone more skilled to help get them rigged up. I was useless after this happened."

"Ah." That made sense, actually. Plus, it'd be easy enough to check his story with Gus if she wasn't sure. "It looks painful. I hope it heals quickly."

"It's already a lot better," he said. "Anyway. Just let me know when you'd like to come back." He picked up the case and went inside, the heavy door swinging closed behind him.

She was on her way to her car when the front door was flung open once more and Sebastian's large fluffy Bouvier bounded out, Winnie close behind him.

She rushed toward Savanna. "Wait! Do you have news? Have they been found?"

She shook her head. "No, not that I've heard. You haven't gotten any updates either?" The dog circled her, sniffing, and then sat at her feet, tongue hanging out one side of his wide canine grin.

Winnie heaved a sigh, shoulders drooping. "Nothing. I don't know what to do. I hate being here without him." Her eyes glistened with unshed tears. "Goodness, Ringo certainly likes you."

Savanna patted the dog's big head. "I like him too. He's a sweetheart. Hey, buddy. Sydney will be so jealous I got to see you." Ringo had become a regular at Fancy Tails & Treats. He had a standing weekly appointment for Syd to brush through his wild double-coated mop of water-resistant fur, and monthly appointments for baths and haircuts. "With Sebastian away, I'm glad you have him for company. And Kyle too," she quickly added, glancing up at the large house. She didn't mean to infer that the happy dog was a better companion than the artist's personal assistant.

"We barely see each other," she said. "Kyle Bishop is my husband's valet, first and foremost. He's not a friend."

Now Savanna noticed what was different about the artist's wife. Winnie was normally made up in full makeup and perfectly done hair, but her eyes bore dark circles beneath them, her blond hair unkempt and oily looking. The flowy gold lounge pants she wore were inside out, the seams showing. The left pocket jutted out near her hip.

Winnie looked down. "Oh." She briefly covered her eyes, shaking her head. "How embarrassing. I'm just—I'm so worried I can hardly think straight."

The poor woman looked as anxious as Savanna felt. She impulsively opened her arms, offering a hug, and Winnie clung to her. The older woman finally let go, stepping back and pulling a tissue from her pocket for her eyes.

"I really think we're going to get good news soon. They're both tough, both good sailors," Savanna said. "Winnie, maybe Chelsea or Griffin might come and stay with you until Sebastian is back?" She nearly added that she and her family were taking shifts keeping her mom company but bit her tongue—Winnie didn't seem as fortunate.

She shrugged. "Maybe. My brother said I should come stay with him. He's in Lake Haven. But I don't want to be gone when they find my Bas."

"I think it's a good idea," Savanna said softly. "We all need someone to lean on right now. It'll be fine if you're with your brother when Sebastian comes home—Lake Haven's only about twenty minutes south of here, right? The police and coast guard have our numbers."

"You're right." She wiped her nose. "I'll call Daniel and let him know I'm coming. I'm sure Chelsea will watch Ringo for me. I can't just stay here crying all day and night. Thank you, honey. You give your mom a hug from me, okay?"

By the time Savanna emerged onto the highway from the woodsy drive away from the Alexander home, she was close to tears herself. She wanted to believe what she'd told Winnie; that the men were fine and would be home soon. She'd tried as hard as she could to stay optimistic. Her heart leaped as her dashboard screen lit up with an incoming call from her uncle.

"Uncle Freddie? Did they find him?" Whenever her uncles called, it was almost always Max reaching out on behalf of both of them. But authoritative Uncle Freddie had made himself the point person since Harlan's disappearance. Seeing Freddie's name on the screen made Savanna certain there was news.

"We have an update, of sorts. Where are you? Can you come by the house?"

"What does that mean?" She made a sharp right turn, heading toward her parents' house instead of home. "Is Dad okay?"

"It's, ah… We'll go over it when you get here. See you soon." Before her uncle hung up, Detective Jordan's voice in the background came through the Bluetooth system, too clear to miss—*county medical examiner's report.*

As quickly as her heart had jumped, it now plummeted.

Chapter Eight

SAVANNA FELT LIKE she was stuck in a bad dream. She stood in the kitchen doorway, fighting the urge to run. Nearly her whole family was gathered in the sunny kitchen, cheerful yellow walls softly lit from the afternoon sun. If not for the presence of Nick Jordan, she might've been here for a Sunday dinner.

"It's not him." Her mother's tone was firm, resolute. Before Savanna could ask, her mom filled her in, taking no time to soften the news. "A body washed up onshore in Charlevoix. It's not your father. I don't give a rat's heinie about protocol, none of us is going up there to identify the body."

"Depending on the amount of time the body was in the water, it's going to be hard to determine—" Detective Jordan began, but Charlotte interrupted, slapping one hand on the granite countertop.

"We are going to let the medical examiner do his thing. That's his job, isn't it? If there are still unanswered questions when he's finished, we'll discuss what's next." Her mother's auburn hair was pulled severely back into a ponytail, her face devoid of her usual light makeup.

But her hair was wet—she'd showered. That had to be a

good sign. That, and the fact that she was arguing with the detective. But she wasn't sure her mom's decision made sense.

"Where's Skylar?" Savanna murmured to Uncle Max. Her parents sometimes took Skylar's opinion more seriously than hers or Syd's.

"We called her. She's tied up at the moment, love."

Jordan pushed the stool back and stood. "You understand, we may not get a definitive answer right away. Don't you think it'd be prudent to rule it out and move forward on a better lead, at least?" His gaze moved from Charlotte to Freddie.

Savanna glanced at Sydney, leaning silently against the sink and looking like she might cry. Her little sister's expression matched her own; they were the children in this scenario. Their mom and uncle were the grown-ups, making the hard decisions and trying to shield them from hurt and harm. They weren't kids anymore, but their strongest link was missing...once again.

Savanna wished for Skylar's voice of reason. "Mom. I think—" she began.

"Savanna, no." The sharp edge in her voice was nonnegotiable. "None of us is going up there. Not now, not for this. Your father is an excellent swimmer. *If* there was some reason for him to have to leave the yacht, he'd still be fine."

Jordan gave up. "All right, then. I'll keep you updated."

"Nick." Her mom's voice stopped him on his path to the door, the familiarity in her use of his first name issuing a reminder they'd all known each other long enough to be frank with each other. "I know you're only doing your job. But it's not Harlan. If it was, I'd know."

He softened, sympathy transforming his features. "I believe you believe that. I want to trust you're right; I do. I'm just trying to cut out any delays in us getting him home."

Savanna followed him out. "Hey. I'll go," she said, stopping on the wraparound porch.

Jordan faced her. "The admiral asked if it'd be possible, but they're still putting puzzle pieces together after that questionable sighting far off the coast. This...new development...is just tough. With no definitive identifying marks to go by, we'll probably be waiting for labs and dental records to know for sure."

Her stomach lurched. "But my dad has that tattoo. On his arm, from when he was in the Marines. Does the body—the person—who washed up onshore have that?"

"The medical examiner isn't able to determine that. There's some, uh, damage."

Images of the vastness of Lake Michigan played on a reel in Savanna's mind. Deadly undercurrents, large fish species, depths of—as her insensitive coworker had pointed out—900 feet.

Her eyes burned with a sudden rush of tears that she blinked back. "I'll go. I hope my mom's right. But I can see how it'd help the focus of investigation if someone could, for sure, take a look now and say it isn't him."

Detective Jordan frowned, holding her gaze. "Right. Or that it is him."

A shudder passed through her. "It won't be." She felt

none of her mother's certainty in her own voice. "Can you send me the address?"

"Will do. You'll be heading to Charlevoix Hospital. The morgue doubles as the medical examiner's field station. It's about a three-hour drive up the coast, but I'd already planned on my deputy taking your mother there. He can take you. You won't need to drive."

"No, we won't." Sydney spoke from behind her. "I texted Finn to ask if he could fly us up there. He's in the middle of a shift; he can't. But he got ahold of Aidan and let him know what's going on. Aidan's driving us."

The queasy bundle of nerves in the pit of Savanna's stomach settled a bit for the first time since her uncle's phone call. Having Aidan and her sister along for the daunting task would help.

Less than twenty minutes later, Aidan showed up with little Mollie and their happy mutt, Jersey, in the car with him. He cleared up Savanna's confusion right away. "We're dropping Mollie and Jersey off at Grandma and Grandpa's house on the way. I heard a rumor that there might be ice cream, if they behave," he stage-whispered, eliciting a giggle from his daughter.

"I always behave, Daddy."

Savanna slid into the back seat beside Mollie, letting Sydney take the front until they reached Aidan's in-laws' house. Aidan had moved to Michigan from New York when he'd gotten married, so his wife could be close to her family. She'd gotten sick when Mollie was only three. Aidan had stayed after she passed so his daughter could grow up with her grandparents in her life. Orphaned when they were teens, Aidan and Finn had no other family left now.

"Hey," Savanna whispered, tipping her head to Mollie's. "Where's your dragonfly today? I saw one on your dad's tie."

Mollie's eyes widened. Savanna guessed the girl was still not used to someone else being in on her secret language shared with her dad. After Aidan had told her about Mollie's morning ritual of choosing a matching item for them both to wear, a habit developed in the early days after losing her mother as a way of keeping her connected to her dad, Savanna had learned to look for the chosen items every time she saw Aidan. Sometimes it was something as simple as rainbow-striped socks, other times it was turtle cuff links for her dad and turtle barrettes in the little girl's wispy, fine blond hair.

Mollie tapped the tiny pink rabbit charm on Savanna's wrist, a gift on the day she and her dad had proposed. She rarely took it off. "Mrs. Fluffypants says she can't tell you. You just have to look."

This was why she loved her teaching job—kids had a way of distracting you from the big, heavy life stuff, if even for only a moment. She sat back, scrutinizing the girl. "Hmmm."

"No hints either," Mollie said. And then crossed one pink Croc-clad foot over the other on the console. Among the unicorn accessories attached to the small shoes was one lone blue dragonfly.

Savanna pursed her lips, pretending not to have seen it. She cocked her head this way and that, lifting a few strands of the girl's hair and finally fixing her gaze on the Crocs. "There it is!"

"You almost couldn't find it." She laughed. "Oh! There's Bandit and Scout!" She squirmed to see over the front seat as they pulled into a long driveway and past a wide green pasture with two horses meandering toward the split-rail fence.

"Bandit and Scout?" Syd asked.

"Bandit is the gray one, and Scout is the brown spotty one," Mollie said, pointing. "They're my horses."

"Well." Aidan raised an eyebrow in the rearview mirror at the girl. "They're Grandma and Grandpa's horses. But they sure love you, don't they, Mol? Come on, I see Grandma on the porch."

While Aidan handed off Mollie and the dog, Sydney swapped front seat for back with Savanna, hanging over the seat with her elbows poking out to the sides. "Dang. I mean, jeez, Savvy. They must have fifty acres here. At least."

She had to admit Aidan's in-laws' place was impressive. "It's nice, I know."

"My manicure is nice," Sydney said, waggling her fingers in Savanna's face. "Ice cream is nice. This is something else. What are they like—the grandparents?"

"I don't know. They seem normal, I guess. I've only been here once before, with Aidan, to pick up Mollie."

"He's got a good setup," Sydney said. "Built in babysitters close by and money's never an issue."

"His wife died," Savanna said, turning to stare at Syd. "I doubt he sees this as a good setup; I'm sure the grandparents don't either."

"Sorry. You're right."

"I really wish you had a filter sometimes," Savanna grumbled.

"Just be careful. That's all I'm saying."

"What do you mean?"

"You're the new wife-to-be. Are they awful to you?"

"No! Of course not, they're always nice. Why would you—" She clamped her lips shut as Aidan opened the car door.

With Mollie gone and Sydney's words ringing in her ears, Savanna fell quiet for a long stretch of road as they headed north. Mollie's grandparents had been nothing but kind to her every time they'd crossed paths. Her sister watched way too much reality TV; she was anticipating problems where there were none. Savanna pushed the off-base remarks out of her mind, but that only allowed earlier intrusive thoughts back in. No matter how she tried, she couldn't stop picturing her dad in a hospital basement morgue on the medical examiner's table, lifeless and pale, devoid now of everything that made him *him*. How had she taken for granted that he'd return to them intact, whole, healthy? He was getting older. He wasn't necessarily the tough, invincible dad she'd grown up with anymore.

Aidan's warm hand enveloped hers, grounding her and drawing her back to the car, the trip, her sister, and her fiancé right here with her. "You were far away," he said quietly. "What are you thinking?"

She shook her head. "Nothing good." She squeezed his hand, holding on. Syd's chatter with Aidan had petered out;

in the back seat, her sister's head was tipped back, her mouth slightly open while she softly snored. "How can she sleep right now? Where are we, anyway?"

"Sleeping can be a stress response. I can't imagine how hard this must be for both of you." He tapped the GPS screen, zooming out. "We're coming up on Cadillac. About halfway there."

"Jordan said there'll be a special agent meeting us at the hospital," Savanna said.

Aidan didn't respond, leaving a comfortable silence between them. Just like her dad. Had she subconsciously chosen a man like her father to spend her life with? If she had, she'd chosen well.

"I feel like I'm never going to see him again. Alive," she clarified, her voice barely a whisper.

He lightly stroked the side of her hand with his thumb. "I think that's a normal reaction to all of this. It's probably why your mother chose not to go." He paused. "She seems very certain he's all right. She seems like a level-headed person."

"She is. She's the practical one between them. Maybe I'm feeling this way because I'm trying to prepare myself...but that's crazy. There's no way to be prepared if it really is my dad."

"True. It probably makes more sense to focus on the likelihood it's not your dad, right?"

She nodded.

After a while, he spoke again, his tone soft. "You're going to draw blood if you keep biting your lip like that."

She hadn't realized she was doing it. "Ugh. Thank you."

"Talk to me. Tell me what you're thinking."

She didn't want to. She was a terrible daughter. She'd taken so much for granted. Most of her friends either had difficult relationships with their parents or had lost a parent. How fortunate she was to have the ones she did. She knew it—maybe she hadn't realized it until she grew up, but she'd known it now for a long time without even thinking about it. Yet she'd never said as much to either of them. "I wish I'd told him I love him," she blurted, her voice cracking. "I should have. I'm so mad at myself for not saying it—I can't even remember the last time I told him."

"Oh, hey, Savanna, it's all right. You're being way too hard on yourself. Your dad knows how much you love him. Do you really think he doesn't know? That's the kind of thing your family says to each other all the time, even when you don't say the words. I've seen it."

She sniffled. "Yeah? For real? I never thought about it that way."

He put an arm out and she leaned in, hugging him sideways across the console. He kissed the top of her head. "For real," he echoed. "Your dad knows, without a doubt."

It was a little after nine when Aidan pulled into the Charlevoix Hospital parking lot. Walking toward the entrance, the sound of waves lapping at the shore was audible beyond the hospital. It was that close to the water. Her thoughts morbidly in line with her anxiety-ridden emotions, Savanna wondered how often the hospital and medical examiner dealt with bodies washing up onshore.

Inside, a man who was clearly military approached, removing his cap and tucking it beneath one arm. "Admiral Moore, ma'am." He shook Savanna's hand. "Ma'am. Sir," he said, doing the same with Sydney and Aidan. "You're Harlan Shepherd's daughters, I presume? Your county sheriff's department let me know you'd be coming in place of your mother."

Introductions were made all around. Moore ushered them away from the reception area, speaking in low tones. "I know this is an extremely stressful situation. We'll head down to meet with the medical examiner when you're ready. It's fine if you'd like some time first to gather your thoughts. There's a family waiting room we can use."

"Can we just do it?" Sydney asked. "We've had hours to gather our thoughts; this is an awful feeling. I want to get it over with."

She was right. But now, faced with the terrifying prospect of getting answers she didn't want, Savanna just wanted to turn and run out of the hospital.

"Savvy?" Syd had that look, the one that always got her way when they were little.

She nodded. "Is that all right, Admiral?"

"Of course." Moore led them down a long hallway to an elevator, which took them to the ground floor and another series of hallways.

They stopped at a set of double doors. A metal plaque on the wall read G108. That was all. Moore pressed a button below the plaque and the doors swung open, revealing a second set of doors, these marked simply as MORGUE. She'd never seen one before and didn't want to now. Beside her, Aidan kept one arm protectively around her shoulders. Sydney sucked air through her teeth, and Aidan placed a hand on her back.

He spoke for the first time since they'd arrived. "Most hospital morgues are very similar. They're set up as a functioning lab, with, uh, storage along one or more of the walls," he said, hesitating before going on. "There's usually a covered gurney or two toward the center of the room if there were hospital patients who've passed away recently. In a small hospital like this, even handling the surrounding area's incidents, this may not be a busy place. There's a medical examiner—different than a coroner—who determines cause of death for the death certificate," Aidan finished, his tone low.

"That's Dr. Jim Andrews today," Moore interjected.

The admiral was as kind and respectful as could be, and Aidan's cautiously worded description was clearly crafted to avoid causing more distress, but all of Savanna's initial bravado had deserted her. She'd been sure this was the right move, but now she felt sick. It couldn't be her dad in there.

Sydney took her hand, and they followed the admiral in, leaving Aidan to wait in the vestibule between the two sets of doors. The smell of formaldehyde and something else— decay or heartbreak or death—assaulted her nose.

Beside the only sheet-covered gurney in the room was a compact silver-haired man who had to be Dr. Andrews. His face was mournful, the corners of his mouth drawn down, eyebrows scrunched up with concern over too-wide eyes behind thick glasses as he greeted them. His features must be permanently arranged into this sympathetic mask.

Moore explained the body had been recovered from the steeply sloped dunes two miles down the Lake Michigan coast. High-pitched ringing in her ears drowned out whatever the doctor said, his focus moving from them to the admiral. The ringing finally quieted and her breath whooshed in and out loudly between her ears. She glanced down to find Sydney clutching her hand with both of her own. Her sister's already pale pink skin was an ashy white. The doctor waited for them to say they were ready and then lowered the sheet to the man's chest. He was older, though how old was impossible to guess. His skin was mottled and bloated with large abrasions over the visible portion of his body. His hair and build were similar enough to Harlan's that she instantly understood why they'd been called here.

Sydney clapped a hand over her mouth, a sob escaping her.

She turned and wrapped her arms around Savanna, thin frame shaking. "It's not him," she whispered. "Oh my God, it's not him."

Savanna forced herself not to look away; they had to be sure. She scrutinized the poor man's face, jawline, ears. Her gaze moved to the edge of the gurney where part of his hand was visible under the sheet. She met Dr. Andrews's big eyes around Sydney's unkempt mass of red hair. "Can you...could you move the sheet? I need to see his hands."

Syd let go of her and stepped back. "It's not him, Savvy. Can't you see that?"

Dr. Andrews carefully moved the sheet away on either side of the body, uncovering the man's hands.

Savanna's eyes blurred with tears as she leaned forward, peering at them. "It's not him. I just wanted to be certain. This is not our dad."

"All right," he said, gently covering the man up. "I'm glad to hear that."

"You're positive?" Admiral Moore asked.

"Yes. I'm sure. We're sure." Her voice sounded calm in her ears, but her knees tried to noodle under her. Relief coursed through her, a sort of elation that instantly induced guilt at being so happy so close to this nameless, unfortunate deceased man. "I'm very sorry for this man's loved ones. I hope you find out who he is."

In the vestibule, Aidan pulled them both into a hug, not letting go until they did.

"It's not him. He's still out there—he's still okay. I hope he's still okay," Savanna amended.

"He's still okay," Sydney said, her words coming out in hitching hiccups. "Mom was right. He just has to come back to us."

The mood on their way back through the mostly empty hallways to the parking lot was like the difference between night and day. Savanna phoned their mom and gave her the good news, such as it was. Admiral Moore updated them on the current search efforts and promised to call with any new developments. In the red glow of the ambulance bay as Aidan started the car for the drive back, Savanna's phone rang over Bluetooth. The digital dashboard screen read

Admiral Sam Moore.

Sydney glanced back at the parking lot where they'd left the admiral when they separated. "Did he forget to tell us something?"

"Probably." Savanna answered the call.

"Ms. Shepherd, wait right there, I'm coming over to you."

She shrugged, Aidan and her sister looking as mystified as she felt. "Okay, we'll wait."

Moore's black sedan parked beside them, and he got out, approaching the passenger-side window where Savanna sat. Sydney rolled her window down.

"Was there something else?" Aidan asked, leaning over to see the investigator.

He nodded once. "Your father's been found. He's still aboard the *Serendipity*. The yacht was located in Wisconsin waters, near Baileys Harbor. The update just posted on our investigation channel. Our flight paramedic and health service techs on-site are working to stabilize him for transfer."

Chapter Nine

"TRANSFER TO WHERE?"

"Stabilize him? What happened? How bad is it?"

"When can we see him? Can he be brought to Anderson Memorial?"

Admiral Moore waited for a break in the rapid-fire questions. "He can't be taken all the way back home just yet. They'll medevac him to Door County Medical Center. Once—"

"Door County, Wisconsin?" Syd shrieked. "He'll be all alone, at least until we can get there. Isn't there something you can do?"

"I'm sorry, I really am. It's the closest critical access trauma center and the safest course of action for your dad. You don't want him on a long flight right now. We don't know the full extent of his injuries—"

"What injuries? What's wrong with him?" Savanna asked.

"Just a sec. Let's do this," Aidan spoke up. "We should get your mother on the phone again, right? So she'll hear the details straight from the investigator. Do you mind joining us for a few minutes, Admiral? You can have my spot." He unbuckled and opened the car door.

"We could head back inside to discuss everything, that might be more comfortable for all of you," Moore offered.

"No! No, that will take too long. We need to get home," Sydney said. She huffed out a breath impatiently. "Please. Please, Admiral, can you just get in and we'll call our mom? I want to get on the road to Dad."

"Of course." With the admiral in the front seat of Aidan's SUV, and Aidan beside Sydney in the back, Savanna got her mother on the phone.

"Mom? I'm sorry it's late. We're with Admiral Moore. We were about to head home when he received news about Dad—they've found him. He's alive," she finished, eyes flooding with tears as her throat swelled.

Charlotte's gasp was audible through the car's speakers. "Oh goodness. Skylar, come here quick."

"She finally showed up," Sydney murmured. "About time."

"Stop it," Savanna whispered. "You have no idea what she's dealing with." She groaned inwardly. She'd promised to keep Skylar's marital issues from their soon-to-be-wed sister; maybe Syd would forget, with everything else going on.

"Admiral Moore, hello. Thank you. What are you able to tell us?" Charlotte asked.

After he repeated the information about Harlan being stabilized for transfer, Skylar's voice came through. "When will you update us on the rest of the findings? The condition of the yacht—did it just go off course or was it something else? And what's the status of owner, Sebastian Alexander? Was he also aboard?"

"The entire craft will be investigated, so I have nothing to share yet regarding what exactly happened. As soon as we know something, you'll hear from us, I promise," Moore said. "Mr. Alexander was not on board."

Charlotte broke the silence that followed that grave news. "How awful. I'll be on a plane tonight to Wisconsin. How might we learn about what's happening with my husband, medically? I'd like to know what we're talking about. Is he conscious? How badly is he hurt? Will he need surgery?" Her voice barely wavered through questions Savanna was afraid to hear the answers to. Her mother was the strongest woman she knew.

Moore cleared his throat and ran a hand over his faint five-o'clock shadow. It was the first time he seemed to falter. "Harlan wasn't conscious when the yacht was discovered. He's dehydrated and may have a fractured wrist, but he is breathing on his own. His vital signs are strong despite the condition he was found in." He paused. "He did suffer some sort of impact to the head. There was some bleeding. The blow likely caused a loss of consciousness, though it's not clear yet when that happened or how long he's been unconscious."

The boost in hope she felt when Moore mentioned her dad's strong vital signs swiftly plummeted with that news. "Is this something Sebastian could have done? Did he do this to my dad?"

"There's nothing to indicate that. The blood loss your father experienced is at the stern of the boat, in the cockpit. At the bow, near the jib sail, my investigators found a concerning amount of blood surrounding a broken deck railing. There's no blood trail from bow to stern. It hasn't rained. Forensics still has to process the yacht, but preliminary evidence suggests Mr. Alexander was, like your father, also a victim."

The car was quiet for the first portion of the trip back. It was decided that Charlotte and Skylar would fly out tonight, with the uncles taking care of baby Hannah and Nolan until Travis could pick them up. By the time Aidan passed the halfway mark of Cadillac, Savanna's mom texted that she and Skylar were boarding their plane.

"I never trusted that guy." Sydney had moved to the middle of the back seat, and leaned forward now, scowling out the windshield. "Pretentious old, rich dude... Did you ever stop to think maybe there's a reason his son hates him? His daughter probably does too; I mean, I would, if Dad married someone my age."

Savanna turned in her seat to face her fired-up little sister. "Dad would never."

"Duh. I'm just saying."

"Sebastian's not who you think he is. There's nothing pretentious about him. He ran away from his fame. And he and Winnie are very sweet together." Rosa's comments popped into her head, and she dismissed them; everybody complained about their partner sometimes. "What makes you think he'd turn on Dad while they're sailing in a regatta together? That doesn't make sense."

She shrugged. "Why are you defending him? He's missing and Dad's hurt. Who knows what happened."

She tried to see it from Sydney's perspective. Maybe she didn't know Sebastian as well as she thought. But... "Syd, Sebastian isn't a big man. Dad probably has fifty pounds on him and at least six or seven inches in height. How do you imagine he'd be able to knock Dad out and get away? What about the blood they found on the bow? I think it's more likely that he went overboard." She pressed her fingers onto her eyelids. "God, though, I hope that's not what happened. I can't even imagine how Winnie and his kids are taking the news." And the art exhibit—she and Britt would have to cancel everything if he wasn't found. And if he was—*when* he was—she had a lot of work cut out for her in his studio. She was glad she'd left her heavy kit there, despite Kyle having to having to carry it back upstairs. That interaction had poked and prodded her all evening; he'd acted so weird about her keeping her tools there. Or had he? Maybe it wasn't that. It was when she'd mentioned coming back to work on the authentication that he'd glitched. There was no better word for it—he'd frozen, not answering her at first. Like it didn't compute that she'd need to come back.

"You're probably right," Sydney said. "Whoever did this will get what they deserve. Dad just better be okay."

"How very zen of you," Savanna said wryly. "I'd rather the police made sure whoever did it gets what they deserve."

"Same. Tell me what's going on with Skylar," she demanded, changing topics without warning.

She groaned, turning to stare out the window. She'd hoped to avoid the question. She pressed her forehead to the cool glass. Dark silhouettes of towering trees rushed by. They were the only car on the road, an eerie sensation, even though she knew it was only due to it being late at night on a random Tuesday.

"Savvy. Do you really think I haven't noticed she's constantly on her own? Or doesn't even show up? Where's Travis been? He's always super-dad."

"I really don't know anything." She turned and faced her little sister, whose wedding was less than two weeks away. She'd never seen Syd as head over heels in love with anyone before Finn. None of her relationships ever lasted longer than a few months, mostly due to Sydney breaking things off.

Then Finn Gallager had blown into town, quite literally. A med flight paramedic and pilot, it'd taken aviator-clad, crooked-grin-wearing Finn less than five minutes to piss off her sister—and reel her in with intrigue at the same time. Savanna and Skylar had known before Sydney did that this time was different.

"Why didn't she come to the regatta?" Sydney asked.

"She was working."

"So, where was she tonight, when we were all dealing with the possibility that Dad was on a metal gurney in a morgue up north?"

"I seriously don't know. I swear," Savanna said. "She's not saying much. It seems like she's just stressed and overwhelmed with work right now." It sounded like a lame excuse even as she said it.

"Which is exactly when Travis would normally be taking care of Nolan and Hannah and handling every little detail like always, so Sky can focus on a case. So, what's up with him? Where was he tonight? Or last night, even, when we were all at Mom and Dad's?"

"I don't know." This conversation was making her sad. "People go through things sometimes. They'll be okay, don't worry. They always are."

"Ugh. When will you two stop treating me like I'm five? Stop trying to protect me. I'm a grown-up."

Savanna snickered, pressing her lips closed in an attempt to squelch it.

"What?"

"Nothing."

Sydney snaked her hand over the seat and Savanna jumped at the sudden prickle of pain.

"You pinched me!" She gripped her arm. "That hurt, you snot. If you want people to treat you like a grown-up, act like a grown-up. And maybe don't say 'grown-up'—actual adults don't call themselves that."

Aidan laughed, eyeing the two of them from the driver's seat. "Sorry. She has a point. Mollie says all the time that she can't wait to be a grown-up."

"Whatever." Sydney slouched into the back seat.

Savanna could feel her glare right through the back of her head. "She's trying not to rain on your wedding. I don't blame her. She and Travis will figure this out. I'm sure it's nothing serious."

"It seems serious. Maybe it's money stuff. Finn and I were reading that money is the biggest thing people fight about, which is so dumb."

"That could be it." She'd gotten the feeling it was much more personal than that, but hopefully she was wrong. "I really don't know anything. She's too private sometimes."

"All the time," Sydney said. "At least we know Travis is a good guy. He'd never do anything to hurt her."

"Right, true," she agreed, not feeling it. Was he a good guy? Nobody really knew what went on inside someone's relationship. Her ex-fiancé, Rob, had presented one version of himself to his family and colleagues, but an entirely different version to her.

Savanna's phone rang, the SUV dashboard lighting up with an unknown number.

"Answer it—it could be the hospital," Sydney ordered.

"No." She frowned at the screen. "That's a Chicago area code. I'm not answering that." Good Lord, what if it was Rob or someone from Kenilworth, calling from a new number? She shivered from the chill that ran up her spine. What creepy timing.

"Oh my gawd, get over yourself. It could be the coast guard or life flight or anyone calling about Dad!" Sydney darted forward over the seat and hit the green accept button. "Hello?"

"Hello, is this Savanna Shepherd?"

She didn't recognize the female voice. "Yes. Who is this?"

"Savanna, this is Maeve Davis. We met at the marina on Saturday. Forgive me for bothering you. I've just heard the good news about your father. I'm wondering if he's said anything yet about Sebastian. I'm going crazy with worry over here."

Chapter Ten

"MAEVE, HELLO! I, um. My dad was unconscious when they found him. How did you—you must've talked to Winnie?"

"Chelsea actually updated me. Did the coast guard investigator share any details with you? They aren't telling the family much, just that there was no sign of Sebastian."

"I'm so sorry. I'm sure this is awful for them—and you," Savanna said. "I don't think the coast guard knows much at this point. If we hear anything new, I can let you know. I really hope Sebastian is somehow okay."

"Please. I'd appreciate it. I hope your dad improves quickly too."

As soon as the call ended, Aidan cocked an eyebrow at her. "That's Sebastian's artist friend, right? That was a little odd."

"Very. Chelsea really did give her my number—I wasn't sure she would. But is it weird that she's checking in with us before Winnie or Chelsea do?"

"A little, yeah. Why didn't you tell her about the blood on the bow of the yacht?" Sydney asked. "It sounds like they have less information than we do."

"I can't share that with her," Savanna said, wide-eyed. "I

trust Sebastian. And Maeve Davis—I mean, she's an icon. But what if you're right? What if this all happened because of something he did? Jordan never shares details in an active investigation; I think it's up to Admiral Moore or his team to update the Alexanders, right?"

"Good call," Aidan said.

A little over an hour later, Savanna and Sydney climbed the steps to their parents' front porch. Aidan's headlights swept across the dark driveway as he turned around to leave; the hospital had paged him about one of his critical patients as they were getting back into town. Uncle Freddie opened the front door, motioning them inside, a finger to his lips. He pointed to the couch as they crossed to the kitchen: Nolan was fast asleep on the couch, and Uncle Max snored softly from the recliner, one hand draped over the edge of Hannah's portable crib beside him.

After he'd carefully pulled the double pocket doors closed to separate the rooms, he dropped into a nearby chair, rubbing his eyes. "Are you all right? I hate that you two had to see whoever the poor man in the morgue was up there."

"We're okay. How are you, though? Why are the kids still here?" Savanna asked.

Normally a robust, energetic mid-fifty-something, Uncle Freddie looked exhausted.

"I'm fine. I've forgotten what little kids are like. Ellie wore us out when she was Nolan's age, and I was a lot younger then. He's inquisitive and curious, just like she was. Uncle Max keeps up with him better than I do—but he'll gloat if he hears that. I'll deny I said it." When Freddie met and married Uncle Max years ago in London, he'd acquired a daughter along with a husband. Cousin Ellie's biological parents had died in a house fire when she was two, leaving their only daughter to their good friend Max Watson. Eloise May Watson-Quinn was a sophomore at University of Michigan now, but Savanna remembered her at Nolan's age. She'd been a precocious bundle of energy herself.

"You two still have the knack. He's out cold in there, and you even got the baby to sleep." She glanced at Sydney, who was midyawn. "Why hasn't Travis picked them up yet?"

Uncle Freddie shook his head. "He called. He couldn't make it back to Carson tonight. I guess he's out of town for business." His expression and tone said more than his words.

"Huh." Her face flushed, cheeks burning with exasperation.

What the hell, Travis? She wanted to go find him and yell at him on Skylar's behalf. Of all the times for him to flake, this was about the worst. Sky needed him; so did his kids. None of this was the Travis they all knew.

Freddie didn't comment further. "Listen, your mother and sister just landed; she texted me. They'll be at the hospital in less than an hour. I have strict instructions from your mom to tell you to go home and try to get some sleep. She'll let us know as soon as she learns anything about Harlan's status, but we've already been notified he's regaining consciousness. That's a great sign."

"I'd figured we'd just get on a plane tonight," Savanna said.

Sydney yawned again. "I'm wiped out. I'm all right with

waiting till morning—he's going to be okay, right?"

Uncle Freddie didn't answer right away. "I don't want to guess at that, love. But yes, it sounds as if he's more stable now than when he was found."

"It's a short flight," Savanna said. "If anything gets worse overnight, we can get there fast. I'm pretty exhausted too." The burst of fear-fueled adrenaline at the morgue had taken its toll; her entire body felt fatigued.

Today had been the longest day ever.

BRIGHT AND EARLY Wednesday, Savanna waited by the coffee bar in Anderson Memorial's lobby. Skylar had called at six a.m. to say the Door County attending physician had cleared Harlan to be transported by medevac back home this morning. Last night's doctor had warned them he could be there for several days before being deemed fit for transfer. When she'd asked what had changed between last night and this morning, Skylar said, "Mom called in a favor."

Savanna could only imagine who could grant such a favor. Charlotte Shepherd worked as an independently contracted business consultant. She'd been flown to nearly every state and worked for dozens and dozens of high-profile companies, helping them improve their work model and increase their bottom line. Their mom leveraging a change in hospital protocol made Savanna nervous. But Skylar had promised Harlan was doing better than last night and had been in and out of consciousness, and the attending doctor there was comfortable with his transfer.

The sliding doors into the ER admitting area opened and the Gallager brothers came through, heading toward her. Finn's navy blue paramedic jacket bore the gold hospital emblem on the shoulder, and Aidan was sharply dressed in a black suit and pale blue Brooks Brothers button-down. They bore a familial resemblance, both tall, both with dark hair and light skin, Finn leaner and lankier where Aidan's frame was more substantial, solid. Finn's eyes were as green as Aidan's were blue. Both brothers possessed striking grins. Finn's quick and confident; Aidan's more reserved and with the power to reduce her to a pile of mush in seconds.

He graced her with a mild version of that grin now, one arm slipping around her waist as he bent to kiss her. "Good morning, beautiful. You doing all right?"

"Yeah," she said, heart beating a little faster. Her manners kicked in. "Hey, Finn. Didn't you just work last night? You're on again?"

"I picked up a day shift. I've got to run, but I wanted to let you know your dad's life flight is five minutes out."

"Thank you!" She checked her phone. "Syd should be here soon."

"I'll catch her later. Give your dad my best," he said, bringing two fingers to his forehead in a mock salute to her and Aidan. "Nice work, big brother."

Savanna tipped her head curiously after Finn had jogged through the doors to the ambulance bay. "What nice work is that?"

"I'm the cardiac consult for your dad when he gets here.

He'll be in ICU stepdown until he's fully conscious and stable, but he was found to have an arrhythmia that your mother says is new for him. Dehydration can be a trigger. The Door County doc thought that's what brought it on but still noted it should be checked."

"Oh." She worked to dissect all of that. "He has an arrhythmia? Is it dangerous?"

"Probably not; try not to worry. I'll be seeing him shortly after he arrives, and we'll get a twelve lead and an echocardiogram. Some labs too," he added, more to himself than to her. "I'm just glad I got the consult. It'll be easier to keep you and your mom in the loop on his status."

"Thank you, Dr. Gallager. You're the best."

He held her gaze as she stared up at him, his lips curving into a half grin. "That's what my fiancée tells me. She's pretty amazing herself."

Her cheeks flushed instantly. Sometimes he left her at a loss for words.

The ICU stepdown unit was on the third floor of Anderson Memorial. They'd just stepped off the elevator when Aidan was called to the emergency department. He left her with a promise to be right back. She was cleared by the young nurse at the horseshoe-shaped nurses' station, who pointed her toward room 312.

Her mother stood and pulled her into a hug as Savanna entered the room. She sucked in her breath at the sight of her dad. There were tubes and IV lines and monitors surrounding him. Colored wires sprouted from the neck and arms of his hospital gown. It took her a moment to register that the soft, rhythmic beeping was his heartbeat on the monitor.

Charlotte let go but kept a hand on Savanna's back. "He's okay."

She bit her lip. He didn't look okay. Her normally strong and sturdy father looked deflated and frail, one side of his face badly sunburned and blistered, the other side a waxy white, startling proof of what the admiral had told them. He'd suffered his injuries at some point Saturday night and had lain in the exposed stern of the yacht for around seventy-two hours before being rescued. Another day or even less could have killed him. Stubble covered his cheeks and chin. His left forearm and hand bore a neon green cast. He was asleep—or unconscious. But he was here.

"Come here," Charlotte said, leading her to the chair at the side of the bed. "Sit. Talk to him. He'll know it's you; the nurses say he can hear us."

She slipped her hand under his good one, lightly curling her fingers around his. "Hi, Dad. It's Savanna." Now she saw the large bandage on the side and back of his head. "What do they say about his head injury? How badly was he hurt?" It pained her to ask.

The father of one of her students last year had suffered a traumatic closed brain injury years earlier, and he and his family still had to compensate for the aftereffects—impulsivity in behavior and speech, difficulty grasping complex issues or multistep instructions, labile emotions. Riley's mom had explained that their family had had to adjust, and some days were worse than others. Would her dad have the same struggles?

"There's a lot of wait and see," Charlotte said. "It sounds like we won't know exactly what to expect until he wakes up. They said he has some swelling but it's improving... So far, he's only opened his eyes a few times. He recognized me and Skylar."

"Where is she?"

"She had to take the kids to school and day care; Freddie and Max said they'd do it, but she wanted to. I told her to get some sleep before coming back. Did you take the day off?"

"I took the rest of the week off." She'd emailed Principal Clay late last night and given a condensed explanation of why she couldn't come in the next few days. He'd already replied and urged her to take as much time as she needed. And where the heck was Travis? This was getting old, and she had a feeling something had already been very wrong in her sister's marriage before Savanna accidentally learned of it. Skylar must be beyond frustrated and upset. She started to ask her mom if she knew anything but thought better of it. Charlotte had fetched a damp washcloth and was gently blotting the dried blood that had been missed on her husband's forehead.

The glass door slid open, and Sydney entered the small room. "Sorry, I didn't think I'd be this late," Syd whispered. "I had to get Willow set up to handle the shop without me today. Kate's going to come run the desk while Willow's bathing and grooming, at least until her afternoon yoga classes start. Are you okay, Mom? How is he?" She hugged

Charlotte and took the chair on the other side of the hospital bed.

"I'm fine—better now that he's home. He's not doing badly." Charlotte kept one hand protectively on her husband's leg through the blanket. "That's great you got Kate to help out today. I'm glad you're both here."

A tall, stern-looking nurse came in, pushing another machine. The badge on her lanyard read TRUDIE KELLER, MSN, RN, CCRN. "Okay, family, there are too many of you in here. Two max, and zero while Dr. Gallager's rounding—he's on his way up. He's ordered labs, a twelve lead, and an echo. The cafeteria makes a great omelet. Let's have you clear out and go get a bite."

"I'm not leaving," Charlotte told Trudie. "Girls, you should go have breakfast. I'll grab something when you're back."

Savanna exchanged a wide-eyed glance with Syd, waiting for the nurse to shut her mom down, but the two women locked eyes for a few seconds, and then Trudie gave a quick, curt nod, and busied herself with setting up lab tubes on the cart.

By the time she and Syd returned from the cafeteria, full from the admittedly excellent omelets and slinking past the nurses' station, hoping to go unnoticed, Aidan had already come and gone. Someone had brought a reclining chair into the small room, and Charlotte was curled up in it beside Harlan, asleep under several layers of thin hospital blankets.

Sydney propped her elbows on the bed and quietly chatted to their dad, filling him in on the wedding cake tasting, the snag they'd hit with the restaurant not having sufficient room for the rehearsal dinner, the little cockapoo puppy that had come into Fancy Tails & Treats this morning as she was leaving, and so many other little tidbits of information that Savanna lost track. Harlan's eyes fluttered open when Syd mentioned Finn's tuxedo fitting scheduled for the day after tomorrow; the appointment was for the groom and grooms-men and the father of the bride.

"Daddy." Syd leaned in closer as their father's lips moved but no sound came out. He gripped Sydney's hand, his fingers curling around hers and knocking his oxygen meter off. His gaze moved from Syd to Savanna, standing behind her; he blinked slowly, once, twice, and then his eyes stayed closed.

A different nurse zipped in and popped the meter back on his finger, adding more tape. "It's the pain meds, don't worry. We'll be weaning those back tomorrow and he won't be as drowsy." She was gone as quickly as she'd appeared.

Uncle Freddie arrived to visit, and Sydney stepped out to make room for him. When Skylar showed up midafternoon, Savanna stood, knowing it was her turn to take a break. They'd been rotating three family members in the room all day, but four would've likely drawn too much attention. Nobody was suggesting that Charlotte leave.

"I'm going to run home and feed Fonzie," she said. "I'll let you visit, especially since Uncle Max just texted that he'll be heading up soon too, when he finishes the last flower arrangement he's working on. I'll be back in the evening, if that's okay?"

"That'd be perfect," Charlotte said, awake after a short nap. "Maybe I can send you a little list of some things I could use from the house?"

"Absolutely." Savanna leaned in and hugged her and then moved to the hospital bed. She carefully hugged her dad, pressing her cheek to the unburned side of his face.

She spoke softly, nervous about leaving him but grateful he'd been found. "I love you so much, Dad. We're all here with you. Mom's here, and she's not budging. We don't know what happened on the boat, but you're in good hands now. I'm sure Sebastian will be found soon too," she added, trying to add a little hope to her message.

She was on her way out the sliding glass door when Detective Jordan rounded the corner of the nurses' station. She shut the door and waited for him outside the room.

"Savanna," he said in greeting. "How is he?"

"He's in and out of consciousness, just opening his eyes now and then. He's still sedated. But he's back and he's alive and in one piece," she said.

"I'm so glad."

She resisted the urge to hug him. He'd done a lot more behind the scenes than he'd mentioned to locate her dad, she was positive. She settled instead for using her words. Nick Jordan was one of those people whose body language spoke volumes, and 99 percent of the time she'd spent around him, even with their history of high-stress situations, that language said *I don't do hugs.* "Thank you so much for getting him back home. We seriously would have been a mess—more of a mess—without you. I know you've worked nonstop with the coast guard trying to find him."

"You don't need to thank me. But you're very welcome," he said. He peered past her into Harlan's room. "He hasn't woken up enough to say anything yet, has he? We're trying to get a handle on what happened, especially with the evidence of violence."

She shook her head. "No. I don't get it either. It couldn't have been Sebastian—I can't see them having a falling out or getting physical. But then what does that mean? Someone boarded the yacht and attacked them? Way out on the lake?"

"That possibility would involve definite premeditation and planning. Without a clear motive, there are more questions than answers at the moment."

The red abrasion on Kyle Bishop's hand popped into her mind. And he'd been at the Sweetwater counter the morning of the regatta...but then what? Did he rent a boat to go attack her dad and Sebastian? For what reason? The valet's livelihood depended on Sebastian being alive and well and productive. Her musings sounded ridiculous in her head—too ridiculous to say out loud to the detective. But someone had gone out of their way to hurt the men, and it obviously hadn't been about stealing the X-Yacht either.

"Well," Jordan said, "I'm going to need to come back when he's awake. Maybe tomorrow will be better for that."

"Tomorrow for sure." She hoped.

Chapter Eleven

SAVANNA FELT LIKE a stalker, watching Griffin Alexander from her parked car in front of Holy Grounds. She should back off and let the authorities do their thing, but there were some local angles she could explore much better than the coast guard or the sheriff's department—she and Griffin were practically peers. They'd graduated a year apart. She didn't know his phone number, and from what he'd said the other day, she doubted he'd be hanging around the family home. This was the only way for her to catch him.

Her phone buzzed with a text from Aidan. *"I'm sorry I missed you when I came to check up on your dad. Are you still here at the hospital?"*

"Shoot! I'm on a coffee run." It wasn't a complete lie, but she still felt guilty telling him a half truth. She glanced at the counter where Griffin was cashing someone out, making sure he was still there.

"I can stop by later to update you on his test results."

"Okay, thank you, that would be great... Should I be worried?"

"Not necessarily. Let me know when you're back up there and I'll try to get away."

That certainly sounded worrisome. What did *not necessarily* mean? She stared into Holy Grounds without seeing, her mind running through scary possibilities. She'd been so concerned about her dad's brain she hadn't given any thought to his heart. He'd always been active and fit, worked outdoors on construction sites most of the time, enjoyed his motorcycle and sailing; if this ordeal had left him with heart damage, he'd likely have to change his whole lifestyle.

Griffin startled her by waving from the barista counter. He was staring right at her through the big front window, his hand lifted in a tentative greeting. The coffee shop had emptied considerably since she'd pulled up. Well. Now she had to make good on what she'd told Aidan, otherwise, she really did look like a stalker. She grabbed her purse and headed inside.

Before she could offer an excuse, Griffin spoke. "I was going to call you. Good timing that you needed coffee."

"I guess so!" She scrutinized the menu on the wall behind him. "I'll take a large iced mocha cappuccino, please. So…what were you going to call me about? Is there any news about your dad?"

"No. Nothing. I just—I know he wasn't on board, but what if a boat picked him up? Or what if—" He clamped his lips closed. "Never mind."

She leaned in. It was just the two of them and a customer at a table against the wall with AirPods in, absorbed in her laptop. "What if what?"

"You'll just think I'm crazy."

"I promise I won't. Nothing makes much sense about what happened. What were you going to say?"

He shrugged. "I don't know. My dad isn't the sweet old sailor dude or spaced-out artist people might think he is.

He's smart. He's always got an agenda."

"What do you mean?"

"What if he wanted to disappear? He and my stepmom were having problems. And he's been back and forth to Chicago a lot lately—for what? You know who's in Chicago? Maeve. Plus, he kicked me off the regatta."

Savanna was speechless. After picking her jaw up from the floor, she struggled with which part of all of that to respond to first.

"I know, I know," Griffin said. "He made it seem like I flaked on the race, right? I didn't meet his criteria to go. He hates that I'm not what he wants me to be. He said if I have time to sail, I have time to get a real job. Like this isn't a real job—he's such a snob. The crappy thing is, I like my job. And I really love being first mate for his regattas. This would've been our twenty-second race—I've been going with him since I was a kid. I helped him place in the Barcolana Regatta four years ago. This year, he decided I'm too old to be a barista, and if I don't become a corporate drone with a full-time job and cancel my art opening, he's done with me. Still think he's father of the year?"

"I never thought—" She didn't even know what to say. "He wants you to cancel your art show? I'm sorry, this all sounds awful."

He shrugged. "I guess he thinks I've had enough time to make it happen. Maybe he's jealous his career's basically over and mine is just starting. Let me get your drink for you." He moved about the small space, brewing the two shots of espresso, setting up the cup with ice first, then her mocha syrup, followed by the shots. Lastly, he steamed the milk into a perfect frothy consistency and topped off her drink with a fine-lined flower of mocha drizzle into the foamed milk. He set it on the counter for her. "I'm just saying, maybe my dad planned on starting over. He wouldn't be the first person to fake his own death."

She stared at the masterpiece he placed in front of her. Was he lying? Why would he lie about an ultimatum Sebastian had issued—everything he'd told her was equally as revealing about himself as his father. But the rest of what he'd said made no sense.

"See. I told you you'd think I'm crazy. Maybe he thought it'd be easier than going through a messy divorce. I'm sure my stepmom would get half of everything if he tried to divorce her. She should just for putting up with him all these years. So, he just disappeared. With Maeve's help, he could pull it off. And maybe that's why he suddenly got so hard-nosed about my job and my art. He knows how tough it is to get by as an artist. Maybe he knew he wasn't going to be around to push me anymore. He knows I usually need help with my rent and whatever."

"I'm trying to wrap my head around what you're saying," Savanna said carefully. He was right—he did sound crazy. "If your dad tried to fake his own death, wouldn't Winnie still benefit once his estate was settled? I'm not sure the idea makes a lot of sense."

"If he dies, his estate gets split between Chelsea and me; at least that was the case when he had us sign as first and second executors last year. He never told Winnie he changed the terms."

She frowned. "He wasn't leaving Winnie anything?"

"No. I don't know what changed a year ago, but he cut her out. But if he'd divorced her, she'd get half of everything."

"Maybe," Savanna said. "Unless he made her sign a prenup when they got married."

"A French model twenty years younger than him? He's smart but he's human. I'm positive there's no prenup. He fell hard for Winnie, especially since our mom had just left him. I was thirteen, I remember. Maybe whatever changed between them a year ago was Maeve. Who knows?"

Savanna's mind raced. Sebastian and Maeve Davis... She'd detected zero chemistry between them, but she hadn't been looking for it. She could see a conversation with Maeve in her future, and that would explain the phone call just an hour or so after they'd learned their father had been found.

Griffin sighed. "I know what you're thinking—everything I just said makes it seem like Chelsea and I would clean up if he died. If I tried to tell the police any of this, I'm sure we'd be instant suspects. But he's my dad. Even if he hates me, even if he's never approved of my life, I love him. I couldn't ever hurt him." He straightened up as the bell over the door jingled, a young couple entering.

"Your dad could never hate you, Griffin. I don't know what to think about any of this, but I know he loves you. If he didn't, anything you're doing or not doing with your life wouldn't concern him at all." She frowned. She didn't mean to sound judgmental; he got enough of that from his dad. "I just mean, he obviously cares about you. I don't think there's anything wrong with trying to pursue our passions, but you have a point about him knowing he's pushing you."

"Thank you, Savanna." He looked over her shoulder. "I've gotta get back to work. Oh—but I almost forgot why I got your number from Chelsea. We wanted to ask if you can make sure my dad's exhibit in a couple weeks still happens? We don't want all the hype the Lansing Museum has generated to lose steam."

This entire fifteen minutes spent with Sebastian's son had left her so unsettled and uncertain. Why would he care about the exhibit? She stepped aside and waited while he took care of the couple's order, and then the woman who came in next.

During the next lull, he propped a chalkboard sign on the counter that read BARISTA ON BREAK, BACK IN 10 MINUTES. He removed his apron and came around the counter to sit with her at the little table she'd taken. He handed her a cinnamon scone. "That's fresh from this morning. It's my own recipe."

She took a bite. "Oh my goodness." She spoke around a mouthful of delicious scone, a hand up to cover her rudeness. "This is amazing. You and Chelsea both have the baking gene."

He smiled. "I guess we do. Anyway, I talked to her last night. She thinks my theory is crazy, but we both agree that if he is alive, he won't be able to stay away from his first exhibit in twenty years. Is there any way we can make sure the show still happens?"

"I'm not sure we could pull that off without his involvement and consent. I'd need to talk this through with my partner at the museum and clear it with the board. I will try. If Britt and Helene are on board with it, we'll move forward. And if not, I guess it wouldn't hurt to finish the provenances. But I'd like to be optimistic and just hope for your dad to be home safe by then. We could even postpone the exhibit if needed." It'd mean she'd need to get back to work on the provenances. "How do you think your stepmom will feel about moving forward without waiting to see what happens with your dad? You seem like you two have a good relationship? I know sometimes that isn't the case with blended families, but you speak of her as if you really care about her."

"Of course I do. She's been my mom for longer than my actual mom stuck around. Listen, I hope my dad is okay. I hope he's found alive and I'm wrong about everything. But, not to sound heartless or anything, people love art even more when it's from an artist who died tragically. Once this story gets out, crowds will be lining up out the door to see his work."

Chapter Twelve

G RIFFIN'S WORDS ECHOED in Savanna's head all the way home. *Crass, disgusting, rude*...none of those really described the depth of how awful his parting comment had been. Heartless was exactly how he sounded. She tried to imagine a scenario, any situation at all, ever, in which she'd say something like that about either of her parents. She couldn't.

Back at Anderson Memorial that evening after she'd fed Fonzie and stopped at her parents' house to pack an overnight bag for her mom, Savanna punched the three button in the elevator. The doors began to slide closed but stopped abruptly; Aidan stepped into the car, letting go of the door.

He grinned at her. "I almost lost you."

"Never." Her voice came out soft and sultry without her even trying. Heat crept into her cheeks.

He slid an arm around her waist and drew her into him. His lips brushed her neck. "We have to stop meeting like this."

She laughed, her breath catching as he kissed her and she melted into him, heartbeat thrumming in her throat. His blue button-down had lost its morning crispness, the suit jacket left behind somewhere in favor of his lab coat. The first hint of his five-o'clock shadow tickled under her nose as she inhaled—hospital antiseptic, coffee, and beneath it, the clean, masculine scent of his shampoo and aftershave.

The kiss ended and the elevator dinged and the doors slid open as they separated. A pair of nurses stepped aside to let them exit. Savanna self-consciously pressed the back of one hand against her lips; she wished they were at her house or his instead of strolling into the ICU. She wished the constant, nagging worry about her dad would soon be resolved, but she was afraid of Aidan's news, and afraid of what it might mean if her dad continued to sleep, and never fully woke up. He wasn't sleeping, she knew that; it was just less terrifying to think of it in those terms.

Entering his room, it was immediately apparent that everything had changed. Her sisters were laughing. Charlotte perched on the edge of the hospital bed beside her husband, curled against him, one arm wrapped around his good one. Harlan graced her with a smile as she stood frozen by the door, knees noodling with relief. "Savanna." His voice was hoarse and raspy, and it was the best thing she'd ever heard.

"He just woke up a few minutes ago," Skylar said. "I texted you."

"Dr. Gallager," Sydney said, smirking. "You have a little something right there." She pointed to his upper lip and tapped her own. "Something pink."

Savanna didn't even care. She pushed Syd's chair out of the way and hugged her dad. "Are you okay? Does anything hurt right now? We were so scared." Unexpected tears sprang up and overflowed, and she swiped them away along with the remainder of her lipstick. "Are you really okay? Say something, please."

He put a hand on his throat, wincing. "Did you pick out your tile yet?"

"Oh my God," she said, laughing. The hundred-pound weight of fear and worry that she'd been wearing like a shawl was suddenly gone.

A doctor entered the room, looking down at the tablet in his hand. "I heard the patient is awake. Let's have you clear out for—oh, Dr. Gallager. You're finishing up your consult? I can come back."

"No, you're fine. We'll step out for a moment, then the family would like an update after your assessment. Sound good?"

In the hallway, Aidan filled them in on the cardiac findings. "I reviewed the results of the echocardiogram and twelve lead EKG. I may still want an MRI. Even though the findings from this morning's tests are normal, the Door County attending recorded an arrhythmia; it happened more than once while he was inpatient there. Severe dehydration can be a trigger, even in someone who's never had a problem before. Harlan's arrhythmia is called atrial fibrillation, or A-fib. There are several treatment options, and there's the chance they might not even be necessary—"

Skylar interrupted. "Why wouldn't we treat it? He can't just walk around with this A-fib happening. He's very active."

"We will absolutely want to treat it if warranted. Sometimes an episode like this will crop up and then never happen again. I've ordered a Holter monitor for him to wear; we'll do a two-day test to start, and he might need to wear it longer depending on what we find, up to three weeks. That's the first step. We also need to talk about a few lifestyle changes. Is he a smoker?"

"Yes—he says he's not, but he smokes these ridiculous little cigars occasionally," Charlotte said. "That'll stop. What else?"

Savanna's sense of relief continued to skyrocket with each new piece of news. The rest of Aidan's instructions were very doable, especially with her mother's supervision. Her dad was pretty fearless, but not when it came to crossing his bride. The ICU physician called them back into the small room and updated them after Aidan was finished. The steroids and diuretics were doing their job on the swelling in Harlan's brain; he was off heavy-duty painkillers and sedation now, Tylenol sufficient for his broken arm and sore head, his kidney function was already heading in the right direction after his bout with life-threatening dehydration and blood loss, and he was expected to be moved to a general medical unit room downstairs tomorrow as long as all continued to improve.

"I'd have expected you to be much worse off, Mr. Shepherd, given the ordeal you've suffered. It helps immensely that you were in such good shape before this happened."

When the doctor had gone and it was just their little family, Charlotte perched on the edge of the bed again. She leaned down and kissed her husband. "You can lose that smirk anytime, mister. We already know you're Superman."

By the time Detective Jordan made it back Thursday morning, Harlan had been transferred to the second-floor medical unit. His private room was double the size of the glass cubicle in the ICU. A nurse had gotten Harlan up and settled in a big reclining chair, he was still connected to a constantly dripping IV, and he was working on his first real food since Saturday—scrambled eggs and toast, bland but a safe option to begin with.

As Thursdays were always Skylar's long days spent in court, she most likely wouldn't be by until this evening. Uncle Max and Uncle Freddie had finally been comfortable leaving Savanna's parents' home, taking the rambunctious pup Daisy with them, since Travis had showed up last night at last to pick up his children.

"One never truly knows what happens within a marriage, except the people living it," Uncle Max said when Savanna groused late last night that Skylar deserved to be treated better. He was always the gentler and more diplomatic of her two uncles.

"A real man stands by his family no matter what," Uncle Freddie had added. "I don't care what's going on in their marriage. Travis being scarce during all of this speaks volumes about his character."

She was glad her sister wasn't there to hear that. Skylar had yet to share anything concrete with them, and Savanna was trying hard to keep an open mind, like Uncle Max.

Now, in the sunny hospital room, she and Sydney

flanked their mother on the leather couch across from their dad. Detective Jordan had his trusty yellow legal pad in front of him on an over-the-bed table he'd snagged from the hallway.

"If you're not sure," Jordan said, "it's okay. We'll circle back to it." He'd asked if Harlan recalled what time they lost power.

"I don't remember much about the day until right around when I was hit. I can't recall having dinner that night or talking with Charlotte, but she says I called her around seven Saturday evening. We must've lost power shortly after that. I know when I came to, the running lights were out and the boom—"

"When did you regain consciousness?" Jordan interrupted.

He hesitated. "It had to have been a while after we were attacked that same night. It was pitch dark, no stars. It seemed like I was in and out. Like I was blinking—but every time I opened my eyes, hours had passed. It was night, or morning, or twilight again. I know that doesn't help."

"It all helps. You must have drifted in and out of consciousness the first day or two. Back to the attack. You said, 'I don't remember much about the day until right around when I was hit.' So, you have some recollection of the incident and the moments that followed? Can you describe what you remember?"

"I was winching the mainsail when I felt the blow. Searing pain. White hot. In the back left side of my head. I saw stars. It's a real thing, not just something from cartoons.

Bright starbursts filled my vision, and I went down. I don't..." Harlan stopped and held up his left arm with the cast on it. "Is that how I broke my arm? Did I fall on it? Maybe I'm lucky I don't remember breaking it."

Beside her, Savanna's mom had clamped a hand over her mouth, her eyes filled with tears. She made no sound and was perfectly still. Savanna carefully hugged her while Sydney passed her a box of tissues.

"Char," their dad said softly. "Hey. I'm all right. Come here." Using his cast arm, he patted the bed next to his chair. She moved to his other side instead, sitting on the register by the window and taking his good right hand in hers.

"I know this isn't pleasant," Detective Jordan said. "Do we need a break?"

"No. Unless you do?" he asked Charlotte.

"No. I'm fine."

Liar, Savanna thought. At least Mom was consistent. Her mom was always *fine*, even when she wasn't. And seeing Skylar working through some unknown stressor lately, powering through whatever fell into her path along with the usual everyday stuff, it was clear her mom's eldest daughter was the most like her. Skylar was always *fine*, too, even when she wasn't.

"When you were knocked down, did you see Sebastian at all?"

"No, I didn't see him after I was hit. He'd gone up to mess with the jib lines."

"Is it possible, and by that, I'm not asking you to make a moral judgment, just asking about logistics," Detective

Jordan clarified before continuing, "is it possible Sebastian is the one who hit you?"

Harlan's frown deepened. His gaze moved toward the door to his left and the ceiling and he was quiet for a long moment. "I don't think that's possible."

"Dad." Savanna spoke up. "I know he's your friend, but sometimes there are things we can't possibly know, even about our friends. How can you be sure he didn't do it?" Griffin's wild theories were running through her mind. What might Sebastian be capable of if he'd gone on the regatta with his own agenda?

"It's not physically possible. He was on the bow—I saw him trying to free the jib line, it was caught on the halyard. He was a good thirty or forty feet away from me. Then I was hit, I went down, and I couldn't see him anymore. But I was also on the floor of the cockpit at that point. I couldn't see much except for the boom and mainsail above me. When I came to again, it was bright out." He closed his eyes. "The sun was too bright, it hurt. The boom was swinging overhead, lines and pulleys and hardware smacking the metal and whipping about. I remember thinking we had to get the slack out of the mainsail, but it'd be impossible with all the lines cut."

"The attacker cut all the ropes?" Jordan asked.

"Seemed like it. Both sails were untethered. The next time I opened my eyes, it was night."

"And no Sebastian. Not through any of this, not since you saw him on the bow while you were...what was it? Winching something?"

"It's a crank handle, used to reel in the ropes attached to the sails, basically. And no, no Sebastian."

"Do you recall hearing a motor? Saturday night, shortly after you were knocked down?" Jordan asked.

"No...I don't think so. Why?"

The detective flipped to a different page. "The *Serendipity* had a dinghy, right? And it was on board when you left the marina Saturday morning?"

"Yes. Was it missing?" Harlan asked. "Cripes; I never once thought to try and get to it." He looked disgusted with himself.

"Daddy. You couldn't even find the strength to get up from the cockpit. For three days. Not with your concussion and dehydration and blood loss. Don't even start second-guessing yourself," Sydney said, her voice sterner than Savanna'd ever heard it.

"Good point." She nodded.

"It wouldn't have mattered anyway," Detective Jordan said. "The dinghy is missing. We still aren't sure whether it was taken by the attacker or by Sebastian, or if they may have been working together."

Harlan pressed a thumb and forefinger over his eyelids. "That makes no sense. You need a better theory."

Savanna's eyes widened; her dad's usual respect for law enforcement had its limits. But Jordan surprised her.

"Maybe," he said. "It's not my theory, though. Admiral Moore's team is looking into all possibilities. Right now, we don't know enough to rule anything out."

"I think we're finished for now," Charlotte said, standing. She pressed the call button. "He needs to rest. His head hurts. You're welcome to come back tomorrow, Detective, if you have any other questions."

He nodded. "Thank you, I may need to. Thank you, sir," he said to Harlan, shaking his hand. "I appreciate your help. Glad you're back in one piece."

Chapter Thirteen

MAKING GOOD ON her agreement to finish the certification process, Savanna promised her parents she'd stop back that evening and headed out to Sebastian's place. Even though she'd called off for her teaching job that week, leaving her classes to be managed through her detailed lesson plans in the hands of a sub, she was feeling stretched thin. If she did make it back to the hospital tonight, it'd be with Fonzie tucked into her oversize tote bag. She'd been away too much lately, and she couldn't even leave her little dog to be babysat by Sydney at Fancy Tails, since Syd had people covering the shop and was stretched thin just like Savanna was. With their dad now in a regular room and out of the ICU, how much trouble could she really cause by bringing a very small, very sweet—very hyper—little dog to cheer him up?

Her mind kept cycling through all the bits of information she'd heard this morning—images of her dad lying bleeding on the yacht, a fall so abrupt that he broke his thick wrist under his own weight, the sun baking his exposed skin, sails slack and whipping around while the large boat drifted on the waves of Lake Michigan, aimless and far off course. Had Sebastian taken the dinghy to escape being attacked? It seemed more likely the attacker had gotten away in it; if Sebastian had, he'd have returned with help. If he'd survived. The more time went by, the less likely that seemed, unfortunately. As long as she'd known him, she struggled now with mixed emotions after learning of an entirely different side of the artist.

Kyle Bishop once again led Savanna through from the foyer up to Sebastian's studio. He'd opened the front door before she rang the bell, expecting her after she'd texted to make sure it was all right to come do some work.

Without Chelsea or Winnie around, the high ceilings and stone and marble flooring made the silent home seem even more cavernous. She was unnerved, remembering her earlier suspicions about Kyle, but the whole conversation with Griffin had muddled up her conflicting concerns about who might want to hurt Sebastian. She'd have liked to ask if it wasn't perhaps a little spooky here alone, in the big house tucked back in the woods.

Kyle unlocked the studio door for her and ushered her in. Everything looked to be as she'd left it, other than her authenticating case on the desk where he'd placed it for her. "I'm supervising the landscapers today; I may be outside for a bit," he said. "But I always carry my phone. Just let me know if you need anything."

"Thank you, Kyle."

She scrolled through the music playlists on her phone, choosing just the right musical theater soundtrack to stream through her earbuds—today's choice was *Hamilton*. She set up her laptop and mini UVA lamp and powered on the

Firefly, her handheld microscope. She got to work. It'd likely take several more hours, over the course of the next few days, to complete the process of creating provenances for each of Sebastian's seventeen canvases. His new paintings possessed an assuredness that his older originals did not. These most recent pieces exuded much more of the artist.

Surrounded by beautiful artwork, especially from a revered artist who had clearly leveled up in the years he'd disappeared from the public eye, Savanna was in her element. She took her time, not rushing the process. Despite the fact she knew Sebastian personally, she still had to be sure to do her due diligence. Using her Firefly, which was synced with her laptop, she carefully investigated the hallmarks of the pieces, Sebastian's unique brushwork technique. She had the microscope set so that she could capture any specific portions of each piece that'd provide confirmation he was the creator.

Sebastian employed a broad brushstroke technique not typical of most postimpressionist paintings. More often, postimpressionists painted using shorter, more blunt brushstrokes and broken color—the practice of leaving contrasting colors on the canvas unblended. The influence of Vincent van Gogh was apparent in much of Sebastian Alexander's body of work. Van Gogh was known for his use of broad brushstrokes and rich, blended colors, the hues chosen specifically to induce or portray emotion. The current painting under inspection by her Firefly scope was an autumn landscape with a couple in the foreground, their backs to the viewer. The figures' hands were linked, seen against warm oranges, golds, and reds, but the sky overhead was a cool pewter fraught with clouds. The combination of naivety and foreboding was unsettling. He'd titled it *Unwritten*.

Savanna added her notes to the document she'd use later to create the certificate for the piece. Her laptop screen went black before she could finish typing. She hadn't even been watching her battery life. She found her laptop cord in her oversize tote and got it plugged in, but before she moved on to the next piece, she stopped and rubbed at her dry eyes, fatigued from intensive focus the last couple hours. She was parched. Yesterday and the day before had been so stressful, she'd barely taken the time to eat, let alone stay hydrated. She'd go grab a glass of water, then work a little longer. She locked the studio door behind her, bringing her phone to make sure she wouldn't miss any important messages about her dad.

She moved past the wing where the bedrooms were, followed by the pretty parlor and the richly decorated home library on her way through the long hallway. If she had a dedicated library like Sebastian's, she'd fill it with her entire collection including her far too long to-be-read pile of books and never leave. Through the second-story windows at the end of the hallway, she saw that the landscaping truck and trailer was now gone; they'd finished up. Maybe Kyle was downstairs; he didn't appear to be outside at the moment. All the better, as she really didn't love the idea of rummaging through cupboards here on her own, looking for a glass.

Her phone rang in her hand, startling her. It was Sydney

on video call. "Hey," Savanna said, holding her phone up briefly to greet her sister. "Is Dad all right?"

"Yes, I just saw him. He's opening his eyes more this morning. His doctor says he's stable. I need your honest opinion."

"Sure, what's up? And where the heck are you?"

"I'm outside Giuseppe's waiting for Finn. We have an appointment to go over the wedding dinner menu with Chef Joe and Remy. But I'm thinking I should postpone."

Savanna frowned. "The appointment? Why?" Chef Joe Fratelli was immensely talented and so was his protegee, Remy. Joe's restaurant Giuseppe's served the best Italian cuisine in the county.

"No, the wedding," Sydney said. "For Dad. I think this is all just too soon now, with everything that's happened. The guys are supposed to get fitted for their tuxedos Friday—tomorrow, jeez—but that's crazy since Dad was just found and he has a bad concussion and who knows if he's even going to be up and around by the wedding because—"

"Syd." Savanna stopped walking. "Stop. Take a breath. Look at me."

Sydney drew in a breath and exhaled slowly, closing her eyes and pursing her lips. She repeated it. When she met Savanna's eyes again through the phone screen, she was visibly calmer. "Thank you. So…what should I do? I'm sure we can get ahold of everyone to let them know we're bumping it out a few weeks. Don't you think that's best?"

"I think you should sit down with Mom and Dad and talk it through. Especially since he's doing so much better already today. Maybe it's not necessary to go through with postponing; Dad might be a lot better by then. It's still a week and a half away."

She nodded. "You're right. I didn't even think of running it by them."

"It'll help, I think. Mom isn't going take any chances with his health, even if Dad tries to act like a hero," Savanna said.

"Yep, you're right," Syd repeated. "All right, then. I'm gonna ask them. Skylar had stopped by on her lunch break when I left but I'm sure she's gone now."

"Skylar came by? Were the kids with the sitter, did she say?"

"You mean, is Travis home with the kids?"

"Okay, yes. That's what I mean. Is he still home or did he flake again?" Savanna asked, knowing she sounded mean but not caring. Much. The truth was, Travis had been her brother-in-law for the last several years and she, like the rest of her family, had grown attached to him. She'd always believed he was a good husband and father. But now she didn't know what to think. It didn't help matters at all that their older sister was such a private person, keeping things to herself until they boiled over all at once.

"I think he's with the kids. She's not talking. She's been extra weird lately."

Savanna sighed. "We need to get her to sit down for lunch with us. She's always so closemouthed. Maybe that's good as a lawyer, but it's not good for her as a person." Skylar and Travis were dealing with something heavy currently, but maybe their big sister needed the reminder that she could always lean on them, that times like this were exactly what sisters were for.

"I'm in. Tomorrow at Fancy Tails? I'll get her there and supply the sandwiches, you do the talking; she still thinks of me as the baby."

"That sounds good, tomorrow at Fancy Tails at noon." Savanna had resumed her quest for a glass of water and had reached the catwalk that stretched across the vaulted marble foyer. "Good luck with the menu."

"Thanks." A deep voice came through her phone and Finn's cute face filled the phone screen momentarily. "Hey there, Savanna."

"Hi, Finn. I'm envious. I'd kill for some of Chef Joe's lobster ravioli right now." She trotted down the wide stairway.

"That's the best," Sydney agreed. "Too pricey, though. Wow, Savvy, you're at Sebastian Alexander's right now? That place looks gorgeous."

"It is. I really hope he's found soon—alive," she said, lowering her voice to nearly a whisper for the last word. "Go do your thing and then go talk with Mom and Da—"

Savanna tripped and fell hard over some heavy, immovable object, phone flying from her fingers and landing with a crack on the hard flooring of the foyer. She whipped around and laid eyes on a still and lifeless Kyle Bishop, sprawled with limbs askew and eyes staring straight up at nothing. She shrieked, scrambling backward and realizing her feet were sliding out from under her as she tried to stand up; the floor was wet and smelled of lemon cleaning product.

From her phone across the foyer, she heard Sydney's distant, tinny voice. She scrambled to stand, slippery floors working against her. She finally found her footing and got to her phone.

"Savanna! Are you okay? What happened? Savvy. Hey. Oh, hey," Sydney said, calming as Savanna's face appeared on screen. "You scared me. What happened?"

Heart racing, she carefully moved back over to the body—to Kyle. A wide red halo had bloomed around his head. He hadn't moved at all. "I think he's dead," Savanna whispered. She turned her phone to show them.

Sydney and Finn gasped in unison. "Who is that? What happened? Savanna, call the police. Wait, no! Don't hang up, stay on with me. I'll call an ambulance from Finn's phone now. Give me the address."

"I um… it's in my map app. Let me look—"

"Nevermind. Your location's on, I've got you," Sydney said. "I'm calling 911. Is anyone else there? Do you hear anything?"

"Kyle was the only one here. I think he fell—" She tipped her head back, looking up at the catwalk and showing them. She cautiously leaned over him, watching his chest, looking for any signs of life. "What do I do? What if he's…what if he's still alive? Should I check? I should check." She needed to check for a pulse. She had to.

Finn spoke, his voice calm and level. "Use the flat pads of your first two fingers, Savanna. You're going to lightly place them on his neck, just under the corner of jaw. Set the phone down if you need to."

Her hand shook as she did what he said. Feeling nothing, she tried the other side of his neck. A low whine that became one short sob escaped her as she touched him, her own heart pounding in her throat. "He's warm. Oh God, his skin is still warm," she said, the tremor reaching her voice. "There's no pulse. He's not breathing. There's so much blood. I know CPR, I took a course through the school. But can you help remind me?"

Finn's face disappeared. She heard bits of a short discussion between him and her sister. Sydney took the phone back, her worried face filling the screen. "I don't think it's safe. You don't know what happened to him or if someone is still in the house. This could be connected to whatever happened on the yacht. You need to get out of there."

"I can't just—"

"Are there neighbors? Go outside, see if you can flag someone down while you're waiting for the ambulance and police," Syd ordered. "We'll come right now."

"He lives in the middle of the woods. There's nobody around. The police will beat you here. It's okay..." She checked behind her, feeling like her head was on a swivel, paranoid now. She sucked in air through her teeth. The house was completely silent. Kyle was dying—or already dead—on the floor right in front of her. "I think I'm alone. I can't just leave him."

She knelt beside him, reaching to prop up her phone so Finn could tell her what she might be doing wrong. Her knees slid out from under her on the slippery floor, forcing her into a painful, skewed version of the splits she could never do in gymnastics. "What the heck, the whole foyer's just been freshly mopped," she muttered.

She struggled back into position and leaned forward over Kyle's chest, heel of one hand with the other on top, fingers laced together, and began chest compressions. "Is this right? How many do I do again?"

Finn's voice was the calming force within the chaotic storm of trauma and tragedy swirling in Savanna's head—

"Move your hands up toward his neck about two inches."

She did so. Had someone done this to Kyle? Why?

"You're going to stop at thirty compressions and move up to his head to give two rescue breaths."

Who mopped the floor just moments before this happened? Why?

"You'll pinch his nose closed and cover his mouth completely so no air escapes. Two breaths in a row."

Had someone washed the floor to get rid of evidence of the attack? Her gaze darted up to the catwalk railing overhead. It looked untouched, no broken spindles.

"Back to his chest now, Savanna, don't lose momentum. You're shooting to manually make his heart beat at least sixty times per minute to circulate oxygenated blood as much as possible."

If Kyle was pushed, the police would find evidence, and that could lead them to her father and Sebastian's attacker. What if she was accidentally erasing evidence with her CPR efforts? She said as much to Finn.

"Don't worry, if there's something to find, the cops'll find it. You're not erasing a thing. Now give another two breaths."

Finn kept her on track for another few cycles while glorious sirens began and screamed closer and closer.

"They're three minutes out," he told her. "You're doing great."

She waited until she'd finished the next two-breath cycle and then ran across the drying floor to the front door and threw it open, leaving it that way, before rushing back to Kyle for the next set of compressions. Her hair was sweaty and stuck to her forehead and she was breathing hard, but no way was she giving up, not with real help nearly here.

The two first responders carrying huge red bags came through the door and she could've kissed them. She scooted out of the way, leaning on the cool wall, while they took over.

Chapter Fourteen

THE AMBULANCE HAD arrived first. Judging by the sirens, more vehicles were approaching. Ten feet in front her on the marble floor, the high-pitched whine of a defibrillator rang in her ears followed by the abrupt, jerking shock to Kyle's body. Savanna stumbled to her feet and sprinted up the steps for her car keys, putting as much distance as possible between herself and images she was afraid she'd never be able to fully wipe from her memory.

She didn't remember walking down the long hallway to Sebastian's studio or unlocking the door; she stared, dazed, at the paintings and headed over to the desk. She couldn't have stayed near the scene downstairs for another second. She grabbed her purse and tote and was heading to the door when footsteps sounded in the hallway. She carefully, quietly, locked the studio door. She backed up, holding her breath. Was it the police? Was it whoever had attacked Kyle?

Noiselessly, she moved to the desk. Where was her phone? In her mind's eye, she saw it on the foyer floor where she'd left it. The only thing between her and potential death was a locked door. It was just a door; maybe she'd seen too many movies, but a locked door wasn't going to keep her safe if someone really wanted to get to her—or to the reasons

Sebastian kept the door locked. The thought suddenly occurred to her. Was it possible that was what this was about? Sebastian's valuable work? She shook her head. It made no sense. If this was a money thing, the artist's ridiculously expensive yacht would have been stolen.

With shaking hands, she quietly rifled through the drawers of the oak desk, one after another, not knowing what she was searching for but hoping she'd know if she saw it. A letter opener or something heavy, anything to defend herself with. Gum, sketch pads, charcoal pencils, paintbrushes upon paintbrushes, old magnets, a discount card for the auto shop in town, a television remote, several cords, and a daily planner. Nothing useful. On impulse, she grabbed the planner and shoved it into her tote, and behind it, her fingers closed around a palette knife thrown in with more random paintbrushes. Pointed but no means an adequate weapon, she gripped it anyway; it was better than nothing.

The doorknob rattled, someone trying and failing to enter. A voice called to her from the hallway. "Hello? Savanna Shepherd? Are you in there?"

That didn't sound like a killer. Though, what would a killer say? She remained quiet.

"Ms. Shepherd, it's Officer Streeter with Carson PD. It's safe to open the door."

Silence from both sides of the door. Then, almost too quiet to detect, Finn's voice floated to her. "Hey, Savanna, this is Finn. That's my buddy, Ace Streeter. You're safe, it's okay to open the door."

Flooded with relief, she opened the door. The tall and

broad police officer handed her cell phone to her, wrapped a blanket around her shoulders, and escorted her out. She thanked Finn—what would she have even done without his help through this awful afternoon? Downstairs, without meaning to, she hazarded a look at the spot where she'd left the paramedics working on Kyle. A third had joined them, an explosion of medical paraphernalia scattered around them.

"You don't have to look," Ace told her. "Come on, let's get some air." He put his large frame between her and the scene as he ushered her past, shielding her from seeing much more.

Outside, she was surprised to see two ambulances and three Carson police cruisers in the circle drive. She'd noticed this overabundant response seemed common in Carson— and according to Finn, most other small towns. Ace walked her over to Kelly, a paramedic she remembered meeting last year at Councilman John Bellamy's house. Kelly flipped her long blond braid back over her shoulder and sat Savanna down on the back of an ambulance while she checked her blood pressure.

"You feeling okay?" the paramedic asked. "You aren't hurt, right? Maybe a little shocky?" Her focus moved from Savanna to Ace, directing the question at him.

"Probably." He nodded.

"Blood pressure's a little low. You feel lightheaded at all?" Kelly's fingers were on Savanna's wrist now, her eyes on the watch face clipped to her stethoscope.

"I feel fine," she said. "I started CPR as soon as I found

Kyle, but I don't know if it even helped. Did they—does it seem like he might be okay?"

"You did everything possible," Officer Ace told her, a nonanswer. The radio clipped to his shoulder crackled. "Basement and main floor are clear," followed by a different voice, "Second floor clear." And then, "Streeter, assist requested in the carriage house."

"What does that mean?"

"Gotta go. Kel, the sheriff's department will want to talk to her. Just sit tight," he said to Savanna and took off around the back of the house.

THE FRONT DOOR opened, and the paramedics rolled Kyle Bishop out on a stretcher, minus his shirt. She couldn't tell, but he appeared not to be moving. Once he was loaded into the back of the other ambulance in the driveway, the vehicle remained in place, lights on, sirens off. She was afraid to ask what all this meant. Was he dead? If he was dead, wouldn't they have covered his body with a sheet? Why were they still here?

Another siren wailed closer and closer, and Savanna's heart lifted as Aidan's SUV pulled into the driveway followed by Detective Jordan's unmarked car. When they'd parked, Jordan jogged up the front steps into the house while Aidan came over to her. He bent and scooped her up, hugging her tightly without a word. Savanna turned her face into his neck and shut her eyes tight, trying to force from her mind the image of Kyle on the marble floor.

When he let go, he searched her face. "Are you all right? What happened?"

She filled him in, shuddering as she described the state she'd found the valet in. "There was a lot of blood. He'd hit his head really hard when he…landed. I don't think he's okay. But don't they cover a body with a sheet if the person has passed away? He wasn't covered up when they loaded him into the ambulance."

"We're taught to try and avoid covering a body if there's a potential crime involved. The sheet or blanket introduces fibers and other particles that can interfere with evidence investigations. You can't really judge by that."

"How are you here?" Now she saw that he was wearing rainbow suspenders under his suit jacket—no doubt chosen by Mollie. She tugged on one, snapping it lightly against his abdomen. She bet he wore the matching socks—he usually did with these. "I'm sorry you had to drop everything for me."

"I didn't *have* to do anything. I wanted to make sure you're okay. I'm in clinic today; a little easier to get away. How was your blood pressure when they checked it?"

She raised her eyebrows. "They said it's a little low. But I feel okay." Kelly had stepped away and was now on the phone.

Aidan used her equipment to check it, meeting her eyes as he inflated the cuff. "Sorry, I know it's tight."

She laughed. "You don't have to apologize."

He listened, head down, and then cleaned the stethoscope earbuds with an alcohol pad from his pocket and put it back. "One-oh-two over fifty-four. It's on the low end. Just be sure to hydrate and try to take it easy the rest of the day."

"Yes, Doctor." She gave him her best demure smile, making him laugh now.

The other ambulance finally left. The sirens remained off. "Do you think it's all right if I leave?"

As if he'd heard her, Detective Jordan trotted down the front steps of the home, joining her and Aidan at the back of Kelly's ambulance. "I might need to start a family discount for you, Savanna. I've been working on your dad's case since this morning. Do you mind if we go over a few questions about what happened here?"

"Sure, that's fine." She perched again on the back of the vehicle. She really wanted to get back to her dad, but this shouldn't take long.

Jordan had her walk him through things step by step, interrupting occasionally to clarify. When she mentioned slipping on the wet floor, he frowned at her. "What do you mean?"

"It had just been freshly washed. It smelled like lemon floor cleaner—it was wet."

"Hmm. Did you see a housekeeper at all?"

"No."

"Did you notice anything out of the ordinary when Mr. Bishop let you in? Was anyone else home?"

"No. Wait—there was a landscaping company here, but they were gone by the time I came downstairs to get a drink."

"Do you recall the name of the company?"

She searched her memory, eyes wide. She could almost see the name on the side of the pickup truck. Ugh. "No, I'm sorry."

"It might come to you. So, you fell on the wet floor, and then what?"

She continued, Jordan stopping her again after a few minutes.

"Why did you leave the scene once paramedics arrived?"

"I didn't...I guess I didn't think of it as leaving anything. I had to get away from the...from Kyle. I went upstairs for my car keys so I could leave; I was shaken up, and I just wanted to get back to see my dad." She frowned, glancing over and meeting Aidan's gaze.

"Speaking of which, Detective," he said, "that about wraps up anything more she could tell you. EMS and police were here by then. Is it all right if she heads back to the hospital?"

He nodded. "Do me a favor. If you think of anything, even a small detail that seems insignificant to you, let me know. You've got my number, call me anytime."

FONZIE GREETED SAVANNA enthusiastically when she made a quick stop at home before heading back to see her dad. Aidan had pressed her to just drop her car at home and let him drive her to the hospital, saying he'd have the clinic reschedule his afternoon appointments. She'd stopped him.

There was no reason to make him miss work. She promised to take it easy, ordering him back to his patients. Even so, his offer meant more to her than he probably knew.

Right now, Aidan's clinic waiting room was filled with sick patients who'd waited and looked forward to their appointments with the best cardiothoracic doctor in the Midwest. She had no right to monopolize his time. She recalled her chat a while ago with town matriarch Caroline Carson, a would-be grandmother figure to Savanna and her sisters. Caroline had given voice to the thing Savanna was afraid to—the challenges of being in love with a surgeon, especially one as in demand as Aidan. He'd shared with her the conflicted regret he'd carried throughout his first marriage related to all the times he'd run late or not make it to planned events when a patient crashed or a surgery ran long. The conversation had left her with a lot to think about, though she still felt what she'd told Caroline—the little absences when he should be there for her but couldn't were far outweighed by all the other times he showed up, fully present, completely engaged. His job wasn't just important, it was lifesaving. She knew what she'd signed up for.

Fonzie yipped at her, jumping and wiggling around her legs so much, she laughed and dropped to the floor, letting him maul her with whiny kisses. She'd left him alone far too often lately, especially with Sydney being absent from Fancy Tails & Treats; her sister was usually a wonderful, free dog sitter, and Fonzie loved his job as shop greeter. Everything had been turned on its head the past several days, but she couldn't explain that to her pup.

She changed into much more comfy yoga pants and oversize sweatshirt that bore the words I AM KENOUGH in large pink Barbie movie font. She emptied her oversize tote bag onto her kitchen table, pushing everything into a pile and adding a package of chicken churro dog treats from Syd's gourmet treat shop, and then lining the bottom with Fonzie's favorite blanket.

"Okay, Fonz, what do you think?" She clipped his harness on, red to match his collar, and scooped him up, gently settling him into the bag to test it out. With it slung over one shoulder, the blanket pulled loosely over the top, it really wasn't too heavy, just the weight of the leather bag plus her twenty-something-pound dog.

At Anderson Memorial, she stopped in the parking lot to prep him before heading through the main entrance doors. She peeked under the corner of his blanket to find her happy little dog staring up at her, tongue out, his mouth in the wide smile characteristic of Boston terriers. "Don't get us in trouble, okay? You have to be quiet. We're just going for a short visit. Dad's morale could use a boost, and Daisy's way too big to fit in the bag. So, it's all up to you, Fonzie."

His tail wagged, shaking the bag, but he stayed in place and let her pull the blanket back over the top.

She probably could've carried her dog in her arms right past the front desk with two volunteers staffing it, helping visitors find the correct room. The two ladies there now were absorbed in a card game, and the few clinical staff she encountered on her way up to the second floor nodded politely to her and completely ignored the tote with the blanket thrown over it.

Savanna was pleasantly surprised to find her dad sitting up in the chair, freshly shaven, arms free of IV lines, eating a dinner of meat loaf and mashed potatoes. She smiled widely and hugged him, realizing what else was different—her mother was gone from his side for the first time in forty-eight hours.

She closed the hospital-room door and set the tote on her lap, letting an excited Fonzie reunite with her dad. They'd always loved each other. She kept a hand on his harness, trying to rein in the Boston's wiggles, but the desired effect was already complete—her dad's genuine smile told her it was worth the risk to smuggle in the dog.

"Oh no, you can't have any meat loaf," Harlan said. He stuck a huge forkful in his mouth, savoring it. "Mom went home to shower and bring back some clothes for me. They're letting me go tomorrow."

Thank goodness her mother had finally felt comfortable enough to leave him and run home. She'd probably feel like a new person after a shower and a change of clothes for herself. "I can't believe how much better you look. And you're actually eating and drinking!"

"I'm starving," he said. He rested a hand on his nonexistent belly. "I don't recommend the lost-at-sea diet." In a final three bites, he cleared the plate, then finished off the Styrofoam cup of water and picked up the fruit cup, the only thing left on the hospital tray in front of him.

"Don't overdo it," she said, knowing it was an unnecessary warning. Her dad was normally a bottomless pit, and he seemed to be quickly returning to normal.

He held the fruit cup up disdainfully. "This dessert is a joke." He tipped it up and drained it.

"I passed a vending machine...what do you want? I'll go get something."

"It's all right. I think I'm full but just don't know it yet. Thank you for bringing my friend here," he said. He had Fonzie settled on his lap, soaking up as much attention as possible.

"Did Sydney happen to stop by this afternoon?" Savanna asked.

"She and Finn did," he said, frowning.

She and Syd had agreed not to share what had happened at Sebastian's house with their dad; not now, with the heart monitor on. He didn't need to add worrying about her to his focus on healing. Had her sister spilled the news about Kyle? Or kept it to wedding talk? "How, uh, did that go?"

"There's no need to postpone. I told them no."

"Dad—"

"I'm too tired to argue. I already did with your sister," he said. "She chose well. So did you, Savanna. I'm glad I'm here to see it."

She was stunned to see tears in her father's eyes. She swallowed around the sudden lump in her throat and wrapped her arms around him. She rested her head on his. He lifted a hand briefly to his eyes and then encircled her again in his arms, neither of them speaking. She didn't know how long they sat that way.

The door opened and she hastily tossed the little blanket

over Fonzie, who'd fallen asleep, sandwiched in between them. She turned to face the door, expecting a doctor or nurse or someone coming in to take away the dinner tray.

Instead, Travis stood in the doorway, baby Hannah in the crook of one elbow, Nolan beside him.

Chapter Fifteen

"HI, GUYS!" SAVANNA sprang to her feet, knowing she sounded way too enthusiastic.

She met Travis in the middle of the room and hugged him hello, planting a kiss on Hannah's forehead. She bent and whispered to Nolan the exciting news about the secret dog visitor, and he gasped.

"Really? Are you kidding me, Auntie Vanna?"

She chuckled; he sounded just like his dad. "I am not kidding you at all. Come here."

Nolan hung back, eyeing his grandfather cautiously. To Savanna, her dad looked a thousand times better than he had just yesterday. But now seeing him through the five-year-old's eyes, the bandage around his head, the blue-polka-dotted hospital gown with the heart monitor wires poking out, and the neon green cast on his arm all made Harlan not look like Nolan's grandpa.

Travis spoke. "Hey, buddy, remember when Evie in summer camp broke her arm and had to wear that pink cast for a while? Grandpa has the same thing. It's a pretty cool color, huh?"

She grudgingly admitted to herself that he'd drawn a perfect parallel. Through the years, Skylar's husband had morphed from the kind of twenty-something tall blond jock you'd see hanging out on a beach to the kind of thirty-something tall blond executive you'd find at a board of directors meeting. There was no doubt he was a good dad. He'd always seemed like a good husband, but only Skylar would know for sure.

"If we can hunt down a marker, you can draw a picture on my cast," Harlan said.

"I can draw really good dogs." He scooted closer. "Grandpa, that's a funny dress." He moved to the chair and touched one of the thin wires sprouting from the sleeve of the gown. "What are these?"

"Those tell the doctor how my heart is beating. It's beating strong, just like yours, see?" He placed Nolan's palm over his own small chest and the boy's eyes widened.

"I feel it! Do I need those too?" He pointed to the wires.

"Nope. They're mostly only for old guys like me," Harlan said.

Fonzie poked his head out of the blanket and Nolan was finally fully invested; he climbed onto the bed beside his grandpa's chair and Savanna snuggled the little dog beside him.

Travis shifted a fussing Hannah. "Is it okay if I sit? She's getting hungry. Skylar won't be home until after visiting hours are over, and the kids and I wanted to come say hello."

Savanna and Harlan both answered at once, Savanna taking the diaper bag from him and setting it on the long leather couch. "Give me this little cutie," she said, stealing the baby from his arms while he unpacked baby food from the bag. She walked Hannah around the room, stopping by Fonzie and leaning in a bit, the tiny girl erupting in giggles at the dog.

"How are you feeling? We were all so worried. It must have been awful for you," Travis said.

Prickles of irritation crept up Savanna's spine. *Were you worried, Travis? While you left your wife to manage your family alone, while not knowing if her father was alive?* She bit back the words.

"I don't remember much. I did come out of it with this really cool suntan." He drew a line with his thumb from his forehead to his chin, grinning at Nolan.

"I'm glad you're home safe. Is there anything you need? Anything I can do?"

Her dad locked eyes with Travis, silent. Neither man spoke for what felt like a very long time, at least to Savanna. "You're doing it, son." That was all. The things he left unsaid hung in the air between them.

Travis nodded once, and turned his attention to feeding Hannah.

Savanna's mother made it back to the hospital just before visiting hours ended, hair clean and fluffy and face freshly washed, prepared for another night spent sleeping in the recliner chair near her husband. The heavy door swinging open and once again making Savanna rush to shield Fonzie from view was her cue. She'd pressed her luck enough for one day. She got the dog packed into her tote, apologizing to Nolan for having to take him away.

Travis stood and said his goodbyes as well. The last thing

she wanted was to walk all the way through the hospital side by side with her sister's husband, when Skylar was clearly upset with him, especially since she knew nothing at all about why. But she and Travis did exactly that—fought the awkward silence down one long hallway after another, through the elevator ride, and all the way out the exit. She wanted to yell at him, but she had no idea what for. And, for his part, he'd been nothing but respectful and humble the entire evening.

As they parted ways in the parking lot, Travis finally spoke. "I love your sister. I hope you and your family know that."

She stared at him. "I know you do."

"I'd never do anything to hurt her. We're…going through something right now."

"Okay." Then, "Dad was glad you came and brought the kids tonight."

He shrugged. "Of course. He's been like my own father for more than a decade. I'm relieved he's all right."

She nodded. She was about to turn and head to her car but stopped. "The thing my dad said…when you asked if there's anything you can do. What about you and Skylar? Is there anything I can do? Anything Syd and I can do that might help?"

He tipped his head back, looking at the sky full of stars. When he finally met her gaze, his eyes glistened, startling her, just as her dad's reaction had done. "I don't think so."

THE BRIEF CONVERSATION with her brother-in-law replayed in her head on the way home. She pulled in alongside her house, barely remembering the drive. Travis had rattled her. If she was honest with herself, her dad had rattled her first. They could have lost him; he was rescued just in time. They were so fortunate that his head injury wasn't worse, that he hadn't suffered more broken bones, that nothing much had happened to the unmanned, adrift yacht other than a severe course change. She knew all that, so of course her dad did too, so why had his tears shaken her up so much?

Wrapped up in a cozy pink blanket, Savanna propped her feet on the wide edge of the firepit her dad had built for her deck. She'd started an inadequate fire, just to shoo away the chill in the air until she went inside. She'd already fed Fonzie, brushed her teeth, and put her pajamas on, but she couldn't bring herself to climb into bed at 8:25 p.m. She hadn't gone to bed this early since she'd had a bedtime as a kid.

Light swung across the deck and dunes, Aidan's SUV pulling into the driveway. He appeared on her deck steps as if she'd wished him here. She dropped the blanket and stepped into his arms, not caring that she was in threadbare mismatched PJs she should have discarded years ago or that her hair was tied up in a messy bun on top of her head.

His fingers glided along her jawline, tipping her chin up as he bent to kiss her. When he drew back, he kept his hand curled loosely around the side of her neck. "Are you doing all right, fiancée of mine?"

She closed her eyes, smiling. He kissed her eyelids. The

entire experience of being engaged to Aidan was completely opposite so far from the last time she was engaged. She slipped her hand into his and brought him over the fire, snuggling against him. "I'm doing great now. Kind of a rough day today."

"I'd agree with that."

"My dad complimented you. Well, he complimented me and you by default. He said Syd and I chose well, and he's happy he's here to see it. And he cried. It was a good thing; it was so nice to hear. So why am I so shaken up? He's human. He has feelings; I've seen them plenty before today."

Aidan sat back, one arm draped along the bench behind her. "Maybe it's not that, maybe it's Kyle. That had to be traumatic."

"It was. But I felt mostly okay until I saw my dad."

He was quiet. "Well," he said after a while, "he's mortal. He's not invincible."

"I know that."

"You know that, but until today, maybe you've never seen your dad process that. Sounds like he's dealing with some very normal post-trauma responses."

"That makes perfect sense. I don't like it; it's not a good feeling. He got choked up about us marrying good men, but he wasn't upset that he had this near-death experience, he was...grateful. Like a powerful, terrifying gratitude."

"It happens when you become a parent," Aidan said simply. "Your heart beats on the outside of your body where it's vulnerable all the time, and even if you're able to keep it intact, the overwhelming moments of pure joy when your kid is happy, when you know she's going to be okay—those moments are so intense they hurt sometimes."

She had no words; she stared at him, awed. He made her want to experience that firsthand.

"Anyway, it's cool your dad likes me."

She laughed. "Wow, Aidan. Uncle Freddie actually said something really similar about Ellie... He became her dad after Uncle Max did, but it doesn't seem to matter; she's their world."

"So, you're interested?"

"In you? Extremely," she teased.

"In having a baby together. Or babies." He raised an eyebrow at her.

Her pulse sped from normal to NASCAR in seconds flat; her breath caught in her throat. She'd allowed herself to think about it, just a little. She'd tried not to think about it too much, since it was a sore point when she and Rob were engaged. She'd tried to talk about kids and what their respective thoughts were so many times, and he'd constantly dodged discussing it. Looking back, she must have known his avoidance was her answer. With Aidan, she'd allowed herself to wonder if maybe one child was enough for him. Mollie was the sweetest little girl; Savanna already loved her like crazy. If Mollie ended up being her only child, assuming Mollie eventually came to see her as *Mom*, she'd be happy with that. After the whole experience with Rob and the way their engagement had fallen apart, a big part of her had been afraid to think too much about her future as a parent.

"I've spooked you." Aidan squeezed her shoulder lightly.

"I'm not trying to push you. Bad timing—there's no reason we need to talk about this right now."

She pivoted on the seat to face him, bringing one leg up underneath her. She cupped his handsome, stubbly face in her hands. "I would love to have your babies, Aidan. I'd love that. And I can't wait to become Mollie's stepmom. Being a parent with you is the most amazing thing I can imagine."

He seized her around the waist, pulling her into him and burying his face in her neck, sending thrilling zings of electric tingles through her. She felt the smile he couldn't suppress as he kissed her.

Later, after he'd left to relieve Mollie's grandparents before it got too late, Savanna sat at her kitchen table with a bowl of cereal and flipped through Sebastian's planner. She'd be sure to put it back right where she'd found it when she went back to finish her authenticating work, but nobody was going to miss it in the meantime. For a retired artist trying to live mostly as a hermit tucked away in the woods, Sebastian was a busy man. In the two weeks before the regatta, in small, neat print in the applicable calendar boxes, Sebastian—presumably—had notated things like:

SUNDAY 7:00 AM TEE TIME HAWKSHEAD

TUESDAY 11:30 AM DENTIST

THURSDAY 9:00 AM BRITT NASH LANSING MUSEUM

FRIDAY BEFORE 5:00 PM GET NEW RIGGING FROM GUS

SUNDAY 7:00 AM TEE TIME HAWKSHEAD

TUESDAY 3:00 PM JILLIAN BLACK—BRING STATEMENTS

WEDNESDAY 5:30 PM TEE TIME HAWKSHEAD

THURSDAY 7:00 PM MAEVE COAST 236

FRIDAY 4:00 PM PRE-CHECK SAIL

SATURDAY 8:00 AM REGATTA

In the days following the regatta were more notations, tee times Sebastian had now missed, another appointment with the dentist, and a few other mundane things like BARBER and ANNUAL PHYSICAL.

She had so many questions. The only thing she knew now for certain was that Sebastian kept a fairly busy schedule, and he'd had every intention of returning Monday night with all the other boats from the regatta.

She knew about the meeting he'd had with Britt, because her colleague had updated her afterward. She'd no idea Sebastian was such an avid golfer, so that was news.

He'd gotten new rigging from Gus at Sweetwater Boats the week before the regatta, which didn't sit right with her. Kyle's bandaged hand flashed into her mind, the red abrasion he'd said was a rope burn he'd gotten after Sebastian charged him with getting a new line set up the morning of the regatta. She should have trusted her gut that Kyle had lied about why he was at Gus's counter. The proprietor might appear to be an unkempt, old sailor but he was a perfectionist. Anytime she or her dad had occasion to use Sweetwater, the outcome was always flawless, whether for repairs or replacements of vital motor or sailing components, or even in the Catalina he'd rented her so she could teach Aidan to sail. She'd go talk with Gus tomorrow.

More than that, though, she might need to share the

planner with Detective Jordan, which meant confessing that she'd stolen—borrowed—it from his studio. Of everything in the week leading up to the regatta, the two appointments that gave her the most pause were Maeve and whatever he was doing at her sister's law firm.

Chapter Sixteen

FRIDAY MORNING BROUGHT two pieces of news, one good and the other devastating. Her mother called to let her know her dad had been discharged from Anderson Memorial. They were on their way home. Over Bluetooth, she heard her dad say something about taking his motorcycle out this weekend, an idea her mom shot down immediately.

"What part of take it easy did you not understand?"

"The doc said to take it easy. He didn't say I had to sit on the couch doing nothing," Harlan protested.

At the risk of furthering their argument, Savanna asked, "Dad, did you and Sebastian ever golf together?"

"Not much. Even with a handicap, I didn't enjoy the few times we went. It's not really a game to him."

"Who does he usually golf with?"

"He and his daughter are pretty evenly matched. They partner quite a bit."

"Interesting. Thanks. And I agree with Mom, I think it's a little too soon to be out on your bike."

"What's that? You're breaking up...didn't catch that. Gotta go," he said.

The call ended abruptly. He was definitely feeling better!

Savanna turned into the Carson Marina parking lot. The

awning was still pulled down and locked on Sweetwater Boats; she'd have to wait for Gus. The shop opened at ten and it was already five past. Her car was too warm parked, and she hated to keep it running. She went for a walk to visit her Catalina while she waited. She pulled up Maeve Davis's phone number, finger hovering above the call button. She'd asked Savanna to call her with any updates, but this wasn't an update, it was a question—one with a glaringly obvious answer that she hoped she was wrong about.

The appointment—date?—at Coast 236 with Maeve Davis seemed incriminating, no matter how she looked at it. Coast 236 was a prestigious restaurant up the coast in Grand Pier that offered high-end dining to anyone who could afford the one-hundred-dollar-plus per plate price tag. Savanna had never been inside, but most folks around here knew of the place. Why was Sebastian there with Maeve, two nights before the regatta, when Chelsea had said Maeve drove in from Chicago the morning of the race? Chicago was a four-and-a-half-hour round trip; she doubted Maeve went home Thursday night and came back Saturday morning.

She couldn't ask Chelsea why her father had dinner with his lovely artist friend at the nicest restaurant on the west coast—or why Maeve likely lied about when she'd gotten into town. Maybe Winnie had been at dinner with them? There was no good way to ask that of Sebastian's wife. She had to ask Maeve.

The artist picked up on the first ring. "Savanna. Is there news? I've heard nothing from the family."

"No...I haven't heard anything either." Did Maeve

know about Kyle? Savanna still didn't know for sure whether he'd survived, but everything yesterday made her think he hadn't. "I do have a question for you, though."

"Sure, go ahead."

"I'm just wondering...in Sebastian's studio, he'd left his planner open on his desk, and I noticed something. I hate to ask, it's not my business...but I feel like I have to ask, with us still not knowing what happened to them. Maybe even small little pieces of information are relevant, you know?"

"What are you getting at, Savanna?"

"I'm not saying one thing has anything to do with the other. And I'm not trying to draw any conclusions..." She could sense Maeve's impatience through the phone. "You said you drove into town Saturday morning for the regatta." She couldn't figure out how to phrase, *Why did you have dinner with your married friend and then lie about even being in town?*

"I didn't drive in Saturday. I was in Carson since Thursday afternoon. Sebastian and I had some business to attend to."

She'd expected a story. Some convoluted explanation. She was surprised at the admission.

Maeve continued, "Winnie has been prone to some...misplaced jealousy. Sebastian didn't want to stir anything up; it was easier just not to mention it."

"Oh."

"Listen, maybe this is something we could talk about in person. I'd be more comfortable with that. I can be in Carson tomorrow, if that works for you."

She wasn't prepared for any part of Maeve's response. "Yes, that will work. I appreciate it. Just give me a call whenever you're in town."

The artist agreed and ended the call. None of the conversation had gone the way Savanna had predicted.

On the dock, having laid eyes on her and Aidan's beautiful sailboat, she headed back toward the parking lot, glad to see Sweetwater now open. Gus lifted a hand in greeting, as he always did. "Hey there, Miss Savanna."

"Hey, Gus. How are you?" She stood across the counter from him.

He shrugged. "Better question is how's Harlan. He okay? Coast guard found him, that right?"

She nodded. "Yes, they did, Tuesday night. He's a lot better now. He was hit over the head. He has a concussion and a broken arm; by the time they found him, he was severely dehydrated." Gus's eyes had grown wide, his skin paling beneath his weathered perma-tan. "We almost lost him. And Sebastian wasn't with him on the yacht. I'm sure you heard that?"

"I did," he said, his gravelly voice quiet. "Shame. Hate hearing that."

She'd known this man forever; he'd been part of her dad's boating life for twenty years or more. She didn't believe he'd knowingly done anything that had contributed to her dad getting hurt—or Sebastian disappearing. But maybe he knew something without even realizing he did. "The morning of the regatta was insanely busy for you, I noticed. But I'm wondering about one particular customer... It might provide a piece of the puzzle to what happened."

"Shoot. Any way I can help, you know that. I been a friend of your dad's a long time. Sebastian too, though Lord knows they ain't the same, him and your dad."

It was more words than she'd ever heard the man string together at once. She was gratified to know her belief in him wasn't off base. "Sebastian's personal assistant told me he'd been sent over here to purchase a set of lines for the X-Yacht the morning of the regatta. His name was—is—Kyle Bishop. Maybe I can find a picture of him." She pulled out her phone and searched the social media app most of the world seemed to use. A search of his name and Sebastian's together yielded exactly what she'd hoped. She set the phone on the counter turned toward Gus, Kyle's profile picture filling the screen.

Gus picked up her phone and held it away from him at arm's length, squinting his eyes. "That's him. Nasty fella. But that wasn't his name, and he didn't need no lines. I already took care of that the week before for his boss. Nothing wrong with any of the rigging he ordered from me."

"Really! He lied to me. I wonder why." She saw no reason to be coy with Gus. Maybe he'd have some insight. "What did he want, then? Do you remember what name he used? You know what, Gus, I'm pretty sure I saw him at your counter here that day, when I waved hello to you. He seemed like he was giving you a hard time."

"He was that. He wanted one of our runabouts, but he wasn't sure he'd have her back before closing. He said..." Gus rolled his eyes skyward. "What'd he say? He might wanna sleep under the stars or something. Ain't no sleepin' quarters on them boats, they're just for zipping around the lake." He opened a thick ledger book spilling over with papers and flipped through the pages. "I'll find the name he used. I keep everything."

"He rented a boat?" Her mind raced. What had he done? She suspected he'd gotten that wound on his hand in an entirely different manner than he'd told her.

"He did. Cabin cruiser woulda served him better than a runabout. But you can't tell some folks nothing. I gave him the twenty-eight-foot bowrider, plenty speedy, but roomy too, in case he decided to keep her out overnight."

"When did he bring it back?"

"I don't know." He unclipped the three-ring binder and handed her a sheet of paper. It made perfect sense to her that Sweetwater Boats wasn't computerized yet. "She was in the slip Sunday morning, key in the drop box. You'd have to ask him when he brought it back, if he'll tell you. Not likely, with him usin' a fake name."

I can't. He might be dead. To Gus, she said, "You don't even know how helpful you've been. Thank you, Gus."

"Tell your dad I got some new lures in, whenever he's back on his feet."

He'd piqued Savanna's hope. She didn't know what or why yet, but between the bit of information from Maeve and now Gus, she finally felt like maybe she could help shed some light on what had happened to her dad and Sebastian.

SAVANNA STOPPED AT her parents' house before heading over to Fancy Tails & Treats for lunch with her sisters. Maybe her mom might feel all right leaving her dad alone for an hour to join them. She was still tumbling around the puzzle pieces in her head of how Kyle was involved in Sebastian's disappearance, nothing fitting together well yet. It wouldn't do to give her dad false hope, but she could see a visit to Detective Jordan in her future.

A car she didn't recognize was in the driveway behind her mother's, a newer model white Escalade. Savanna went around to the side entrance and came in through the kitchen, out of habit. Her mom sat at the counter with Winnie Alexander, two mugs of coffee and a box of tissues in front of them. Winnie blotted her eyes and added her tissue to the small pile in her lap. She turned her makeup-streaked face to Savanna in the doorway.

"They've scaled back the search. The coast guard investigator said the likelihood of Sebastian being found alive is slim, and they have to conserve resources." Her face crumpled and new tears rolled down her cheeks.

Chapter Seventeen

S AVANNA WAS THE last to arrive for lunch at Fancy Tails. The CLOSED sign on the door displayed a cartoon of a big drooling St. Bernard with the words, NEVER TRUST A DOG TO WATCH YOUR FOOD. WE DON'T! CLOSED FOR LUNCH. As the little bell over the door jingled, Skylar and Sydney looked up from the red and chrome café table by the large front window on the pet bakery side of the shop. Savanna passed the reception desk and, behind it, windows looking through to the grooming area and joined her sisters. She dropped her tote onto one of the overstuffed aqua chairs. The cozy waiting area offered complementary pop or water from a mini fridge and comfy seating where patrons could sit and observe Main Street while waiting for their furry companions to be primped and pampered.

She found it awkward meeting Skylar's eyes, as if her older sister would somehow know about the appeal of sorts Travis had made last night. "Oh, wow, that smells amazing."

Sydney had provided a deep-dish pizza from Giuseppe's down the street. It was still steaming hot. "This side is vegetarian and dairy free." Syd pointed, as if she needed to specify that the half missing its cheese was not meant for Savanna. "And this is your side, plus your stinky feta you love so much."

Savanna slid a piece of mouthwatering pizza onto a plate, sprinkling parmesan cheese on top. "You're just jealous. Enjoy your veggies and sauce." She smiled sweetly and popped a pepperoni into her mouth.

"I will." She took the spatula. "Which kind do you want, Sky?"

Skylar looked up from her phone. "What?"

"She wants the good kind," Savanna said.

"Yes, please. Savanna's side." She returned to her phone, finally dropping it into her purse as Sydney handed her pizza to her. "What? Stop staring at me."

She was exasperating. "Do you know why we're here? Because we're both worried about you. Something is clearly going on, and you need to stop trying to be all stoic or independent or private or whatever. It's not healthy. Talk to us."

Skylar stood, pushing her chair back. "I'm going back to work."

Savanna stood with her. "Sit down. Right now."

Skylar blew her breath out impatiently and dropped into her chair, sitting back with arms crossed over her chest.

"If one of us was going through something, crying in our car, fighting with our husband, you'd be all over it. You'd want to know what it is and how to fix it," Savanna said, taking her seat again.

"You can't fix this. And no offense but neither of you has a husband yet; you can't possibly imagine how I'm feeling."

"Offensive," Sydney said. "I don't have to have been

married for years to know what it feels like when the person I love hurts me. Metaphorically. Right? Not physically, or I'll personally find him and kill him."

Skylar rolled her eyes. "Not physically. You don't even need to ask that. You know Travis. He'd never hurt me."

"He said that."

Skylar stared at Savanna. "What do you mean? When?"

"He brought the kids to visit Dad at the hospital last night. He stopped me as we were leaving to tell me he loves you, he hopes our family knows that, and that he'd never hurt you."

"I can't believe he came to the hospital," she murmured. "What did he tell Dad?"

"Nothing. Well, he asked if there's anything he can do. Like, to help Dad recover or whatever. Dad just said something like *You're doing it.* It took him a minute. I thought Dad was going to lay into him, but he didn't."

Skylar sighed, leaning on the table, and dropped her head into her hands. "That's not his place. Dad's smarter than that."

Savanna exchanged a look with Sydney. How much should they press her? "Since we're talking about it, everyone's noticed he just sort of flaked. He hasn't been around. And Travis is normally *always* around, involved, stepping up, you know that. So, it's been weird."

"Oh my God, this family." She shook her head. "It's not his fault he wasn't here during all this with Dad. Not entirely. I told him not to come home."

She had their attention. Neither of them spoke.

"Don't judge me. You don't even know. It's hard to explain. He has this huge opportunity at work; it would change everything for him. His title, his salary...his location. It'd mean we'd have to move. Or, if we didn't, I'd just never see him. He took off without telling me Monday night to meet with the CEO of the company that's absorbing his, even though we decided he was going to pass on the promotion. He just...went anyway. So, I told him to stay there."

"What does that mean?" Savanna asked.

Travis had never complained about his job as a civil engineer. He'd taken advantage of the ability to flex his hours once Nolan was born, so that he could work around Skylar's busier schedule. It let them limit day care and babysitters to a bare minimum, and he seemed to enjoy his shorter workdays when he had the kids. While there was nothing wrong with him wanting to advance his career, going behind her sister's back to do it wasn't the way.

"He's taking the job anyway?" Syd asked.

"I don't know," Skylar admitted, smoothing a hand over her stick-straight hair. "We haven't really talked about it. I haven't seen him enough to talk about it; he got back and then I had a twelve-hour day yesterday, between prep work and kid drop-off and court. This morning, he was already gone when I left."

Sydney scooted her chair over and hugged her. "I'm sorry. I don't know what to say."

She nodded. "Me neither." Skylar rested her head on Syd's shoulder.

Savanna joined them, smothering their older sister with

sibling affection. "We love you, Sky."

She patted both their backs. "I know. It'll work out, one way or another. Okay, give me some air."

Savanna picked up her pizza, now cool enough to eat. "What can we do? There must be something."

Sydney handed them each a Mary Ann's soda. "I got brownies from Main Street Sweets for dessert," she said. "Not that that will help."

"Chocolate always helps," Skylar said.

"I saw Winnie. She said the coast guard thinks it's unlikely that Sebastian is still alive, and they're cutting back on the search," Savanna said, abruptly changing the topic. The mention of Chelsea's bakery had reminded her she'd been here a whole ten minutes and hadn't filled in her sisters yet. "Winnie's with Mom. They must have just told her."

"It's been less than a week. How can they do that?" Skylar asked.

"Winnie said the coast guard still hasn't found any sign of the dinghy from the *Serendipity*, and they should have by now unless it sank. They think Sebastian must have used it to escape the attacker who hurt Dad. Winnie said with the temperature of the water and the length of time they've figured since he left the yacht and no sign of him... I guess they're just following protocol and scaling back."

"Ugh, I feel so awful for them," Syd said. "Chelsea must not have known yet when I saw her. She seemed fine."

"Skylar," Savanna said, "you're off work tomorrow right, and so is Travis?"

"Mostly. I have a case to prep for on Monday. And I

don't know his plans." Her mouth was set in a thin line, her face drawn. The stress was coming off her in waves.

"We'll babysit. Aidan and I," she clarified as Sydney started to protest. "I know you work tomorrow, Syd, don't worry. I'm supposed to meet with Maeve Davis sometime tomorrow, but it won't take long, and Aidan will be fine with Nolan and Hannah while I'm gone."

"You're sweet," Skylar said. "And obviously Aidan is fine with kids, he has one. He's a great dad. But I can't commit until I check with Travis. He may not be around, and if he is, he might have no interest in figuring things out. I thought we already did that, but then he just made his own decision."

"Back up, Savvy," Syd said. "Why are you meeting with Maeve Davis? And where? Doesn't she live in Chicago?"

"She's driving in. She didn't want to talk over the phone. Listen, there's a lot to catch you guys up on, but it doesn't have to happen right now. Skylar's marriage is more important. That day I saw you outside your office," Savanna told her, "I really thought Travis had done something...terrible. Like, unforgivable. I couldn't even imagine it—probably because it's impossible. You know he loves you, right? I don't think he'd ever prioritize anything above you, Sky."

"I thought that too. Now I don't know." She looked from Savanna to Syd. "Eat your pizza and tell me what led to you talking with Maeve Davis."

In the half hour they had left before Skylar had to cross the street back to work, Savanna covered as much information as she could, starting with finding Kyle in a pool of blood below the catwalk. She backed up from there. Savanna filled them in on spotting Kyle talking with Gus the morning of the regatta, Kyle's hand and his lie to her, Gus sharing that he'd rented a boat to Kyle under a pseudonym, her conversations with Griffin and Chelsea, her chat with Maeve this morning, and Sebastian's high-end dinner at Coast 236 when Maeve was pretending to be home in Chicago, to keep Winnie's jealous streak at bay.

"She probably suspected they were seeing each other," Sydney said. "That's so shady of Sebastian. And Maeve."

"I'm inclined to agree with you," Skylar said. "That's pretty manipulative...keeping secrets from your spouse to prevent them from getting upset, when finding out she's been kept in the dark is guaranteed to make Winnie jealous and upset."

"Well," Savanna said, "in the spirit of full transparency, the reason I know all these things about Sebastian is because I borrowed his planner."

"Oh snap," Syd said. "Borrowed?"

"Stole," Skylar said. "I need a brownie if we're going to do this."

Sydney quickly cleared away the lunch debris and pizza box and set a pretty bakery carton in the center of the table with some napkins.

"Goodness, that lady can bake," Skylar said, savoring a large bite of caramel sea salt brownie.

Savanna seized her chance. "Okay, so, yes, I stole Sebastian's planner. Temporarily. But in my defense, I'd just tripped over the bleeding body of Sebastian's assistant, tried to save him, and then locked myself in the studio because I was afraid the killer was still in the house. I panicked. I was looking for something to use as a weapon in his desk and found his planner."

"And slipped it into your bag." Skylar shook her head. "That could invalidate it as possible evidence if there's something incriminating in there."

"I didn't think of that. But look." Savanna placed the planner on the table, open to the week before the regatta.

"What the heck. I didn't see that," Skylar said. She was looking skyward.

"Skylar. Look, I need your help. I'm going to talk with Detective Jordan today. If you don't think I should bring him the planner, I'll go put it back. I'll tell him I saw it open on his desk when I was working for him and couldn't help seeing some of what's jotted in here." She pointed, drawing her sister's attention to one particular notation on Tuesday before the regatta, two days before Sebastian took Maeve to Coast 236:

3:00 PM JILLIAN BLACK—BRING STATEMENTS

"What is this?" Savanna asked.

Skylar looked from the page to her sister. "Did he have one of our senior partners on retainer?"

"I have no idea. Did he? For what?"

Skylar stared again at the calendar notation. "You want me to find out."

"Can you?"

"Not ethically."

Savanna groaned. "I figured you'd say that."

"Jillian Black handles two types of cases. Divorce and estates," Skylar said.

"Oh *snap*," Sydney repeated. "Sebastian met with a divorce lawyer?"

"Or an estate lawyer. Maybe he revised his will. All right, Savanna, your idea isn't bad. You've got to put this back where you found it—leave it open on the studio desk like you said. When exactly did you plan on sitting down with Jordan to go over all of this?"

"Soon? I think it might help. Plus, I remembered the name of the landscaping company that was there the day I found Kyle. I promised to let him know if I did." The landscaper's logo on the side of the truck had popped into her brain this morning. LAKESIDE LAWN AND GARDEN in bold font cut diagonally across a large tree and root system that created a circle.

"Make sure you put the planner back first," Skylar warned, her voice stern. "Get Aidan or someone to go with you. I've gotta run. Love you guys."

"Love you," she called to Skylar, heading out the door. "Aidan's in clinic. Syd?"

"We're overbooked this afternoon, plus I'm leaving early so I can be at the tux shop when Dad and Finn and the guys get there tonight."

"The fittings are tonight? I'm so excited for you," Savanna said, smiling. "When will your gown and ours be ready?"

"Tuesday," Sydney said. "I thought we could go for our final fitting after work Tuesday, Mom too. If you and Skylar are free."

"If I'm not, I'll make myself free. Don't worry."

Syd smiled. "Oh—we're still doing Sunday dinner this weekend, right? It's your turn to cook."

"We'd better be. I'm making crepes Ensenada. Aidan and Mollie are coming. Will Finn be able to make it?"

"I think so. Oh my God. Do you realize I'll be married for all the Sunday dinners after this one? That's crazy."

"I can't wait. For your wedding and for everything that's coming for you guys. I'm so happy for you," Savanna said.

She meant it. One of her less-than-tactful coworkers had asked her if it was strange having her little sister get married before she did. The question had made her feel like she'd stepped into a Jane Austen novel. She was enjoying every minute of Syd and Finn's wedding prep. A year ago, she'd have guessed her youngest sister would never marry; she'd never had a smidge of interest in the idea. Meeting Finn had changed that.

BEFORE HEADING TO the sheriff's department, Savanna mustered all the bravery she could and drove back to Sebastian's house. With Kyle gone, she expected to see no one. She mentally walked herself through typing in the lock code to the front door, getting upstairs to the studio, displaying Sebastian's calendar open, in plain sight, on his desk, and getting the heck out of there.

She did exactly that, even thinking to grab her laptop in

case she bumped into anyone. She'd only stopped by because she needed her computer.

As she was leaving, the landscaping company was pulling in. The man driving the pickup waved her through, letting her leave so they wouldn't block her in. She stopped alongside them and rolled down her window, double-checking the snapshot of the logo in her memory—she'd had it exactly correct.

The man at the wheel did the same. "Hi there."

"I just wanted to let you know, Mr. Alexander's assistant isn't in today. I'm not sure when he'll be back; in case you were looking for Mr. Bishop."

The man nodded. "Thank you. We shouldn't need anyone today. We're still working on the sprinkler system repair. We won't need the water on until next week."

"Sounds good! Hope it goes smoothly. I came by to get my laptop." She held it up, feeling instantly weird and suspect. Like they cared why she was there. At least now she could go bounce some of her ideas and information off of Detective Jordan without a guilty conscience.

She stopped by the sheriff's department before heading home, but Detective Jordan wasn't in. She left a message with the desk sergeant, and he called her as she was pulling in her driveway.

"Hey, Savanna, what's going on?"

"I was hoping to catch you... I had a few things I want to run by you when you have time."

"I've got time. Is it urgent? I'm on my way home now, but we can sit down tomorrow or Sunday, what's best?"

The perks of your family being friends with the best detective in town, she thought. "Sunday would be great, if you don't mind."

"I don't mind. I was meaning to give you a call. You might have been wondering... Sebastian's assistant, Kyle Bishop, didn't make it."

Chapter Eighteen

SATURDAY WAS A picture-perfect beach weather day. Savanna had spent much of the previous evening trying to erase from her mind the images of Kyle on the marble foyer floor, blood spread out in a wide circle around his head. She hadn't succeeded. She wished she'd been more effective, been able to save him, but she had a feeling Jordan was right. The nature of his injuries from the fall made it impossible. Now, she wondered how much it even mattered that Kyle might have rented a speedboat the day of the regatta. If he'd had anything to do with sabotaging her dad and Sebastian on the *Serendipity*, then who pushed him from the vaulted catwalk to his death? She couldn't make sense of it.

On her way to pick up her niece and nephew, she stopped at Happy Family grocery store in town and stocked up on kid-friendly snacks, juice boxes, sunscreen, and a fun multicolored beach umbrella and sand toy set she found on clearance in the end-of-season section, across from an entire aisle of Halloween decorations and candy that had appeared last week. Fall in all its color-changing glory was her favorite, and she loved Spooky Season. Her dad had started a pumpkin patch several months ago in the backyard, and now, one by one, bright orange pumpkins had begun to make their appearance, promising excellent jack-o'-lantern carving next month. She hadn't thought much beyond that, as every time she did, her stomach was filled with flutters. She and Aidan had talked about a winter wedding but had made no plans as of yet. Her head was filled with beautiful ideas, but they still needed to decide on a venue and a date.

The back of her car full of beach paraphernalia, Savanna scooped up her niece and nephew from Skylar and Travis early Saturday morning, catching her sister still in pajamas, though Travis had gone for a run. She warned Skylar that she didn't plan on returning Nolan and Hannah until Sunday morning. Driving away, glancing in the rearview mirror at the siblings strapped into their seats and her sister's house behind them, she said a little prayer for compassionate, open communication and good memories of all they'd already built and weathered as a couple. She knew they loved each other, but that wasn't always enough.

"Nolan," she said, "I'm just wondering, do you think Fonzie might want to come with us to the beach?"

"Yes!" The shriek from the back seat was ear-piercing, startling baby Hannah and making her burst into giggles.

"Okay, but I don't think he has a swimsuit."

"Dogs don't wear swimsuits, Auntie Vanna." Nolan was giggling now too.

"Seriously? But what if he wants to? That's not really fair."

He was quiet for a beat. "Well, he has fur. We just have to tell him he'd be too hot if he also had to wear swim trunks."

"What about swim fins for his feet? So he can swim faster?"

"He doesn't need 'em! He has four feet, and I only have two. He's already gonna be faster than me."

"Oh my gosh. You're right. It's a good thing we brought your fins, so you can keep up! But will he need goggles?"

"I don't think so. He has big bug eyes, I bet he can see good underwater. But I'll let him try my goggles if he wants," Nolan said.

He was such a sweet kid. "Fonzie is lucky to have such a good cousin," she said, smiling. She was only half joking. Her little Boston terrier really did seem to think he was just one of the kids.

Aidan and Mollie showed up around noon for their beach day, Aidan in aqua swim trunks with goldfish all over them. Savanna had already trekked twice from her house down the sandy path through small dunes and tall crab grass to the waterfront, Hannah strapped to her chest in her carrier. She'd pulled the beach wagon behind her with towels, new umbrella, pails and shovels, and a small cooler of drinks and sandwiches. She was so fortunate to have found this house in the shape it was in last year. The former couple renting it had to move out of state abruptly, and it had been years since the landlord put any money at all into updates. She'd expected to have to fight for it, but there wasn't even any competition. No other buyer wanted to sign up for the kinds of repair and renovation needed to make the place livable. Now, a year later and a huge team effort between herself, Aidan, and her dad and his contractors, she was in love with the place and the location. Aidan hadn't yet brought up the topic of where they'd live after they got married and neither had she; she was dreading that conversation. It was a no-brainer that they'd want to live in Aidan's house so Mollie wouldn't have to go through more changes than she already had.

But they'd broached the terrifying subject of having children; she was sure they'd figure this out too.

In her new pink halter swimsuit, Savanna soaked in the warm September sun. Her little niece was shielded by the umbrella, chubby baby toes kicking around in the sand. Aidan helped Nolan and Mollie with their sandcastle village. The lake was dotted with the white triangles of sails and a dozen or more other boats, taking advantage of the late season summer weather.

Fonzie bounded up the beach to her, sniffed her face, and then shook vigorously, water spraying everywhere. "Fonz!" She tried shooing him away and he flopped down on his back, rolling around and spreading muddy sand on the blanket. She carried Hannah to the shallow water and dangled her over the slow rolling waves breaking onshore to rinse her off. She'd never get enough of her happy, squealing giggles; it was impossible not to laugh with her.

She sat down on the soft sand, Hannah on her lap, and inspected the detailed city of sandcastles and moats. "You guys are talented. I can't believe you've made so many!"

Aidan dropped onto the sand beside her. The moment he did, Nolan and Mollie seized the opportunity and began dumping bucket after bucket of wet sand onto his long legs.

"Nice," he said, laughing.

He swiped some sand off, bits of it sticking to the hair on his legs. He let them continue until he was piled with mountains of sand, and then abruptly stood, shedding clumps of sand. He raised his arms, tipped his head back, and roared—and then reached for the kids.

"Sand monster!" Mollie sprinted down the beach, Nolan close behind her, until Aidan scooped them up, one under each arm, both kids pedaling air and laughing.

Midafternoon, feeling sun-fatigued and lazy, she and Aidan trailed behind them on the way up the path to her house, laden with beach gear and gallons of sticky sand. On the far side of the deck, they took turns in the outdoor shower her dad had installed before heading inside to get dried off and changed. When she left them to go meet Maeve, Hannah had gone down for a nap in her portable crib, and Nolan, Mollie, and Aidan were cozied up on the couch with popcorn, trying to decide which movie to watch.

SAVANNA JOINED MAEVE Davis at her table toward the back of Giuseppe's. "I appreciate you driving all the way in. I think the phone would have been fine, but this is nice," she said.

The artist was dressed simply in all black, a sleeveless chiffon top complementing toned arms and straight silver bob. "With the questions you asked, I wanted to fill you in on some...sensitive information. And I wanted you to hear it from me first." She pushed a black folder across the table.

Inside was a several page document titled LIVING TRUST AND ESTATE OF SEBASTIAN ALEXANDER, with the firm BLACK, JONES, AND SYDOWSKI listed as the preparer. So that question was answered—estate prep, not divorce, Savanna thought. Maeve reached over and flipped to page seven. "Read this."

In the midst of a lot of legalese Savanna struggled to comprehend, the last paragraph was crystal clear. Sebastian's estate was to be divided equally between Chelsea, Griffin, and Maeve Davis, with Griffin's held in the trust for the first year following Sebastian's death. At that time, he'd only receive the sum if specific conditions were met. The criteria allowing Griffin to realize his share of the estate was basically what he'd described to Savanna earlier in the week when he'd complained about Sebastian kicking him out of the regatta— he'd need to have secured and kept a full-time job sufficient to support himself for a minimum of one year before receiving his share. If he didn't, his inheritance would revert to Chelsea. There was no mention of his art endeavors.

"I'm sure you have questions," Maeve said.

"Winnie isn't in here. At all. So, Griffin was right."

"Griffin and Chelsea knew their dad removed Winnie as a beneficiary last year. But this is a new revision. I tried to talk him out of it. I don't want his money. This makes it look like we're something we aren't."

Savanna couldn't keep the surprise from her expression or tone. "You aren't?"

Maeve sighed. "No. Never. The idea of it is ridiculous.

You have to remember, he and I have been friends for going on thirty years. If there was one iota of attraction between us, something would've happened a long time ago. He wrote me into his will because he's always felt guilty his career took off before mine, after he connected with my agent. I've told him for years how happy it made me, seeing his work gain global recognition. He's trying to even things out, but it was never a race. To be honest, I believe he also included me because he knows I'd never let Griffin become destitute. He's so worried that kid will never grow up—kid. I'm saying kid, but he hasn't been that in fifteen years. I agree with Sebastian on that point. Anyway, he came to Chicago a few times last month so we could sit down and hash out details. He got the revised estate papers drawn up last week and made a point of getting me in front of his attorney to witness and sign as new executor."

Everything she said made a lot of sense, even Sebastian's trips to Chicago. Griffin suspected his dad was seeing Maeve, and he was, though not in the way his son thought.

"One thing," Savanna said. "Griffin said his dad was pushing him to cancel his art opening. There's nothing about him not being allowed to work as an artist in the estate papers, though."

Maeve shrugged. "Why would there be? Sebastian's goal isn't to dictate Griffin's life. But I think they both know Griffin isn't the artist his father is. Sebastian always wanted to save him the heartache he endured trying to break into the art world, but he knows no one could have convinced him to quit; Griffin will have to figure it out on his own."

"So, you don't think he tried to make him cancel his

event?"

"He wouldn't do that. Griffin told you that? It sounds like his own sour grapes, knowing his dad doesn't support his art."

The server took their orders and returned with drinks, an iced tea for Savanna and a cucumber martini for Maeve. They chatted about postimpressionist artists, including their mutual friends, and the conversation worked its way around to Maeve's contemporary pieces and then to Sebastian's exhibit, which might need to be postponed or canceled. Maeve waited while the server delivered their dinner to share her thoughts.

"Personally, I think he'd want you to move forward with it. But you'd know better than I would the legalities involved. Even if his wife gave permission, does she have the authority to do that? He isn't dead—hasn't been declared dead, I mean," Maeve corrected herself.

"There's been a huge marketing push for the event. Lansing Museum of Fine Art has been promoting it since July, with international sponsorship offers and plenty of interest from gallerists and collectors. It might be less complicated to go through with it than try to cancel it," she mused.

"Well, Sebastian will reap the rewards of the exhibit eventually, if or when he's found, and if he isn't, I supposed it'll all be rolled into his estate."

She had to ask. "Winnie really doesn't know he took her out of his will? She seemed open to the show going on without him when I saw her yesterday; I gently brought it up. I couldn't help wondering if her decision was financially motivated. She knows there's plenty to gain with this exhibit."

Maeve sighed. "I don't think Winnie truly sees Sebastian. She sees the version of him she wants him to be, even when that version has nothing to do with reality. She'd be completely shocked to learn she's not in the will."

"What happened a year ago that prompted him making that change?" She'd come into this meeting convinced Maeve was Sebastian's lover—and probably had been for a long time. The artist was believable and seemed genuine in her description of their platonic relationship. But what if the simplest explanation was the truth?

Maeve tipped her second martini glass up, finishing the last of it. She smoothed an already smooth strand of silver hair; she seemed to be stalling. "Sometimes things change in a marriage. Sometimes people change; what they want can shift. I can't say exactly what prompted him to change his will, but he felt he had no other choice."

AIDAN LEANED IN the doorway to Savanna's bedroom, one hand on the frame over his head. "So, do we get a sleepover too?"

She found the pajama set she was looking for in her dresser and straightened up, coming over to stand in front of him. "I don't think so. I'm all out of sleeping bags; I gave Mollie and Nolan my only two." The space between them was charged. She crossed her arms to avoid temptation.

"Auntie Vanna! I need my Bluey blanket." Nolan's voice

carried from the living room, where he and Mollie were set up in their blanket fort.

"I'll be right there," she called. "I suppose, if you really want to, you could sleep on the couch," she suggested. "In the living room."

"All by myself?" He ducked his head, gazing at her with so much smolder her cheeks burned. "Where's the fun in that?"

She leaned forward, pressing her head against his chest. "Holy cats, man. This is a G-rated evening. You're pushing PG-13." She looked up, meeting his eyes. "Don't make me wish it was R."

He raised an eyebrow. "You're reading my mind."

She took a deep breath. "Okay, then!" She thrust a pillow and blanket into his chest. "Take these. You'll be on the couch, and I'll be on the love seat. All very proper."

"If you insist." He turned to head back downstairs, hanging his head.

"Wait!"

He turned back hopefully.

"Here, give this to Nolan, please. I'll be right down after I change."

"Right." He took the Bluey blanket from her. "How about a G-rated kiss good night, before we join the slumber party?"

"If you insist," she copied him. She stepped into his arms for a very PG-13 kiss.

Chapter Nineteen

SUNDAY AFTERNOON FOUND Savanna in her parents' sunny kitchen assembling crepes Ensenada. Tortillas, shredded cheddar cheese, slices of ham, and a light coating of flour on nearly everything covered the island countertop. The crepe recipe required a good amount of prep and effort; making them was always a labor of love. Today, she was making them because they were her dad's absolute favorite dish.

She couldn't believe the way he'd bounced back. He'd humored her mom and hadn't yet been out on his motorcycle, maybe out of respect for the heart monitor Aidan was still having him wear as well. But he'd been working in the garden, coordinating jobs to get things back on track for the coming week, and had gone to the driving range that morning. To a trained eye, he seemed down. He was not quite back to normal. He brought Sebastian into every conversation. She knew he was worried—and *worried* was probably not a strong enough word.

Harlan came through the kitchen door with an armful of zucchini, depositing it on the counter. "You need to take some home later; you all do. We've got more." He pinched some shredded cheese from the counter and popped it into his mouth. "I love your crepes. Can't wait; I'm starving."

She laughed. "I think you've said you're starving at least ten times since Friday."

"I am. I can't imagine what Sebastian is doing for food. I keep hoping someone picked him up. The dinghy might have held up, but there's no navigation. And he's been saying for years that he should add a food cache to that thing, but we never did it."

She nodded. She didn't want to upset him by asking anything, but she didn't want him to think she didn't care or hadn't noticed he was struggling. "Want to sit and help me, one-handed?" She nodded to the stools on the opposite side of the kitchen island.

"Sure." He crossed to the sink and washed his hands before joining her.

She set up an assembly line for the two of them, directing him on how to roll the tortillas with the ingredients inside so that she could then add the custom cheese topping from the roux she'd made. "Have you heard anything from Admiral Moore?" she asked. "Any updates?"

"Not a word. I guess I should call him tomorrow. In a way, it's better not knowing than knowing he's gone." He shook his head, about to say something else but then changing his mind.

"Dad? What were you going to say?"

"I just wish I'd done something different."

"What do you think you could have done? You had no idea what was even happening when you were knocked out."

"Yeah. I don't know. I could've been paying more attention. Maybe he gave me some sign and I missed it. I should've been able to get to him, help him. I keep thinking of him in the water, hurt the same as me or worse." He frowned. He scowled at the tortilla he was awkwardly rolling using his right hand and just the fingertips of his left.

"He had the dinghy," she said. "I want to think he was all right, at least for a while. Maybe he still is."

He nodded, but his expression said he didn't agree.

"Do you want to call Admiral Moore now? I have his number. He might answer on a Sunday, you never know."

He looked up from the tortilla he held. "You're sweet, Savanna. Yes. I do. It'd help."

She washed her hands and pulled up the admiral's number in her phone, putting it on speaker. Maybe he could give them even a small update, something so her dad would feel bolstered. The call went to voicemail. Harlan took the phone and left a brief message, asking for a call back with any news. At least they'd tried.

They finished with the first pan of crepes Ensenada and began the second, Savanna absorbing as much of the prep as she could. The point wasn't for her dad to end up aggravated from working with a cast on; she just hoped to distract him from his worry about Sebastian. When both pans were full and covered, she got them into the oven and set the timer for an hour.

She brought two glasses of lemonade out onto the deck for them; her dad didn't sit well. It was unusual to find him holding still. So, she took advantage of it now.

She set a glass in front of him, joining him in the shade

on the two-person glider. "Hey, Dad. Did you know Sebastian's assistant very well?"

"Not really."

"Detective Jordan let me know he didn't make it. I was really hoping he did."

He pushed off the deck flooring with the tip of his shoe, getting the glider moving, a relaxing, swaying motion. "From what you told me it doesn't sound like anything could have been done. That's a wicked fall."

"This is a weird question, but just humor me, okay?"

"Sure."

"You and Sebastian were up around Glen Arbor last Saturday evening, right? Like, twilight-ish? Just before dark?"

"Yeah."

"Were there lots of boats around you? Or had they all sort of spread out by then?"

"Not too many. There are always a few that are visible, even several hours into the race. It does get tougher to see fellow competitors once it gets dark, though."

"Did you notice any boats around that night that weren't part of the regatta? Speedboats or cruisers, maybe?"

His brow furrowed. "Not that I recall."

She pressed. "Would you have been able to tell the difference between a sailboat and a motorboat in the dark? Like, by running lights or something? Or would they look the same from a distance?"

He looked at her. "You're trying to get a handle on who attacked us. It's been on my mind too. I saw nothing, heard nothing, but you know what it's like. We had the stereo on, and we were struggling with the sails, shouting to each other. Probably the perfect opportunity if someone was waiting for the right time to come aboard."

"But you didn't see anything unusual, lights that didn't seem like a sailboat, nothing like that?" She added quickly, "Gus said Kyle rented a boat, a quick little runabout, from Sweetwater under a fake name last Saturday. I have to fill in Detective Jordan on that, if he doesn't already know. The question is, why? Did he do this?"

"Savanna—" he started.

But she cut him off; she could hear a reprimand coming. "Sebastian was on the bow, dealing with the jib, yelling back to you. Right? He's crouched or standing, but either way, he's elevated above you; he's got a view of the entire cockpit and the diving platform in the back."

"Well…yes and no. He'd have seen the cockpit, me, the winch I was cranking, the stern of the yacht, but no, there's no way he could have seen the dive platform. At least, not the bottom three or four feet of it. I hadn't thought about it, but that's probably how they boarded."

"But when you were hit, was Sebastian facing you from the bow? He'd have seen your attacker. He'd have had a clear line of sight since he could see you and basically the whole stern."

He considered. "I'm not sure. He might have seen. The jib was caught on the left halyard, I remember, and it was whipping around, which is what sent Sebastian up there in the first place. He might've seen who hit me, or the sail might've blocked his view at the right moment."

"And then, presumably," she said, "once you were down, your attacker went for Sebastian. Dad, I'm sure he knows who did this."

"Yeah. You're probably right. But…water temps that far north this time of year have been between fifty-seven and sixty-two degrees. A handful of hours in water that cold is about all a body can take. I'm holding out hope he's somehow survived this long in the dinghy, or washed up somewhere, maybe injured. But if anything happened to the dinghy, there's no way he's still alive."

She didn't know what to say to that.

"Listen. I've learned these last couple years—and before that, when you were a kid—that this is just your mind at work. You notice details, small things other people miss. It's a valuable skill or talent or whatever you want to call it, Savanna. It's why you work so well as an art authenticator, the ability to spot subtle nuances or flaws. I believe you do it often without even meaning to. But it doesn't obligate you to take risks. It doesn't mean finding out who did this is on your shoulders. You could've been thrown over the railing on that catwalk right after Kyle. I don't think you realize that—"

"I do, Dad. But I promise," she said, scooting over and wrapping her arm around his, "all I'm doing is talking. Thinking. Puzzling things through. I'm not taking risks."

"That's not all you're doing. I don't want you back over at Sebastian's house, not alone like you've been. I don't want you running around tracing movements and motives, trying to catch a killer. I accept that this is how your mind works; you can't help it. But you control what you do with the things you notice. Call Admiral Moore again. Get Detective Jordan over here and lay out everything you know for him. But then let them take it from there." He stared at her, his stern face serious. "Got it?"

Chapter Twenty

SAVANNA TOOK HER father's advice literally. Detective Jordan had mentioned Sunday as an option to sit down and talk, but she'd woken up that morning not wanting to bother him on a weekend, not for a conversation that could wait until Monday. She had a bad habit of seeing the detective the way her students thought of her—as someone who lived and breathed her profession, slept at the school, was teacher Ms. Shepherd and nothing else. She tended to think of Jordan as law enforcement and only law enforcement, always in uniform, always at the sheriff's department. But she'd seen Nick Jordan off duty; the Sunday version of the detective looked more like backyard-barbecue-sports-and-leisure Nick Jordan. At least the last time she'd seen him on a Sunday.

Her dad was right, though. And they'd already tried Admiral Moore, which just left Jordan. Hitting send on her text message to him, she told herself it had been several months, maybe even a year, since she'd had to bug him on a weekend.

He responded right away: *"I was just about to call. There's a bit of an update. Are your parents around?"*

He arrived just as the crepes Ensenada came out of the

oven. Savanna invited Jordan to stay for dinner; it didn't make sense to delay and let the food get cold. The big dining table at her parents' house was already set, but Skylar's family of four had dropped out last minute with a nonexcuse, stirring the worry already settling into the family—the tension between Skylar and Travis hadn't escaped anyone's notice.

"What did she say, though?" Syd asked.

"Almost nothing. Just that they were dealing with something and can't make it."

Charlotte harumphed, an impatient exhalation. Her features were painted with concern. "This is crazy. They're both so stubborn, they've lost sight of what matters."

Uncle Max spoke. He and Uncle Freddie had arrived with homemade apple dumplings and French vanilla ice cream for dessert, another of Harlan's favorites. "How did they seem this morning when you brought the kids home to them?"

Savanna shrugged. "I don't know. I only saw Skylar. She was as closemouthed as always."

"Maybe Dad and I need to go over there and talk with them?"

Harlan covered her hand on the table with his larger one. "We can't. We have to trust them to work this out." He turned to Jordan. "Detective, sorry, we'll get down to business. Sometimes strife in a family like ours affects our whole family. Anyway, Savanna brought up a fair point today in talking me through the attack on the yacht."

"Don't apologize. You all must know how fortunate you

are to have a close-knit family. It's nice to see. What're you thinking, Savanna?"

"I talked to Gus, the guy who runs Sweetwater Boats at Carson Marina. He showed me the rental agreement from Kyle Bishop for a speedboat he took out last Saturday. He didn't return it till early the next morning. And before anyone here says lots of people rent boats from Sweetwater, and lots of people were out on the water the day of the regatta, including me, Kyle used a fake name to rent the boat."

"Gus is sure it was him?"

"I showed him Kyle's social media profile. Yes, it was him. And I'm sure you've thought of this, but Sebastian has to have seen the person who attacked Dad and then him."

"Admiral Moore's team is working with a theory that Sebastian staged the attack and then fled in the dinghy," Detective Jordan said.

"That's a stupid theory," Harlan said. Charlotte stared wide-eyed at him. "What? It is. No offense to the coast guard, but they aren't factoring in almost twenty years of friendship between me and Sebastian. There's no way he'd hire someone to knock me out and leave me for dead. Not possible." His tone challenged Jordan to argue.

"The sheriff's department is inclined to disagree with the investigator's theory," he said, nonplussed. "The problem is, we can't ask Sebastian who he saw attack you. The dinghy from the *Serendipity* was discovered this morning in a small cove near Door County, Wisconsin. But Sebastian's still missing."

"But the dinghy made it to land. Which must mean Sebastian did too?" Savanna asked.

"Maybe. After a week though? Even if he lasted that long in the elements without food, he'd have died of dehydration in half that long."

From the corner of her eye, Savanna saw her dad wince.

She spoke. "But he didn't. If he died, then where's his body? Kyle lied to me about what happened to his hand. He had it bandaged right here"—she tapped her own hand—"Sunday when I saw him at Sebastian's house. Then I saw the big abrasion a few days later when he had it uncovered. He said it was a rope burn from Sebastian sending him to get a new line from Sweetwater and set it up, but Gus didn't sell him any rope. He hurt his hand attacking my dad *and* Sebastian. Why else would he lie?"

"But he's dead," Sydney said. "If he attacked Dad and Sebastian, then who threw him over the catwalk railing?"

"And why was the floor freshly mopped?" Savanna asked.

"We do have a theory about that," the detective said. "Keeping in mind the goal of finding and prosecuting the person or people who did this to Harlan...and Sebastian...and possibly Kyle. Kyle may have been the pawn used on the yacht; we assume an attempt on Sebastian's life. We're investigating who was working with him; who would benefit from Sebastian's death. Anyone with access to the house could've used the element of surprise to force someone over the railing. The catwalk railing isn't up to code. It's four inches too short."

"And whoever pushed him then mopped the floor to

cover something up. Footprints maybe? Maybe there was mud or dirt or something they had to get rid of," Savanna said.

"They didn't use a maid service," Charlotte said. "Winnie took care of the cleaning. They'd tried out a few companies, but nobody was up to her standards."

"So, we're talking about relatively few options for Kyle's accomplice," Savanna said. "The people who stood to gain something from Sebastian's death are Chelsea and Griffin Alexander, and Maeve Davis."

"And his wife," Detective Jordan added. "Who's Maeve Davis?"

Savanna was mildly gratified she had a potential puzzle piece that Jordan didn't know about. "Maeve is Sebastian's longtime artist friend. They go way back; their careers started at the same time, and then Sebastian's took off. He's been seeing quite a lot of her. She lives in Chicago. And also, just so you know, Sebastian removed Winnie from his will a year ago. And then added in Maeve two weeks ago."

Every eye on the table was on her. "I had dinner with Maeve last night. She kind of filled me in."

"You...had dinner with Sebastian's mistress?" Charlotte's eyes were huge.

"I don't think so. Maeve swears they're platonic. She says Winnie has some misguided jealousy but that they've always just been friends."

"Maeve saying they're just friends doesn't make it true," her mother said. "I cannot believe that man cut Winnie from his estate. How cruel."

Savanna sighed, gaze moving from her mother to Detective Jordan. "Honestly, even after spending two hours with her, I'm still not sure I believe Maeve. Even if she's telling the truth about herself and Sebastian, she's hiding something. I am sure of that. She knows what prompted Sebastian to revise his will last year, but she wouldn't tell me."

"I need to go talk with Winnie," her mother said. She put a hand up as more than one person at the table protested. "I *won't*, not about any of this. I'll wait. But I can't believe what she's been through. I'm sure she could use a friend right now."

"Maeve knows how it looks, that Sebastian is leaving a third of his estate to her. She isn't happy about his decision. And then there's the thing with Griffin…and Chelsea."

"Savanna," Jordan interrupted her. "You've made more headway in some of this than we've been able to. I hate to admit it. What pointed you in the direction of Maeve? What made you check into the estate papers? I'm missing something."

She was caught. She looked to Sydney for help, but Syd shrugged, giving her a wide-eyed look. What would Skylar say? Where was her big sister when she needed her? "I saw something. In Sebastian's art studio. You know I've been there creating certificates for his new work, authenticating his existing pieces—"

"What did you see?"

She got up and fetched her phone from her purse. She pulled up the photo she wanted and handed her phone to the detective, showing him the two weeks of entries she'd snapped. "Sebastian's planner was wide open on his desk. I didn't mean to look at it. But then after Kyle's accident—or murder—I looked. I guess I thought it might help. He had several things written in there that I had questions about. So, I took a quick picture and then got ahold of Maeve. And Gus. Gus confirmed he'd set Sebastian up with all new rigging before the regatta, so Kyle's lie didn't make sense to me."

"And what about Sebastian's kids? Griffin and Chelsea?" Detective Jordan asked.

"Sebastian's been supporting Griffin for years; they have a strained relationship. There's a condition in the will that Griffin's inheritance will be given to Chelsea after one year if Griffin can't get and keep a full-time job sufficient to support himself."

Chapter Twenty-One

SYDNEY BEING WITH Savanna this time at the Alexander house was a huge relief. She couldn't remember the last time she'd broken a promise to her dad. This might not technically count as breaking a promise. He didn't want her at Sebastian's house alone, and she wasn't alone. He was right, as usual; she understood his concern. But with Winnie staying at her brother's place, Kyle dead, and Sebastian missing, she couldn't justify neglecting her work here. She still had a job to do, whether the Lansing exhibit kicked off as planned next week or not.

She'd enlisted Sydney to come with her Monday after work. She'd done as much of the provenance research as possible at home, leaving only about an hour and a half's worth of work left to do here before the collection was fully authenticated, old and new pieces alike. The front door code hadn't been changed, and the police tape had been removed from the front door a few days earlier. In Sebastian's studio, she focused on getting a few of his smaller pieces organized and then set to work with her Firefly handheld microscope and the mini UVA lamp.

While Sydney worked on thank-you notes for her wedding shower earlier this month, Savanna dove into the final two new paintings she had yet to authenticate. His methods had evolved since his original works, as had his palette preferences. She marveled at the brushwork, the expert variations in portions of each piece depending on scenery and mood, the first painting calling for shorter, unblended brushstrokes, characteristic of his original style, while the second one employed the use of both blended and staccato strokes to fit the imagery he portrayed.

When she was certain she'd finished everything that needed to be done on-site, she packed up her tool case and she and Syd headed down the side staircase to the foyer. Sydney stood looking up at the catwalk, standing in the spot Kyle had landed. Someone—Winnie or Chelsea, most likely—had arranged for a cleaning company to come in and take care of the large pool of blood on the marble flooring. Savanna thought she could see a trace of discoloration left behind, but maybe not.

"Do you even get how lucky you are that you were locked inside Sebastian's studio when someone was in here shoving Kyle over the railing?" Syd asked.

"Yeah. It's sinking in," Savanna said. "Being here still creeps me out a little."

Sydney turned in a slow circle and then drifted over to the wide doorway leading to the dining room and kitchen. "I mean…yeah, but wow. This place. It's fancier than Caroline's."

Their would-be grandmother figure, Caroline Carson, the town matriarch, occupied a gorgeous turn-of-the-century Victorian home on Lake Michigan, just past the end of Main

Street. "I don't know, they're too different from each other to compare. This place is ultra-modern. Caroline's is warm and inviting; we always feel at home there."

"True. Oh my gawd, look at the kitchen! Wow. Uncle Freddie would be in paradise making his famous bacon-wrapped filet mignon in here." Syd stopped in front of the stainless oven across from a set of French doors leading onto a stamped concrete patio. "Savvy."

"Hey, I'm allowed to be in the studio. You're getting out of hand. Let's go." Savanna set her heavy case down and crossed the smooth tiled floor to her sister.

"Wait. Look. It's probably the only time we'll see one of these. This is a Miele range." Syd made a sweeping flourish with one hand over the appliance.

Savanna laughed. "Okay."

"No, seriously. This thing is worth more than my car. Easily. Dang."

"So, you're saying this is what I should get you for your wedding?" Her little sister was ridiculous. "You barely cook."

"But I would on a Miele."

"All right, sure. I'll pick one up for you, no worries. I'll make sure to gift wrap it too," Savanna said, rolling her eyes. She rounded the expansive island to peer through the French doors on her way back to the foyer.

"Yes, please. Definitely. As if!" Sydney turned. "Okay. I'm ready. Sorry, just got distracted."

Savanna narrowed her eyes, trying to decide what she was looking at. "Syd. Do you see that?"

Sydney glanced through the glass panes. "Yes. It's a gorgeous patio with a smoker and bilevel dining complete with wet bar."

"No. That—" She needed a closer look. She almost grasped the door handle to step out but thought better of it. She wrapped the edge of her shirt around the handle and slid open the door. "Come on." She'd dropped her volume to a whisper without meaning to.

Sydney followed her through. "I thought we were leaving. What are you doing?" She was whispering now, too, even though they were outside surrounded by forest.

Savanna dropped to her knees, crawling along the patio. She pulled her phone from her back pocket and snapped a photo. "Hold on. I see more." She rose and moved to the edge of the patio, crouching down again and taking more pictures. "Stop!"

Sydney froze, one foot off the ground, panic in her voice. "What?"

Savanna pointed, coming back over to her. "Don't step there. Look. Do you see this? What does this look like to you?"

Scattered across the patio, almost too faint to see, were small blots of red. There were a few just outside the French doors, and then a single splotch here and there, and more leading off the patio. Savanna carefully took a photo of each one, thinking after the first few about scale. "Do you have a coin? A quarter or penny or something?"

"No, why would I?"

"Ugh." Savanna patted herself down, checking pockets, and coming up empty. She stared at her engagement ring.

She couldn't. It would be far too disrespectful, wouldn't it? But... She grabbed Sydney's hand. "Give me your thumb ring." Having a stylish, boho-chic fashion maven of a sister was finally paying off.

Sydney removed the sterling silver and turquoise ring from her thumb without question and handed it over. She knelt on the patio while Savanna snapped photos of the ring beside each red splotch. "They're paw prints," Sydney said in wonder.

"Not all of them." She pointed. "This one looks like a dog's nose, doesn't it? Like a dog walked through blood—Kyle's blood—and maybe sniffed it, too, and left across the patio."

Sydney scrutinized the specific looking blot. "I think you're right. It's a noseprint. From a big dog. This guy wasn't small. This nose belongs to a large breed, like a Bouvier. There's another one." She pointed, moving to the edge of the patio that led to a stone path.

"A noseprint, wow."

"Dog's noseprints are like our thumbprints. There are no two alike," Sydney informed her.

"Oh, *wow*," she repeated. "We have to call Jordan." But she didn't; not yet. She handed Sydney's ring back to her and followed the trail of fainter and fainter red until she could no longer see the prints. In front of them, across the driveway, was the guesthouse. The large carriage house loomed behind it. The Alexanders kept three or four cars in there; she'd seen them the day Kyle had been killed. The garage doors had been standing wide open when she and

Aidan left. She remembered that friend of Finn's, Ace Streeter, leaving her with Kelly the paramedic because help was needed in the carriage house.

A much smaller version of the main house, built in the same style, the guesthouse appeared either very inviting or else lived in. Before she could think better of it, she crossed the drive and stood on the front porch, peering in through the door. "It's a mess." She turned to summon Sydney, but her sister was right behind her.

"Someone lives here."

Savanna agreed. There were dirty dishes still on the kitchen table. Three pairs of men's shoes were in a pile by the front door, along with a jacket and a sweatshirt on the hooks above the shoes. "This has to be where Kyle stays." She wiggled the doorknob through her bunched-up shirt hem, but it was locked.

"Where Kyle stayed," Sydney corrected her.

"Chelsea has Ringo. Winnie left him with her since she's been staying at her brother's house. Was Chelsea here when Kyle died?"

"So, she's the one who pushed him?" Syd asked.

"Why, though?"

"No idea."

"What if she paid Kyle to kill her father?"

Syd was quiet, hand over her mouth.

"She's the one who cleaned the floors," Savanna said. "Because of the dog. Ringo must have walked through Kyle's blood after he fell, and Chelsea hurried to clean it, so it'd look like an accident. It did seem like no one was here when it happened."

"And she cleaned the floors, but she didn't notice the patio. She was probably rushing to get away. Oooh!" Sydney pointed at Savanna. "Good call, Columbo, not touching that door handle. Chelsea left through the French doors. I bet they'll find her fingerprints."

"Which doesn't really prove anything. Sebastian's daughter's fingerprints are probably all over the house."

"But you're right about the dog; Ringo must've walked through the blood right when it happened. Because you said Kyle was still warm when you found him; it hadn't happened too long before you came downstairs. Then paramedics and police arrived."

Savanna nodded. "There'd have been no other opportunity for Ringo to track fresh blood through the house and patio, except for right when it happened."

Sydney groaned. "Chelsea can't be a murderer. I like her. Plus, she makes the most amazing carrot cake."

Savanna left the porch of the guesthouse and walked around to the large carriage house. She tried the handle on both the tall overhead doors but they were locked. The family was apparently vigilant about locking everything up, even in the middle of the woods. Sydney followed her around to the side door, and the doorknob turned easily. "I've gotta call Jordan," she murmured.

They stepped into the darkened garage. Savanna found the lights. A vintage red Corvette, a black F350 truck, and a sensible navy blue hybrid filled the oversized garage, with two empty spaces. "Look." Near the entrance, Savanna bent and pointed to a bright yellow evidence marker on the concrete floor. In front of it was a small red smear. It had to be blood. The police had obviously thought so, but they wouldn't have known it likely came from Ringo's paw when Chelsea rushed him in here to get away. There were no other blood stains in the thirty feet or so between where Savanna stood and the parking spaces against the far wall. This must've been the last trace of blood left on Ringo's paw.

She dialed Jordan. He instructed her to stay where she was unless she felt they were in danger. She and Sydney agreed to wait. They headed over to the patio to watch for Detective Jordan.

"How old was Kyle?" Sydney asked.

"Maybe early forties? Why?"

"And Chelsea, she's older than you, right? What is she like thirty-six? Thirty-seven? Never been married, no kids?"

Savanna nodded. "I think her bakery is her marriage. She's there all the time. She must be thirty-five-ish, if Griffin's thirty-three."

"All right, you're going to say I watch too many reality shows, but what if Kyle and Chelsea were involved? Or maybe Kyle thought Chelsea was into him, but Chelsea just wanted her inheritance and needed someone to get rid of her father for her."

"I don't know," Savanna said. "Sebastian and Chelsea golfed together. It sounds like they had a good father-daughter relationship."

"Maybe. But since they're close, she'd for sure have known about the changes to his will, like you said. What's his net worth, do you know? Is it enough to kill for?"

Savanna shrugged. "I don't have a clue. A lot, probably."

Sydney turned her phone toward Savanna. "Your guy must be a brilliant investor. His original worth has grown—without him even releasing any new pieces—to four hundred million."

"WHY DO YOU need a warrant to check out the Alexanders' Bouvier?" Savanna asked. She and Sydney had taken the Detective Jordan on a tour through the house, starting with the foyer for the full effect, into the kitchen, out through the French doors where the dog paw and noseprints now seemed glaringly obvious—even though Syd hadn't even spotted them the first time—down the stone path and past Kyle's house into the carriage house.

"We can't touch him or Chelsea Alexander's car without a warrant, Savanna. I'd go right now and get the impressions we need if I could. She'd mostly not allow me to do so, and if I tried while Ringo is at a grooming appointment, as you suggest, the court could toss it out as evidence collected without cause. I have to do this by the book."

"Because there's a book for what to do when your dog tracks blood from a crime scene to the killer's car," she said, smirking.

He nodded. "The circumstances are unusual, I agree. You are correct, though. Dog noseprints can be used to definitively confirm or deny the presence of a particular canine."

"I know dogs," Sydney said.

"So, you'll get a warrant and then go get Ringo's nose-print. Assuming it matches, is that enough to prove Chelsea and Kyle did all this?"

He shook his head. "I don't know. We'll have to wait and see how it goes."

Cryptic Nick Jordan, Savanna thought.

"I don't have to keep you here. We're all set. I'm just waiting for my evidence techs to come back. They need a refresher on making sure to capture *all* the evidence," he said.

Savanna stopped on the way down the driveway, Sydney in the passenger seat.

Savanna rolled down the window. "I just thought of something."

Jordan came over to her car. "Yeah?"

"If Chelsea really did this, and it seems like she did, what if she goes after Griffin? What if she's not satisfied with a third of the estate?"

The detective nodded. "One step ahead of you there, at least. I've got an officer keeping an eye on Griffin, don't worry."

Chapter Twenty-Two

S KYLAR SAT BACK in the chair in her office, waiting for the senior partner across from her to leave for the day. Jillian Black typically ended her workday from her home, to be present for her three teenagers. So, it figured that on the one day Skylar really, really needed her to take off, she was at her desk just tapping away at the keyboard, no sign that she'd wrap things up anytime soon. Skylar wasn't giving up. She needed to do this; it was too important to her dad. He'd do the same for her.

Maybe she'd just close her eyes for a moment. She hadn't slept in days. At least it felt that way. She'd hoped she and Travis could spend Saturday talking things through while Savanna had the kids. It was the perfect opportunity. Instead, Travis had volunteered to be one of three engineers flying down to Florida to vet the site and permits where the new office would be built. He was avoiding her.

Greenway Environmental Engineering had operated out of Grand Rapids for thirty years. Travis had been there for half that; it was the first and only civil engineering company he'd worked for. His loyalty was tied to the fact that Greenway had put him through school in exchange for a two-year commitment after graduating. He wouldn't have been able to get his degree at all if it weren't for Greenway. There was no money in his family for tuition. His dad had been in and out of his life while being in and out jail, mostly due to substance use issues. His mom tried hard to be both mother and father to him and his two sisters; she'd done her best. But college wasn't an option until he convinced the new company he'd started working at straight out of high school to let him intern there while going to school.

Skylar knew his work ethic. She had never doubted his loyalty to his career, but more importantly, to their little family. In the eleven years they'd been married, he'd become the best father to her children she could have ever imagined. She wasn't sure how he did it without a role model growing up. She'd told him once that he seemed to have used his own father as a reverse example of the father he tried to be. He was everything his own father was not.

She couldn't imagine breaking her family apart. She couldn't envision it if she tried. But she saw no other option. He was moving forward with plans, with or without her.

Oh thank goodness—Jillian slung her laptop bag over her shoulder and turned off the light, locking her office door behind her. Skylar raised a hand in a small wave, and the senior attorney waved back.

"Staying late again?" Jillian gave her a thumbs-up. "Our most valuable asset. Thanks, Skylar. Have a good night."

She waited a full five minutes longer, after she was sure Jillian was out of the parking lot. Zach had left two hours ago along with the rest of the office, while she and Jillian faced off, waiting each other out—though her boss had no idea that was what was happening.

She fished the key to Jillian's office from the top left drawer of her receptionist. Nicole always put it back in the same spot; Skylar had watched. In the senior partner's office, Skylar rifled through two tall filing cabinets against the wall. Jillian insisted on paper copies of every single case, and today Skylar was thankful for that. She found what she was looking for and carried it down the hall to the copy machine, making just one copy and then slipping the paper back into its file and the file back into the cabinet. Mission accomplished.

With the key put back in the top left drawer after she'd locked up, Skylar locked her own office as well, eyeing Zach's desk outside her door. She supposed anyone could do the same thing she'd just done to break into one of their offices. Not that it mattered; there was nothing in her office that anyone would find exciting or scandalous.

Pulling into her driveway alongside the babysitter's car, she was hit with the guilt that plagued her all the time and probably plagued every mother ever. She should have been home hours ago, but she'd needed to take care of this tonight. Tomorrow night was their final fitting for the bridesmaids' gowns, and more importantly, Sydney's final fitting, and Skylar still hadn't even seen Syd's wedding gown. When had life gotten so busy that her baby sister was getting married in five days and Skylar didn't know what Sydney's gown looked like?

She would give Savanna the document she'd copied when she saw her tomorrow. She'd considered bringing Nick Jordan up to speed, but that was even more likely to blow back on her. As it was, she was trusting her sisters to use the information without throwing her under the bus.

Skylar was snoozing on the couch at nine when Travis finally made it home. Carly had been paid and relieved, Skylar had made chicken nuggets for Nolan and fed Hannah her favorite, turkey and sweet potatoes, and fed herself a bowl of cereal. Baths for Nolan and the baby worked wonders to get them both to sleep, and she'd settled under a blanket to try to wait up for her husband.

Travis set his garment suitcase by the door and came over to her, dropping to his knees to wrap her in a hug, his face turned toward her neck. He smelled like Florida sunshine and sweat and airplane food.

"I missed you," she told him.

"I missed you too."

"We have to talk, Trav."

He nodded against her neck. "I know."

Outside, on the patio he'd built, they sat side by side on a lounge chair. He opened a cold beer and handed it to her, opening a second for himself. "I shouldn't have gone. I just...I didn't want to stay here and keep fighting."

"I get it. I'm tired of fighting."

"So, I've been thinking about everything you said. And you're right. It's not fair to ask you and Nolan to leave everything and start over. You've built a career here. Your family is here."

"You're my family."

"I went for the interview last week because it was something I needed to do. I needed to see if the new role is even something I want. Money isn't everything." He gave her a small smile. "You know I've dealt with having none, so turning down a raise isn't the end of the world. We have enough. I've always known that. I guess I just got a little too full of my own ambitions. I told them I'm staying. They'll move on to the next candidate."

Skylar dropped her head into her hands. She hated fighting with him, but she also hated how much she'd cried lately; it just made her mad.

"Hey." Travis rubbed her back, between her shoulder blades where she was always so knotted up.

She picked her head up, smoothing a hand over her hair. "You can't turn it down. I was…" She wiped her face on the sleeve of her robe. "Ugh. I was wrong. I was mostly thinking about myself." The truth in that made it painful to admit.

"I don't think you were," he said kindly.

"We live here where my family is. In the five years since having Nolan, you've passed up promotions, avoided stretch projects, allowed your peers to outpace you so you could be here, instead of at work."

"You've done the same, babe. I know that."

She sighed. This hurt even more to admit—"No, I really haven't. I've taken pretty much every opportunity that's been handed to me. I took on the late court day no one else wanted because I thought it'd make me look good to the partners. I cut down to part-time to be here more for Hannah, but if I'm being honest, even when I'm here, half my brain is reviewing cases and prepping for tomorrow's clients."

"You're a lawyer. It comes with the job. Listen. We were doing fine before this merger, before the offer. Let's get back to normal. It'll be good," he said, hugging her around the shoulders.

She met his eyes. "Take the job. I mean it, Trav. Take it. It's two years. Two years of our lives, two years for Nolan and Hannah to get to know their other grandma. Two years to spread our family's wings in Florida and create new adventures, new memories." The gravity of what she was saying hit her full force. Her eyes filled with tears again, her throat thick. "Take the job."

He stared at her, speechless.

"You can still accept it, can't you?"

He nodded. "Probably. Sky—"

"I'm sure," she said.

"You know my mother is nothing like Grandma Charlotte. With her memory issues, I can't promise how any of that will go."

She wrapped her arms around his waist, hugging him. "That's even more reason for us to do it now. While she might still be able to enjoy the kids. Oh my goodness, she's going to freak out when you tell her. Is the new building far from Tampa? I don't even know where Venice is. Is it nice?"

"We'd be an hour from Mom. Venice is on the Gulf side of the state. It's pretty...but I only saw the commerce loop the new site is on. I haven't looked into houses or schools or anything. I don't know much. But if it's not nice, we'll find somewhere that is." He paused. "Do you want to sleep on it, in case you change your mind? I love you, babe. I'm not going anywhere without you."

She laughed, tears running down her cheeks. "Good God, I'm a mess. No, I don't want to sleep on it. I want you to call Harold and tell him you want the job. Right now."

He kissed her, arms around her, her tears wetting his stubbly jaw. "Let me go get my phone." He stood.

She grabbed his arm. "Wait. How much more money are we talking? Because you can negotiate. Never accept the initial offer."

He smiled and bent to kiss her again. "Trust me. Nothing I could negotiate would outbid the offer on the table. It's all good. I promise."

Chapter Twenty-Three

TUESDAY, AT CARSON Elementary, Savanna stopped outside the main entrance before heading in to start her day. She'd missed a call last night from Britt, and another one this morning while she was at Fancy Tails dropping off Fonzie for the day. She called them back.

Britt Nash's smiling face appeared on her screen. Their shock of white-blond hair was nearly as bright as the sun shining behind them, giving her friend a halo of sorts. "Hello there, my friend! Are you doing better now, with your dad back home, safe and sound?"

"So much better. It was really such an awful few days. He's doing great—back to his normal, stubborn self. How's everything going there?" She knew why they'd called. She just didn't have any answers so far.

Britt delivered the biggest news first. "We've got sponsorship interest from Pemberly's."

"Pemberly's as in Pemberly's Auction House? In New York? For real?"

"The realest, lady. We updated the info on the exhibit page with the private collector pieces that will be on loan, along with your preliminary details about his new work. They want to send a rep out later this week to take a look.

Helene is setting up a meeting." Helene was Britt's partner—at work as the museum's curator, and outside of work since they'd started dating a few months ago.

Savanna couldn't breathe. She put a hand out to steady herself against the wall and missed, almost falling. "Okay, hold on. Wait." Pemberly's being involved with Sebastian's exhibit would be surreal. She leaned against the brick wall of the school, bending over at the waist.

"Deep breaths, darling. There you go. All right now? Because there's more."

"There's more? Sure, of course there is. You know he's still missing, right, Britt?"

"I'm aware. We're keeping that quiet for now. Helene got confirmation late last night that Archibald Renfro has agreed to lend us Sebastian's *Rebirth* from his original Paris collection."

"Britt. Shut up. Renfro doesn't lend pieces. He never has." Savanna's head was spinning. Sebastian's show was going to be phenomenal, if it actually came to fruition.

"Well, he is for this exhibit." Britt looked quite pleased with their exciting news.

"You're amazing," she said. "Tell me what to do. Oh no—that's the second bell. I have to run, I'm so sorry. In five minutes, there'll be twenty-seven six-year-olds waiting for paintbrushes."

"Sounds terrifying. I'll let you go. And don't worry. All you need to do is get me access to move Sebastian's collection before Friday. I'll be the one with the fancy museum transport vehicle and a couple buff handlers. Call me later and we'll talk details." They blew a kiss at her and the call ended.

Savanna rushed inside and down the hallway to her room, beating Mr. Slate's first graders by three minutes. She didn't know who she'd need to contact first in order to make this happen, Detective Jordan, Winnie, or Sebastian's children.

After school, on her way to Lyla's Bridal twenty minutes outside town, she called Jordan. She'd thought through strategy all day, but she wasn't sure she could truly impress upon him the magnitude of what was happening with Sebastian's show. As impressive as it was, to folks not into art, it might seem trivial, or worse, unnecessary to jump through hoops just because Pemberly's was involved.

The detective's voice came through her speakers. "Detective Jordan here."

She smiled. "Hi, Detective. Do you not have my number saved in your phone after all this time?"

"I do. It's just habit. What's going on, Savanna?" He was always super serious. Before she knew him well, she'd spent a lot of time assuming he was irritated with her. Now she knew it was usually just his normal tone.

"I have a very important question. You know Sebastian has an art exhibition planned for next week at the Lansing Museum of Fine Art, right?"

"I recall you sharing that."

She dove in. "I don't know if you know this, but his work was huge years ago, so there are a lot of collectors and galleries expressing interest in his upcoming show. His most famous piece from twenty years ago will be part of the exhibit, on loan from a private collector we were positive wouldn't contribute. And this morning I learned that Pemberly's Auction House has offered sponsorship, a newer concept that can really help out the artist, the museum, and the auction house."

"Sounds like there's a lot riding on Sebastian's show," Jordan said dryly.

"Yes. Pemberly's would like to see his new works by Friday this week...in Lansing."

The long pause told her Jordan actually was irritated this time. "Savanna, you're asking me to allow a fortune's worth of creative property be removed from the home of a man who's been missing for nine days."

"Yes, but removed only so it can be on display. It can't be sold without Sebastian's consent. If he isn't found, all his work will come right back to his studio until his estate is worked out."

He sighed loudly. "Tomorrow is the last chance to locate him."

"What does that mean? They're giving up?"

"If he isn't found by tomorrow evening, Admiral Moore plans to sign off on ending the search. It'll be ten days in water not conducive to sustained survival—the admiral's words. I'm sorry. I know he's your friend," Jordan said.

Now she was at a loss for words.

"Let's get to the end of the day tomorrow. I'll try to look into whether there's any precedent for this type of situation; I doubt it," he grumbled. "We'll have to figure out if his next of kin has the authority to release his work—and who is next of kin is. It'll fall to Chelsea or Maeve. Should be fun to navigate all this with his wife in the mix."

"Yeah. I can see how complicated it is. I appreciate your help, seriously. Did you get the warrant for Ringo's nose-print yet?"

"Judge McKinnon is reviewing the affidavit. No warrant yet. But I'm pretty confident we'll get it."

THE LYLA'S BRIDAL assistant held the door open for her, issuing a welcome and asking if Savanna preferred a glass of white wine or sparkling beverage. She eyed her mother and Skylar already in the fitting area, each holding a wineglass, and asked for the same. She pushed all her Sebastian concerns away, or to the furthest corner of her mind she could get them to, and joined the women in her family. Her sister had asked them to choose a pink bridesmaid gown—the style was left up to them. They'd left their chosen gowns with Lyla's seamstress last month, each needing a couple small alterations. Tonight's try-on was to make sure everything fit perfectly.

Her cousin Ellie stood on one of the pedestals surrounded by mirrors while the seamstress zipped up her sparkly pink spaghetti-strapped gown. "You look so gorgeous, honey," Charlotte said. "The fit is just perfect, too, isn't it?"

Ellie spun this way and that, her newly close-cropped dark hair and big brown eyes complementing the dress for a lovely pixie vibe. "I love it. Oh my gosh, my dads are totally going to swoon when they see all of us."

"Ellie, turn my way," Savanna said, snapping a few pictures for Uncle Max's wedding collage—because she was positive he'd make one. He created a shadowbox for every major event. She'd already signed him up to make one after her wedding for her and Aidan to display.

The double doors of the bride's suite fitting room opened and Sydney emerged, her cheeks flushed with excitement. Her wedding gown was beautiful, an off-the-shoulder silk and chiffon confection with a sweetheart neckline, generous off-center slit, and delicate appliques on the modest train. Sydney piled most of her long red waves on top of her head, a few long tendrils escaping, securing it messily with the elastic on her wrist.

Their mother gasped, hand hovering at her throat. "Sydney. My baby."

"Mom, don't cry. You'll make me cry," Syd said.

"You look like a goddess," Savanna told her. "You really picked the perfect gown."

Sydney did a slow twirl on her pedestal, looking down at her skirt. "It's so pretty. I love it."

Skylar lurched from the couch to Sydney and hugged her, stunning them. She kissed Syd's check and backed up. "Sorry. I don't want to muss the dress. But, Syd. Baby sis. I'm so happy for you." She sucked in a breath and pressed the back of her hand to her lips, tears spilling over.

Savanna could count on one hand the number of times she'd seen her older sister cry, and one of them was last week.

"Are you okay?" Sydney asked her.

Skylar nodded. Normally, a question like that during a moment of perceived sappiness would elicit a snotty retort, like *Yeah, are you okay?* Or *What? I'm fine!* Today's Skylar just smiled and brushed a hand across the tears on her cheeks.

"Skylar?" The girl who'd brought Savanna's wine called Skylar into a fitting room now and she went without another word.

The remaining Shepherd family women exchanged glances with each other.

Is she okay? Syd mouthed the words.

Savanna shrugged, hands palm-up at her sides.

Their mom scowled and hushed them. "She's fine. This is an emotional day for all of us."

Skylar came out in her pink gown, an elegant short-sleeved A-line dress that fell just past her knee. After the fawning responses from her family, Savanna was called next.

Savanna's pink gown had crisscrossing spaghetti straps with a plunging back and high neckline, the fabric faintly shimmery.

Ellie squealed. "Wow, I love it! You look so pretty."

"I love how different they all are," Charlotte remarked, stepping into the fitting room for her mother-of-the-bride gown. She emerged with the seamstress still zipping her into a lovely gold gown with a few elements that mirrored Sydney's, like the sweetheart neckline.

"Oh, Mom. Oh my goodness," Sydney said. "Look at us. I love you guys."

On the way home, each of them in separate cars, Savanna skipped her own turn and instead followed Skylar to her house. She pulled in the driveway and met her older sister between their cars.

"Hey, what's going on?" Skylar looked concerned.

"I just need to know. Are you all right, Sky? And honest answer, not just 'I'm fine.' I've been worried. Syd and I have both been worried."

She nodded. "I really am all right. I promise."

"Can I ask," Savanna said hesitantly, "did you and Travis get a chance to talk things through this weekend?"

"We talked. I, uh." Skylar looked over her shoulder at her house and then back at Savanna. "I was planning on talking with you guys after Saturday. Next week…maybe next month. I seriously don't want to put any kind of damper on Syd's day. It's not like things will be changing right away."

"What's changing? You're going to make me worry until after the wedding about what's happening with your situation? You guys have to deal with this. You know that, right? You're gonna have to talk and come up with a solution you can both live with."

"We did…"

"Oh no." She touched her sister's arm, searching her face. She seemed okay, but Skylar had the best poker face she'd ever seen.

"I'm sorry. I don't really know how to say this. We did talk. Last night. I told Travis to accept the offer. The job is in Venice, Florida."

Savanna stared at her.

"We're going. We're giving it a try. It's a two-year commitment."

"Oh my goodness, I'm so glad you were able to work things out!" She wasn't sure what she'd been expecting, but what a relief; she couldn't imagine her sister and Travis splitting up. Not with Nolan and Hannah in the mix, and not over a change in career or location...then her selfish side took over. "But I just got back! Not just, but you know what I mean. It's been so wonderful being back with you guys only a few minutes away."

"It has! I wouldn't trade the last couple years for anything. This is something I need to do. Did you know flights start at ninety-nine dollars? Think of it as a new, free vacation destination."

She nodded. "I can do that. That's how you should sell it to Mom and Dad too. It won't be that different." Even as she said it, she was abruptly so sad, yet simultaneously happy for her sister. "You're really waiting to tell everyone?"

"Yes. Now so are you. Right?"

"Yeah, yeah, of course." She threw her arms around her sister. "Jeez. I'm gonna miss you way too much."

"Same, sister. I can't really wrap my head around it yet," Skylar said. She let go and pulled a folded piece of paper from her bag. "I need to show you something."

"What is it?" Savanna moved into the glow of the headlights so she could read it. "What the heck? What the heck! So, when we were guessing whether Sebastian was using your firm for estate help or divorce help, we were right on both counts?"

Skylar took the copy from her, folding it back up. "No matter what you do, Savvy, you cannot share that you got that information from me. I'm shredding this when I get inside. I don't care how we explain knowing Sebastian was divorcing Winnie, as long as it doesn't come back to me stealing confidential information from my senior partner."

Chapter Twenty-Four

WEDNESDAY MORNING, BEFORE her second graders came in and she got too immersed in helping them paint and decorate wings for their latest project based on the Eric Carle book, *The Very Lonely Firefly*, Savanna crafted a carefully worded text to Nick Jordan. She'd slept on the wild news from Skylar, making sure she'd come up with a way to update Jordan without throwing her sister under the bus.

"Good morning! I heard something through the grapevine that you might want to look into. Sebastian was in the process of divorcing Winnie."

He replied right away. *"Morning. Who told you this?"*

"I can't say. I was in line at Happy Family and heard it; I have no idea."

"So just some random speculation at the grocery store?"

"Seemed like more than that. The two people talking sounded like they knew them."

The three little dots appeared on her screen, indicating Jordan typing his response. Then they disappeared. Then reappeared.

"All right, thanks for the tip. I'll check it out."

After school, Savanna found herself on the long rural road through the woods again to Sebastian's house. If Jordan was able to give her the okay, she'd need to have all of

Sebastian's work ready for Britt and his handlers by tomorrow. She'd been up late last night completing the rest of her authentication research on the provenances already in existence for the older original pieces. As she'd hoped, there were no snags. Since they'd never changed hands and had been in Sebastian's possession since he created them, the provenance history was nil with him listed as original and still current owner.

She'd completed, filed online, printed, and validated each certificate for his nine new pieces and eight older works, each provenance stamped with her raised seal and placed it its protective sheath. Including the physical provenance with a work of art upon purchase wasn't required, but it reflected good faith and protocol on her part. When Britt came tomorrow, as she hoped would happen, Sebastian's entire collection in his studio would be ready to be wrapped and transported. She'd thought about going the extra mile and preparing them, but museum handlers were trained at that and more efficient than she'd be.

A black Chevy sedan with rental plates was parked in front of the guest house when she arrived at Sebastian's. Rolling slowly past the small house on her way by, she noted a couple boxes and a suitcase on the porch. Savanna parked in the back of Sebastian's house rather than her usual spot in front, wanting an excuse to get a closer look at who was going through Kyle's things.

"Hello?" She stood on the steps, peering inside but not wanting to intrude.

A petite blonde woman poked her head out the door.

"Hello?"

Savanna gave a little wave. "Hi there! I work for Sebastian. I, ah, hadn't seen anyone over here in a bit. I was just curious." She kicked herself internally. If she and Syd were right about the occupant of the house, this woman was probably Kyle's grieving sister or wife. "I was so sorry to hear the news," she added.

"Thank you. I'm Sara, Kyle's sister." She came out on the porch.

"Savanna. I'm really sorry for your loss. I only met him a couple times, but he was always nice to me."

Sara pulled a tissue from her pocket and patted her brow and neck with it. "He was a sweet man. I can't believe he's gone. I'd just talked him a week earlier." She fanned herself. "I didn't know Michigan was this warm in the fall. North Dakota's already in the fifties most days."

"I've never been there. Michigan weather is hot one day and cold the next this time of year. Totally unpredictable. Can I help with anything? Are you trying to clear out his things? Looks like a big job." It seemed like a huge job for one person; she hoped there was someone else with Sara to help her.

She shook her head. "Sorry. I just got in this morning and I'm already exhausted." She sat on the top step. "I'm not clearing out the house, no. I came to find something for him to wear—for the funeral home to use. The service is this weekend back home. I found a nice suit and tie but then got involved in trying to find cuff links, and somehow just started packing up some of his things to ship home before I leave. I'm gonna have to come back next week with my husband to take care of all this."

"It must be overwhelming," Savanna said sympathetically.

She nodded. "Too much tragedy. He told me about Sebastian going missing. What a mess. A landscaping company was here this morning, and the guy said they haven't seen Sebastian or anyone around. What do you think happened?"

"I don't know. The coast guard doesn't seem to know."

"The police said that catwalk Kyle fell from wasn't up to code; they think he fell because the railing was too low or the walkway was higher than it should be, even with the vaulted ceilings. They said the lady that found him did CPR and tried to save him." She dabbed at her eyes, sniffling. "But the hospital said he hit his head too hard; he didn't suffer. They think he passed right after it happened."

"I'm so sorry." A part of her wanted to share that she'd been the lady doing CPR, but it wouldn't help Kyle's sister to know that. It was very interesting that the information his family was getting thus far was that he'd fallen. To her knowledge, Jordan was leaning very much the other way, with everything pointing to someone pushing him off the catwalk and then covering up evidence—dog footprints and noseprints?—but missing more on the patio. The detective had been poker-faced when she suggested that Kyle rented a boat to follow the *Serendipity* and attack the sailors, but it didn't seem crazy to Savanna.

On the porch step, fresh tears were now rolling down Sara's cheeks. She pulled more tissue from her pocket and wiped her eyes and blew her nose. "I'm so sorry. You just stopped to see who was in Kyle's house, I'm sure you have work to do. I just really thought I knew my brother. We weren't close, but he called me almost every week. Why didn't he tell me he was going to propose to his girlfriend? And I can't even find her to tell her what happened or share the funeral arrangements with her. There's nobody by her name on his social media friend list. There's nothing in his house, like a birthday card from her or pictures or anything. Did he lie to me?"

Savanna stared wide-eyed at her. "What do you mean?" She hadn't thought about Kyle's personal life or a girlfriend, but why would she have? "How do you know he was planning to propose?" The tiny hairs on the back of Savanna's neck stood up; this was not what his sister thought it was. Too many small details were trying to add up. Who was Kyle seeing?

Sara got up and went inside, coming back with her purse. She produced a small aqua-blue box, holding it on her outstretched palm for Savanna to take a look.

Savanna opened the box. A stunning princess-cut diamond ring sparkled up at her. "Oh my," she breathed. "This is gorgeous."

Sara took the box back and dropped it into her purse. "I'm sure it's real. He must've saved for months to afford it. But unless his girlfriend, Gina, just isn't on social media, I'm starting to think he either lied about her name or lied about having a girlfriend at all."

"But—" Savanna pointed. "That ring. That's a serious

ring. He never sent you a picture of her or of them together?"

"No. I asked. He hated the camera. But you're right— it's a serious ring. It's not like I can ask Sebastian, and I don't know his kids, not even after all these years. Do you think Mrs. Alexander might know who my brother was dating?"

"Maybe. It's worth asking her. I'm so sorry you have to deal with this," she said, meaning it. What a mess to step into.

"I appreciate that. My poor brother. I know Sebastian was good to him; he made it worth staying with him all these years, but sometimes I wish Kyle had never done that study abroad program. He'd have graduated college and stayed in town, and he'd still be with us."

"I'm sorry. I have sisters; I'd be a wreck if something happened to one of them. I wish I could do something to help somehow, Sara." She started down the steps. "I'll be here for a little while. If you need anything just come ring the doorbell, I'll hear it."

When she was back in the driveway, Sara called out to her. "Savanna, wait. I have Sebastian's phone number, in case of emergency, but I don't have his wife's phone number. Would you mind giving me Mrs. Alexander's number? I hate to bother her with all she's going through. But Kyle's funeral is this weekend. She might want to know, plus maybe she can help me with contacting his girlfriend. She should have the chance to come, if she wants to."

"I can do that. I don't have Winnie's number, but my mom does. Let me call her. Will you be here for a bit?"

"I'm spending the night and then flying back home in the morning. I'll be here."

Savanna let herself in with the code and then entered the studio upstairs with the key, calling her mom on the way.

"Savanna! Are you stopping by? I'm not home but I will be soon," Charlotte said.

"No, I'm finishing up the job for Sebastian's artwork. Britt called, they're coming to transport everything tomorrow, assuming Jordan allows it." A thought occurred to her. "I'm calling to ask you for Winnie's phone number, if you don't mind."

"Of course. Just a sec, let me put you on speaker." In a moment, she read the digits and repeated them for her.

"Got it, thank you! Jordan mentioned we might need permission from Winnie to move Sebastian's collection, I'm going to give her a call." She'd share the number with Kyle's sister too; Winnie wouldn't mind.

"We have plans tomorrow," her mother said. "I'm taking a few casserole dinners and some flowers down to her brother's house; she shouldn't have to think about cooking right now. She's struggling."

"Poor Winnie."

In the studio, Savanna carefully went through the delicate process of attaching her copies of the provenances to the backs of each of the paintings, similar to a COA or certificate of authenticity. The difference between hers and a COA was the history—the process of validating a painting's travels, both from place to place but also each time the painting changed owners.

She completed the nine new works, and six of the eight older pieces. The final two paintings that she had provenances for, ready to be attached, were gone.

Had she left them in a different part of the studio? Sydney was here with her Monday, chatting about her wedding veil, their fitting appointment, how hard it'd been to find the cake topper she and Finn really loved for the red velvet wedding cake they'd chosen, whether or not Fonzie and Daisy would behave for their role in the ceremony, and probably a lot more that Savanna had unintentionally tuned out. She'd been distracted. There were plenty of other times when she'd be multitasking, or her focus was off, and she'd put things away and then completely forget where she'd put them. Was this one of those times? Her stomach flipped over as the beginnings of panic set in. She couldn't have somehow lost two of Sebastian Alexander's original works of art. She truly couldn't have. It wasn't possible. The studio was only so big, with almost no closed storage. She circled the room twice just to make sure she wasn't missing them sitting in plain sight or tucked behind another painting. They were smaller than his current works; it was possible.

They weren't here. Based on the provenances, the two that were missing were *Mercy* and *Betrayal*. They were gone, and she was sure they'd been here on Monday.

When Kyle instructed her to keep the studio locked at all times, handing her the single gold key, she hadn't thought to ask who else had one. He did, Sebastian did, maybe Winnie. She doubted Griffin and Chelsea had a key; there'd be no reason they would.

Would lack of a key have stopped someone who really wanted to get their hands on a painting? The lock hadn't been tampered with. But two of the people who had a key to the studio were now gone—one dead, one missing. Which left their keys up for grabs, hypothetically, though Sebastian's had likely gone with him on the yacht.

Savanna took the two provenances for the missing pieces, locked the studio, and went back outside to the guesthouse. Sara met her at the door.

"I have the phone number for you," she said. "I'll jot it down, if you have a pen and paper." She hoped the woman wouldn't just put it in her phone, as Savanna had when her mom gave it to her. She wanted a closer look at the keys hanging on the hooks in the entryway.

"Sure, come on in," Sara said, holding open the door. She went around the corner into the kitchen, leaving Savanna in the entryway.

Carefully, quietly, Savanna plucked Kyle's key ring from the hook. "Sara," she called, "I'm so thirsty. Could I get a glass of water?"

"Of course! Now where does he keep his glasses?"

Savanna heard cupboards opening and closing. She held up the gold key on Kyle's key ring and pressed her studio key against it. "With ice, if you don't mind." Sara would think she was a pain in the neck, but that was all right.

"No problem," Sara answered.

The studio keys matched. No one had stolen Kyle's.

She drank the entire glass of ice water and jotted two phone numbers on the slip of paper Sara handed her. "I hope

Sebastian's wife is able to help. This is her number, and this is mine. If I can help at all with anything as you're working on getting things tied up here, let me know; I'm always around."

It wasn't exactly the truth. She planned to come back here one more time, tomorrow, to help Britt, and that was all. But she hoped to hear from Sara. She was dying to know who Kyle was dating. She expected Winnie to tell Sara one of two things. Either that she didn't know his girlfriend's name, or else the same name Sara already had, which she suspected was a pseudonym Kyle had made up to hide the fact that he was dating Chelsea.

Chapter Twenty-Five

"**W**ANT TO COME to an art show with me?"

"Not really," Detective Jordan replied. "Is that why you stopped by?"

She stepped into his office, rather than try to explain from the doorway. "Can I close this?"

He nodded. "Please. Sit."

She did. "Griffin Alexander's art opening debuted last night at J. Sinclair Gallery in Grand Pier. It runs through the weekend. I have reason to believe he may have been in Sebastian's home studio and taken two of his original pieces from 2005. I'm not sure if he'd try to pass them off as his own or sell them, but I want to go check out his show and see what there is to see."

Jordan sat back in his chair, mild surprise in his expression. "Really. What makes you think Griffin stole his father's paintings?" When she'd explained, he admitted it was worth the drive to take a look. "Tonight?"

"If you're free."

Jordan drove them in his unmarked car. Grand Pier was an hour away, which meant they'd arrive shortly before the gallery closed for the night. On the way, she filled him in on the fact that Kyle Bishop's sister had discovered a newly purchased engagement ring while looking for a funeral suit for him but hadn't found a way to contact the girlfriend yet.

"Don't you think it's weird that he died, but whoever he was dating hasn't shown up, asking where he is? Has anyone been calling or texting his phone?" she asked.

"I'd have to check. It's in evidence. Our forensic IT guys went through it but didn't find anything unusual; most of the activity was work related, within the Alexander family. I'll have them pull records from the past week if they're not already monitoring for that."

"Well, if the girlfriend isn't an outsider and already knows what happened, it'd explain why no one's shown up. And why his sister is having trouble contacting his girlfriend. It supports my theory about Chelsea."

"About Chelsea and the Bouvier? We'll have an answer back by tomorrow on the warrant. It shouldn't take this long, but it's an unusual request. The judge had no knowledge of dog noseprints being unique. I didn't either."

"Me neither. Sydney told me. But no, that's not what I meant. I'm not talking about the dog now. What if Kyle was dating Chelsea? What if the two of them wanted Sebastian gone so she could get her inheritance? Do you even know how much he's worth?"

He nodded. "I do. That's an interesting thought. So then, what happened? Chelsea shoved him off the catwalk so she wouldn't have to share?"

"Maybe she was only using him. He had constant close contact and access to her dad. Plus, I don't think Chelsea has the stomach to actually hurt or kill her father. She needed

Kyle for that."

"It's a stretch."

She sighed. "Maybe. But combined with her having Ringo and the dog being there the day Kyle died…maybe it's not a big stretch?"

"I'll be able to move on the Ringo angle tomorrow, I hope. We'll know more after that. Let's focus on the art show," Jordan said. "I've gathered there's some bad blood between Griffin and his father, is that correct? Griffin trying to follow in Sebastian's footsteps, Sebastian trying to steer Griffin away from the art world, right?"

"Basically. I had a chance to chat with Sebastian's friend Maeve Davis, who was in the Paris art scene when he was back in 2005. She filled me in on what really happened that made him retreat into anonymity and quit painting. Just before his work exploded on the art scene, he'd lost nearly everything. He was drinking too much. He was never home with his family. He'd spent every cent he and his wife had trying to get his work noticed and seen by the right people. His house went into foreclosure and his wife left him—and left the kids with him.

"And then he hit big; his work was discovered with help from Maeve's agent. He was in high demand. Interviews, appearances, sponsorship deals, everything he'd been toiling to make happen suddenly did all at once. He met Winnie around that time. He opened his namesake gallery, and the money flowed. But a year after it opened, he learned the gallerist was stealing from him, falsifying sales receipts, selling forgeries, and using Sebastian's work for his own gain.

Maeve says it was too much for him. The sudden fame, the betrayal, all of it, when all he really wanted to do was paint. So, he ran away. He came back home, here, and hasn't released a single piece to the public since 2005."

Jordan took his eyes off the road to look at her, eyebrows raised. "That's some story. Be careful what you wish for, huh?"

"Pretty much," she agreed. "He seems to be trying to shield Griffin from having to go through what he went through."

"What kind of artist is Griffin? Did the father's talent get passed down to the son?" Jordan asked.

Oof. That was a tough question to answer without sounding mean. Savanna tapped her phone, pulling up Griffin Alexander's website. She scrolled through several images, turning the phone toward the detective for a few of them. "Griffin's style is very different than his dad's. He's more...pop-culture oriented, like Andy Warhol, while Sebastian's work is inspired by van Gogh and other postimpressionists." She hated to say it, but she needed to prep Jordan for what they'd see. "Griffin's work lacks imagination and confidence. His paintings are in the same vein as Warhol, but he possesses none of that talent or his father's." She checked the detective's expression, but he'd barely reacted.

"He's not good." He looked at her. "That's what you're trying to avoid saying? So, Sebastian was shielding him to save his son's ego."

Leave it to Detective Jordan to cut through the crap and get to the point. "Yes. Exactly."

J. Sinclair Gallery was situated among the boardwalk shops on the south end of Grand Pier. The venue was elegantly lit with mini chandeliers hung from high ceilings over pale ash hardwood flooring through a glass storefront. With an hour until closing time, Savanna expected a thinning crowd, but she was instantly let down on Griffin's behalf when she and Jordan entered. The gallery was empty except for two patrons chatting in front of a large colorful canvas depiction of multiple cats in trees.

She headed to the left, meaning to make a loop and try to discover what, if anything, Griffin had done with Sebastian's *Betrayal* and *Mercy*. Detective Jordan kept pace with her, not speaking. There was no theme, other than bright, vivid colors. In the paintings with people, the figures were cartoonish. One wall held four pieces with muted colors and fewer elements and brushstrokes. She wondered if these were Griffin's earlier works, or if they were the result of him trying to grow beyond the initial pieces they'd already seen.

Halfway through their tour of the gallery was a freestanding half wall that bore Sebastian's two missing paintings. Beneath each one was a card bearing the title of the work and the narrative. EARLY ORIGINAL WORK, C. 2005, BY THE LATE SEBASTIAN ALEXANDER, FATHER OF GRIFFIN ALEXANDER. PRICE UPON REQUEST.

Griffin rushed over to them; they'd been spotted. "Savanna. How great to see you here. Thank you for coming. And you are?" He held out a hand to Jordan.

She realized at that moment that Griffin had only had contact with Jordan's partner, Detective George Taylor, who'd been dealing with the Alexander family while Jordan had handled the Shepherd family.

"Detective Nick Jordan." He ignored Griffin's outstretched hand. "Tell me about the decision to remove these from your father's studio."

Savanna was silent, lips pressed together. Griffin was lucky Detective Jordan was so chill. A different law enforcement officer might've slapped handcuffs on him. Griffin looked like he might throw up. His face had gone pale.

"I thought it'd help promote his Lansing exhibit next week. You know, get the word out. I wasn't going to sell them."

Jordan raised a single eyebrow at him, not speaking.

"I figured if I got any offers, I could, um, pass the buyer's info on to my stepmom or whatever." He lowered his volume, leaning toward them. "And you know art gets hotter if an artist is dead. My dad would appreciate the ingenuity if he was around—I'm happy to let him know what I did if he's found. I was trying to help."

Nick Jordan sighed loudly. "Those doors—is that a supply room?"

Griffin turned to look. "Yes—"

"Go. Now. We need to talk."

Griffin gave her a wide-eyed, terrified glance and did as he was told, following the detective through the set of double doors at the back of the gallery, Savanna close behind. The three of them were in a small, dimly lit storage area.

Jordan looked like he'd reached his capacity for aggravation and then had an extra helping piled on. "Do you know something I don't?"

"I don't think so. What—"

"Have you received word that your father is dead?"

"No." His face flushed red. He looked down at his shoes.

"Eyes up. Look at me." He waited until Griffin did so. "Let me tell you how this is going down. When we go back out there, you'll get rid of the customers. I don't care what you tell them. Savanna will then remove your father's two paintings and place them in my car out front. I will escort you to my car and you will get in the back seat."

"This is just a misunderstanding—"

Jordan's scowl deepened. "Tell me I don't need to handcuff you to walk you out of your art show."

"You don't." Griffin's voice shook. "I'll go."

"Griffin Alexander, I'm placing you under arrest. Anything you say—"

"No!" Griffin's eyes filled with tears. "I said I'll go, okay? I'm sorry."

Jordan nodded. "So am I. I still have to read you your rights."

Savanna hadn't expected to feel sorry for Sebastian's son, but she did. He looked scared and younger than his years. Jordan finished issuing the Miranda warning and allowed Griffin to go splash some cold water on his face at a utility sink and compose himself before following him through the doors back into the gallery.

The patrons left easily when told the gallery had to close up a little early. Savanna got the two paintings settled in the trunk of the unmarked cruiser, everything going as Jordan said it would.

On the way back to Carson, she turned around to look through the partition at Griffin in the back seat. She had to ask. "How did you get into the studio?"

"Dad kept an extra key in his top dresser drawer."

"When did you come take the paintings? Yesterday?"

"You don't have to answer anything you don't want to yet," Jordan told him, looking in the rearview mirror.

"Thanks. Yeah, yesterday morning before my show. I wouldn't have kept the money." Even as he said it, his words lacked conviction. "I might've kept enough to cover the cost of my show, but then I'd have split the rest with Chelsea and our stepmom. Or just put it back in the studio for him in case he does still get rescued."

Chapter Twenty-Six

T HURSDAY AFTERNOON, SAVANNA led Britt Nash and the two museum handlers they'd brought through the stately foyer and up the curving stairway of the Alexander home.

"Stunning," Britt said. "Is there none of his own work on display?"

"There isn't. Sebastian said once that the creative process brings him joy, but he finds too many supposed flaws in the final product," she said.

"I'd read that about him—that he's a perfectionist."

"Yes. An artist is his own toughest critic—that holds true for Sebastian."

Britt paused at the catwalk, looking down. "I can see how it might be possible for a person to go over the railing. It seems low, no? It wouldn't take much," they mused. "I expect it'll be the first thing your artist remedies when he's back home."

She agreed. She'd noticed the way Britt referred to Sebastian as if he was simply out for a stroll and would arrive home any moment; Savanna appreciated that. Last night, Griffin had said *if* his dad was found, rather than when. She'd caught herself a few times as well, thinking of Sebastian in the past tense, as if he'd passed. What a loss, and a loss to the art world with his reemergence already in the works. She didn't want to think in those terms...not yet. Hopefully not ever.

The coast guard disagreed. Admiral Moore had informed Winnie this morning that the search and rescue efforts had ended—Savanna had heard through her mom.

Britt watched as Savanna found the correct key on her key ring to unlock the studio. "So, the police must have been fine with the signed contract we faxed them?" they asked. "We wouldn't be here otherwise."

"I talked to the detective running the investigation," Savanna said. "He said it's perfect. It's all they needed to see to let us clear out the studio. I can't believe I didn't think of it, Britt. I've been out of the game too long."

They laughed. "You were only out of the game for two years, and then right back in it with me since June. Your help this summer was invaluable. Besides, I wouldn't have expected you to think of the contract Sebastian signed with our curator when we set the exhibit plans in motion. It took me a minute too. But the verbiage is clear. We're legally able to transfer to the museum the bulk of his current and past work on-site here."

"Perfect," she said.

Now inside the studio, she walked Britt through the pieces, making sure they saw the certificates attached to the backs. Everything was exhibit-ready, including the two pieces Griffin had stolen. She'd kept that little fiasco to herself; Britt didn't need to know about mission she and Jordan had gone on last night. She had no idea whether Griffin would be charged and prosecuted. If Jordan decided against charging him, assuming his family wasn't interested in pursuing anything, he'd obviously be relieved, but she couldn't wrap her head around how a grown man older than she was had such an air of entitlement.

Her dad had set her straight the only time she could remember throwing a tantrum over not getting what she was positive she deserved. Eighteen and upset over losing out on a scholarship she'd put all her effort into winning, she'd groused to her parents how unfair it was. It'd taken her two weeks to write her essay, she'd jumped through all the required hoops, met all the criteria, but hadn't been chosen.

"Life's not always fair," her dad had said. "None of us are owed a thing, even if it's something we think we're entitled to. The trick is appreciating what we already have."

"But I have no scholarship. How am I supposed to be thankful for nothing?" she'd argued, mad at her father for giving unrealistic advice.

"You have the ability to work and earn money for school. You have two parents who are able and willing to help you. You're blessed with a sharp mind and the drive to succeed. How is that nothing, Savanna?"

He was right. Griffin seemed to be laboring under the idea that he was owed success—that it should be handed to him by his father or the art world or the universe. She wasn't sure what needed to happen to help him overcome that idea. He seemed like a nice guy. Hopefully, he'd figure things out.

"What a beautiful setting to create in," Britt remarked,

perching on the edge of Sebastian's desk. "He's got just the right light, tons of space, plenty of quiet. And he's only gotten better since Paris; look at that one."

Savanna followed their gaze to *Untethered*, the largest of Sebastian's new pieces. Sea and sky sliced the painting horizontally, the water and air blending into dark pockets and shadows in some places and expanding into bursts of vivid color in others, reflections of a jut of land in the background. Painted with a heavy hand and thick, choppy brushstrokes, the seascape demanded attention, drawing focus from the other pieces in the room. "It's so...striking," she said.

"Emotional. Fluid. Sadness and elation at once, I think," Britt said.

"That's it." She shuddered.

She'd thought while examining it and even more so now, with another set of eyes seeing what she saw, how surreal the imagery was given Sebastian's current situation.

"He titled it well," Britt added. "Each of his pieces has only a one-word title, going all the way back to before he found fame. Kind of cool."

She nodded. "Pretty cool." She leaned over and bumped shoulders with them.

She forgot sometimes how long they'd been friends, since meeting years ago at Kenilworth. Britt Nash had become a well-known name in the last few years among artsy types. Savanna loved seeing it.

She supervised, standing sentry at the door to Sebastian's studio, while the two handlers made several trips to carefully carry each wrapped and secured painting outside to the museum transport van. Britt hovered, directing them and ensuring everything was firmly unmovable for the drive. When all the pieces were cleared out, Savanna locked the studio door and went to ask Britt if she could do anything else to prepare for tomorrow's visit from the Pemberly rep.

Britt flashed a grin at her. "We've got it in hand. Don't worry. The hard part's nearly over. Now we just need the artist to turn up."

She promised to let them know the moment she heard anything.

SHE STOPPED BY the sheriff's department on her way through town.

The desk sergeant shook her head. "Detective Jordan's out in the field, Ms. Shepherd. Do you have his number?"

"I do. I'll try him again, thank you." She was sending a text to Jordan while walking back to her car when she heard her name.

Finn raised a hand in greeting from outside Fancy Tails.

He met her halfway, jogging across to her side of Main Street. "Hey there, I'm glad I caught you. I'm waiting on Syd. She's finishing up her last dog. Is tomorrow night still happening? I want to make sure I have the time right."

Savanna threw a glance toward Fancy Tails & Treats. "She's in the back right now? Come over here, just in case." Finn followed her, stopping when they were partially concealed behind the large maple tree in the center of the town offices. "We're definitely still planning on tomorrow. I'll come pick her up at five. Does that work?"

He nodded. "Sounds good. I'll be at her place to make sure she's ready without knowing it." His quick grin appeared. He shook his head, scrubbing a hand through his hair—so similar to Aidan's mannerisms. "Y'know, I just have to say, I figured cold feet would kick in for me by now, two days out. But I don't think they're gonna. Before Syd, I was positive I'd never get married. God, no. Never wanted to. But now…"

She smiled. "Sydney's pretty one of a kind."

"This'll sound sappy as hell, but I can see us. Like, five, ten, thirty years from now. I see it. She's my future. Craziness, huh?"

"The good kind of crazy. She was the same as you before. I guess you two were just waiting for each other."

"I like that," he said.

"You're going to be a good brother-in-law, Finn, I can already tell."

"Brother-in-law twice over," he said.

"Now that's crazy!" Her phone dinged; it was a return text from Nick Jordan. "I've gotta go."

"See you tomorrow," Finn said.

When she was almost to her car, she turned back, calling across the street to him. "Finn. Use that. What you said about Syd, about your future. Put it in your vows or something. She should hear it."

He gave her a nod and his trademark salute. "Yes,

ma'am. Great idea."

Savanna answered Jordan's call the same way he answered hers. "Savanna Shepherd."

He was silent on the other end. "Uh…"

"Hi, Detective." She smiled to herself. "Just trying it out."

"Funny." His voice said he did not find it funny. "I promised I'd keep you in the loop. We got the warrant—took long enough. We're heading over to Chelsea Alexander's for Ringo's noseprint in a bit."

Chapter Twenty-Seven

"CAN I GO with you?" She knew the answer but still had to ask.

"No, you can't go with us."

"Chelsea and I are sort of friends. It might make it less awkward."

"Why would I be concerned about it being awkward?"

"You wouldn't," she said. Awkward was his middle name. He seemed very comfortable with that. "It was worth a try."

"You and Sydney are the reason we're collecting a nose-print from a dog; I'm just updating you as a courtesy."

"What about Chelsea? What if she was involved with Kyle and that engagement ring was meant for her? Did your team find any fingerprints on the catwalk railing?"

Jordan was quiet for a beat. "You know I can't discuss details of an active investigation, Savanna. Trust that we're looking into every angle. And keep in mind, the entire family was frequently in and out of Sebastian's house. Even if we had pulled prints off the handrail, saying definitively that they belong to the person who pushed Kyle over the edge is tougher than you'd imagine."

"Oh. That makes sense. I do trust you and the process,

by the way. Good luck at Chelsea's. Ringo's a big baby, just so you know. He looks scary but he's sweet."

On her way home, Savanna stopped at her parents' house to drop off the little care package she'd put together for her dad. He wasn't back to work yet, not technically. He was coordinating projects and visiting job sites, checking in on his subcontractors involved in the actual building processes, but he'd promised her mom he wasn't lifting a finger himself. Aidan hadn't cleared him yet to get back on his motorcycle, not with a broken arm or the random episodes of dizziness and headaches still happening. That meant a lot of downtime. Her father didn't sit well. She'd packed a big plastic toolbox with a few of his favorite snacks, three fancy new fishing lures to replace the ones he was always losing, and a home putting practice game she'd found online for him. He always enjoyed fishing, and even though his cast prevented actual golf, he could still fill time by improving his short game.

Daisy met her in the driveway, all fluffy blond fur and wagging tail. "Hey, pup! What're you doing out here? Where's—"

The screen door into the kitchen slapped against the frame as her mother came out, a large box stacked high with casserole dishes in her arms. Savanna rushed over and took two off the top before they fell. "Thank you! I have a few more inside too," Charlotte said.

"What're you doing?"

"I'm taking these down to Lake Haven for Winnie and her brother. I made enough for them for about a week.

Daniel doesn't cook, and she shouldn't have to think about where meals are coming from right now."

"Wow. That's so nice," she said. She hurried ahead and opened the back of her mother's SUV and Daisy leaped inside. "You aren't invited, Daisy, I'm sorry." She shooed her out and helped get the dishes arranged strategically so nothing would spill on the way.

Harlan met them halfway up the walk to the house with the remaining three pans. "Will you let Winnie know the steaks are from me? I used that marinade Sebastian told us about last summer. Hey there," he greeted Savanna.

She took the pans from him, leaving her mom's hands empty. Charlotte stepped into Harlan's open arms for a hug. "I'll tell her. I bet he'll be home safe before they get to that one. You're sure you won't come with me?"

He shook his head. "I want to finish the tune-up on the fishing boat motor. Still time left in the season."

Charlotte stood on tiptoe, placing her palm on his un-shaven cheek. She kissed him. "Sounds like a good idea. I'll only be gone a couple hours. And just so you know, the neighbors will tell me if you try to take your bike out."

He didn't crack a smile. "I wouldn't dare. Don't worry."

"I have to grab my purse," her mother said, jogging back into the house.

Savanna stood quietly near the tailgate of the SUV, observing her parents. Six ample casseroles were loaded and secured into the vehicle. Her dad stood still, watching after her mother, who'd just gone back inside. He was not himself.

Savanna grabbed the forgotten toolbox with the blue bow that she'd set in the drive to help her mom. "Dad," she said, capturing his attention. "I brought you a present."

The half-hearted smile he graced her with didn't reach his eyes. Even flipping open the top and rifling through the items didn't elicit near as much of a response as she expected. "Thank you, honey."

She hadn't seen this much beard growth on him since...ever. She'd thought the sadness she'd picked up from him last Sunday might have gotten better by now, but it seemed worse. Not that she didn't get it. He was, at least in part, blaming himself, against all logic. Nothing that had happened was in his control. But maybe this would take more than just time to improve. "Dad, are you okay? I mean, you're probably not really, right? What can I do?" She squeezed his arm.

What an odd feeling, asking this tough, self-sufficient man how she could help him feel better.

"I don't want you worrying about me, Savanna. I'm all right." She must not have looked convinced, because he tipped his head closer to hers. "I promise. Things'll get better."

She nodded, and was about to ask if she could hang out and help with the motor—not that she'd actually be helpful—when a work truck turned into the driveway. She recognized Mike, a subcontractor, as he lifted a hand in a wave to her.

Her dad pulled her into a brief hug before going over to meet the worker. "I never thought that sail would end with me coming home but not Sebastian. It's hard losing a friend; I'm hoping I haven't." He let go, nodding to himself. "But we have a world of blessings to be thankful for, don't we?"

"Savanna, would you mind moving your car?" Charlotte called.

"I'll come with you," Savanna said on impulse.

When she'd moved her car and Charlotte steered them toward Lake Haven, Savanna voiced her concern. "Is there anything we can do to help Dad through this? He just seems kind of lost."

Her mother nodded. "He is."

"Should he see someone? Maybe go back to his doctor, or talk to someone?"

"Yes. Absolutely." Charlotte glanced at her. "He knows we're worried about him and that just makes him feel worse...but he's not okay. Of course we're worried. He's starting therapy on Monday."

Savanna's eyebrows rose. "Really? I think that's great."

"I think so too. I don't know if he'll stick with it, but he needs to." She sighed. "I just really hope something happens, some piece of information or news or, God willing, Sebastian himself being found, so he'll stop blaming himself."

"I hope so too. I'm glad he'll be talking to someone." She shouldn't have doubted that her mother would be on top of things.

"It was his idea. Your father never ceases to surprise me. And, hopefully, Sydney and Finn's wedding will cheer him up a bit in the meantime."

"I hope so!" Savanna agreed.

Tomorrow after work, she, Skylar, their mom, and Ellie were kidnapping Sydney for a few hours to celebrate her impending nuptials the next day. Ellie had helped her come up with an itinerary Syd would never expect.

The remainder of the drive passed quickly with the two of them chatting about plans and the wedding itself. The route to Lake Haven was south on US Highway 31, a Blue Star Highway that ran along Lake Michigan from Holland down to South Haven. It wasn't quite dark out yet. At dusk, the commuter traffic had thinned, but now daredevil deer were the biggest threat to drivers this time of night, especially as their route became more rural. Daniel's dirt road was a bumpy two-lane ride for the last half mile to his house. The rustic cabin sat in the center of dense stands of thick pine trees; each residence looked to have an acre or more each.

Winnie threw open the front door, embracing them each one at a time around the casserole dishes in their arms. "Come in, come in! Oh my goodness, what did you do? This is enough to feed an army!" She ushered them through a large living room done in dark tones and leather furniture, Savanna's head turning at the sight of the stone hearth. Over the fireplace were the mounted heads of a multipoint buck, a coyote, and a large black bear. It made sense, given where the man lived; it was probably easy to hunt in this area.

Winnie caught her looking. "Daniel's an avid hunter. Our father taught him. Those are from around here, except the poor bear—he took that one way up north a few years ago." She motioned them into the kitchen. "Set those down, they must be heavy. You must've been cooking for days!"

"You could freeze these three," Charlotte pointed out, "and these will keep fine over the next several days. Have you eaten yet? Because the tuna casserole is straight out of the oven if you'd like that one for dinner tonight. It's still almost hot."

"I haven't even thought about dinner," Winnie murmured.

She wore a beige lounge set with fuzzy house slippers. Her face was bare of makeup, hair pulled back into a ponytail, but her outfit matched, and everything was on right side out, unlike a week or so ago right after the yacht had gone missing. Charlotte helped her set a table for four.

They dug in, Winnie insisting they not wait for her brother. "Daniel's out checking his traps, but he loves tuna casserole. He'll just be glad we don't have to figure out dinner. This is so sweet of you both."

"It's all Mom," Savanna said. "I can't take any credit. How are you doing with everything, Winnie? It must help, being away from the house?"

"It does help, but that's my home. I miss it. I miss him— I'm planning on going back home next week. I needed to get away, but now I just want to be in the place where Bas was. I should be at the house in case he comes home. I can't really believe he's gone."

Charlotte reached over and took Winnie's hand, giving it a squeeze. "He's tough. I don't blame you for not wanting to give up hope. We don't know what a person is capable of, truly. Did Admiral Moore have any thoughts on how to proceed when you talked to him this morning?"

"Not really. It's all so hopeless. I'm not dumb." She sat back, gaze going from Charlotte to Savanna. "The water is too cold for him to survive for long. So now what? They want me to just move on, like it's over? Without any answers or resolution?"

"I don't know," Charlotte said softly. "I don't think you have to decide anything right away."

"Admiral Moore said I could request a presumptive death hearing, if I want to."

"What is that?" Savanna asked.

"It'd be a way to get closure. He mentioned it when I asked what I'm supposed to do now—the state typically won't declare someone...deceased...until after they've been missing for seven years. Unless there are circumstances that'd make it very unlikely the person survived."

"And...in Sebastian's case...the admiral thought it might be an option for you, given the circumstances? Oh goodness, Winnie. I'm so sorry." Charlotte got up and hugged her.

Winnie sniffled. "I guess so. It's not a certainty, just asking for the hearing doesn't mean they'd do it. It can end up being a good thing, so estates don't get tied up in limbo for years. I don't want to think about it." She shuddered. "I'm so glad you're here. Thank you both," she said, gaze moving to Savanna.

"Of course," Savanna said.

She couldn't get a good read on Winnie. Her emotions were all over the place. But that was probably normal, given the situation.

"Have either of you heard anything about Griffin's art

opening? Chelsea says she and a coworker got there last night a little before closing, but the gallery was locked up and Griffin was gone. I haven't been able to reach him all day."

Griffin hadn't told his family yet what had happened.

Charlotte spoke up. "I haven't heard anything. That's odd, but I'm sure he'll call you back."

"I'm not," Winnie said. "I'm not sure of anything! I must've tried getting ahold him ten times today. He always answers the phone when I call. What if something happened to him too?"

Her words pained Savanna. One more loss was the last thing the woman needed to worry about right now. She couldn't let Winnie think something had happened to him. "Griffin was fine last night when I went to the gallery. The crowd thinned out a lot in the last hour before closing and he said something about leaving early to get dinner," she lied.

Winnie would eventually learn what Griffin had been up to. There was no reason to bring that on sooner.

"Oh, thank God. I can't handle one more thing," Winnie said. "Let's move out on the deck. I'll open a bottle of wine."

She knew it was rude, but her phone had been buzzing from inside her purse by the front door for several minutes. "I have to grab my phone," Savanna said. "I'll be right there. Just a half a glass for me, please."

She fished her phone from her purse, turning her back on the three mounted game heads watching her from over the mantel. She paused by the entry table to see who she'd missed. Nick Jordan had called, and Aidan had texted. She swiped on the text from Aidan.

"Stepping into a triple bypass. Hope all went well with Britt. I'll call you later." A small heart emoji followed his words.

She texted back. *"I'm with Mom visiting Winnie in Lake Haven. Hope surgery goes well."* She added her own heart emoji to match his.

On the deck, behind her mom and Winnie, the sky was a brilliant pink through tall pine trees. Savanna dialed into her voicemail for the message from Detective Jordan:

"Savanna, Jordan here. You'll learn of this anyway, I'm sure, so I'm letting you know. That evidence collection ended up being a no-go tonight. Will have to get a revised warrant and take care of it tomorrow. The dog isn't with Sebastian's daughter. Chelsea said her mother never dropped him off. The dog's with Winnie Alexander."

As she hung up, the sound of heavy footsteps carried through to her from the front porch. The door opened and Ringo came bounding through it, mussed black curls flopping over his eyes and long pink tongue hanging out as his greeting nearly knocked her down. Savanna raised her gaze to Daniel in the doorway. With a shotgun slung over one shoulder and the red-and-black-plaid button-down shirt he wore he conjured an image of every oversize film lumberjack she'd ever seen. Her mouth went dry, and she struggled for words.

He tipped his head, puzzled.

"I'm—uh—Winnie's friend—well, my mom—she is—" She gestured toward the deck, his gaze following.

"Charlotte," he said, nodding. "We've met. I'm Daniel." He stuck out an enormous hand and she shook it, hers disappearing within his. "You are Charlotte's daughter?"

The sliding door out onto the deck opened at Ringo's pawing, whining insistence.

Winnie poked her head in. "Daniel, that's Savanna. She and her mom brought us so much food. You should make a plate and come join us."

The big man moved to the kitchen, doing as his sister suggested. Savanna quickly tapped her phone screen. She had to let Jordan know the dog was here.

"Savanna," her mother called from the deck. "You have to see the sunset."

"I'll be right there!" She smiled at Winnie and snatched up her purse, digging around furiously. "I'm just looking for...my...glasses. They must be in the car. I'll only be a minute."

She took her purse and shot out the door and down the porch steps, firing off a quick text to Jordan on the way. *"The dog is at Winnie's brother's place. She's had him the whole time."*

He'd get it. He'd know exactly what that meant. Ringo had been in no one else's care except for Winnie's since before Kyle landed on the marble foyer floor. Savanna became aware of her mom and Charlotte on the deck to her far right, overlooking the property. She flung open the car door and ducked down, pretending to search—though why she'd need her reading glasses to sip wine and watch the sunset, she couldn't fathom. It was a quick lie but not a good one. She checked her phone. A series of dots from Detective Jordan appeared in the text box and then went away. She reread her text. She'd completely left out the most important part.

"Mom and I are at Daniel's cabin with them in Lake Haven."

Three bubbles appeared and disappeared again. Then, *"Don't jump to conclusions. Technically nothing has changed. If you're concerned, make an excuse and leave."*

He was infuriating. She momentarily wondered if there was anything at all resembling a weapon in the car. And on the heels of that came the realization that Jordan was right. Nothing had changed. Not technically. But—if Chelsea hadn't had Ringo, if she hadn't been involved with Kyle, what if Winnie was? Could Winnie have convinced Kyle to kill Sebastian under the guise of eliminating him so they could be together? It was clear Kyle had fallen hard; he'd been about to propose. She'd thought Chelsea had used him as a pawn, but too many things now pointed at Winnie. And with Kyle's age falling in the middle between Winnie and Chelsea, neither pairing seemed unrealistic as a couple.

She headed back up the steps and inside, not given a choice as Winnie was motioning her over. Winnie's words during dinner replayed in Savanna's mind. First, she'd said she couldn't bear to think of her husband as really gone, then she'd mentioned wanting a presumptive death hearing. If Harlan was still missing—if Aidan had gone missing that way and was still gone—there'd be no way Savanna would be pushing an agenda to have them declared dead. Not even to gain closure. Winnie's husband had been off the radar one week longer than Harlan. If it was her own husband, she'd be ramping up search efforts, even if it meant funding it herself somehow, not pursuing a declaration of death. And the Alexander family certainly had the means for an extensive, privately paid search effort. Why was no one even considering that? Griffin was broke, and Chelsea didn't necessarily have a pipeline to the family money, but Winnie presumably could have kept the search efforts going.

Joining the trio of her mom, Winnie, and Daniel on the deck, Savanna plunked her purse down and sat, ignoring her phone buzzing now and then. Jordan was probably elaborating on why she shouldn't panic. Ringo came over and placed his head in her lap, making her smile. If the situation turned abruptly dangerous, would this sweet dog spring into action to protect his owner? He seemed nothing but docile every time she'd seen him.

"He really likes you," Winnie said.

"He's a sweetheart." Her phone rang, long buzzes impossible to ignore. She improvised. "I'm sorry, this is my colleague from the museum. I'd better take it. Hi, Britt, what's up?" she answered, casually stepping back inside the kitchen.

"Got it," Jordan's voice came through, so quiet she could hardly hear him. "Can you get somewhere to talk?"

"Yes, the certificates are with each painting," she said, sliding the door closed behind her. "I'm alone. Why on earth are you calling?"

"I take it you haven't seen your text messages. The judge granted the revision to the warrant almost immediately. We're going to head there now to get the dog's nose and paw prints. I need you and your mother out of there."

Her heart raced. "So, you believe me now?"

"It's not about what I believe. It was enough for the

judge to issue the revision without delay. But we have to do this by the book. Think about this," Jordan said, speaking quickly. "Kyle's strolling across the catwalk. Someone, anyone, pushes him to his death. The thing is, if it's an outsider, for instance, a landscaping company worker, how do you know their dog wasn't with them that day? How do you know Ringo wasn't already at the house; maybe Winnie left him there overnight when she left for her brother's house and came back for him the next day. There are a lot of variables. See?"

Her mind raced. "If there was an outsider," she whispered, "like the landscaper, you'd have found fingerprints on the railing."

"Maybe. Maybe not. Bottom line is I need you out of there, just in case you end up being right about everything."

"Oh boy," she breathed. This was one time she really hoped she was completely off base.

"Savanna. You have time. We're lights on sirens off. The county sheriff's post at South Haven has four deputies on standby for us within a mile of the address. The deputies have been brought up to speed on the dog and the possibility of Winnie being a person of interest in Bishop's murder. This will be over soon. If you can't get out of there without being obvious, then just sit tight. I'm not going to let anything happen to you or your mother."

"Okay." An idea occurred to her, a way to extract her mother and have it look as organic as possible.

She hung up with Jordan and sent a quick text to her dad. *"Dad, Mom and I need some help. Can you text her right now and say Daisy ran away and you can't find her? Say you need her to come home. Text, don't call. Please. I'll explain later."*

"Everything all right, Savanna?" Winnie spoke from behind her, and she gasped, spinning around. Sebastian's wife stood uncomfortably close, worry written in her features.

"I didn't even hear you, Winnie. You startled me," she said, a nervous laugh escaping her. Where had she come from? More importantly, how much had she heard? Or seen? She slipped her phone into her pocket.

"The deck wraps around the house. You seem like something's wrong."

"No, everything is fine. Britt just had a couple questions about Sebastian's newer pieces."

"Hmmm. Well." She held the door open and followed Savanna through.

Chapter Twenty-Eight

"YOU REALLY HAVE a gorgeous view," Savanna said, smiling at Winnie and Daniel as she took her seat beside Charlotte.

"Dessert," Charlotte said. "I nearly forgot. I brought all the fixings for strawberry shortcake."

Savanna began to follow her in, seeing a chance for escape. "I'll help, Mom." Why hadn't she gotten the text yet from her dad?

"No, sit," Winnie ordered, her tone stern, eyebrows drawn together. "Your mother and I will do it. You just relax."

"Oh—Thank you." Her mom hadn't gotten a text out here on the deck yet, because her mom's phone must be somewhere in the house, in her purse. "Mom! Wait."

Charlotte turned back.

"When you go in, can you get your purse? I need some of your hand lotion."

"Sure," she said, giving Savanna an odd look.

Left alone with Winnie's brother, she racked her brain for bits of conversation she might use. "Winnie says you're a great hunter and trapper. What do you see the most of around here?"

"Coyotes and deer," he said.

"Interesting. No wolves this far south, right? Are they only in the UP?"

"Yep."

She carried the bulk of the conversation volley for what seemed like forever before her mom and Winnie returned with four servings of strawberry shortcake. Charlotte hung her purse on the back of her chair and handed Savanna the lotion.

"Mom—is that your phone?"

Her mother pulled out her phone. "No! Oh no." She gripped Savanna's arm. "Daisy got out and ran off. Your father just texted. Winnie, Daniel, I'm so sorry, but we have to run. Our puppy is gone. Oh my, I hope she's okay." Savanna was on her feet, purse in hand, ready.

They made it to the front door. Flashing blue and red lights filled the living room. Several things happened all at once.

Winnie turned on Savanna and Charlotte. "What did you do? What is this?"

Ringo leaped onto the back of the couch, loudly barking at the window.

Daniel shouted at the dog, then at Winnie, ignoring Savanna and her mom.

Winnie sprinted toward the closed door between the living room and kitchen, jerking it open—basement stairs descended into darkness.

Daniel shoved Charlotte away from the front door, stopping her before she could touch the doorknob. "Not a chance," he growled.

The sight of her mother's terrified face gripped Savanna's heart. Savanna's upper arm pinched as Daniel's large hand closed around it, squeezing and jerking her toward the kitchen. She snatched up a heavy glass paperweight in the shape of a large egg, curling her fingers around it.

A crash came from below. She spun around, trying to follow the noise, and caught sight of more red and blue lights now through the trees and out to the dirt road. *Oh, hurry up, hurry up, hurry up* ran through her head.

Daniel shoved her mother into the basement stairwell, dragging Savanna after him. Savanna tried to grab on to the railing to no avail. She fumbled for her phone, getting it out of her pocket. Her shoulder banged against the wall and the phone slipped from her fingers, hitting the stairs and tumbling down.

Winnie shouted from somewhere below and Daniel let go of Savanna's arm, his heavy footsteps pounding down the steps. Where was her mom? Savanna couldn't see a thing.

Her mother's voice cut through the air. "He's got a gun! Get out, Savanna. Run!"

A dark shape rushed around the L-shaped corner of the steps straight up toward her and her heart stopped—and then started again as light from behind her illuminated Ringo running up the stairs, barking and tail wagging. Without conscious thought she sidestepped him, letting him run out. She slammed the door after him, now frozen on the stairs without a plan. In the dim light, she could only make out shapes of storage racks and bulky boxes.

Heartbeat thrumming loudly in her throat, Savanna started slowly down the steps once more. "Winnie," she called, "we don't have to do this. Nothing bad has to happen." She set foot on the dirt floor of the Michigan basement, similar to a cellar. "Please don't hurt my mom. You've been frien—"

The wind was abruptly knocked out of her, the whole room flipping upside down as someone hit her like a freight train, grabbing her around the waist and throwing her over his shoulder. Daniel was far too strong. She screamed and kicked, fingers of one hand grappling for purchase, searching for anything to grab on to. The cool, heavy glass of the paperweight in her right hand registered as she realized she still held it. She renewed her efforts, twisting her body around and trying to change her angle so she'd reach him.

From the corner of her eye, she spotted Charlotte darting toward her. Daniel must have as well—his grip on her loosened just enough. Savanna hauled her arm back and swung, willing the heavy glass to meet its mark. It did, with a sickening thud against the side of his head. He dropped her and grabbed his head, roaring.

The basement was bathed in bright light, a high-powered, blinding flashlight at the top of the stairs held by whichever law enforcement officer had gotten here first. "Freeze!"

Savanna put her hands in the air, noting the big man who'd picked her up, who'd been behind her a second ago, was gone. Deputies rushed down the basement stairs, passing her and fanning out. A deafening shot rang out, followed by two more. Savanna dropped instinctively into a crouch behind the stairs, covering her head.

"Officer down!" A shout from the far side of the basement. Oh God, someone was hit. What if it was bad? She'd never forgive herself.

"Calling it in now." Another voice spoke, this one from the top of the stairs.

"She's gone," a deputy shouted, and Savanna's vision narrowed, the basement becoming an endless tunnel, the deputies small the other end.

Who's gone? she tried to ask. *She's not gone, she's okay, she's fine* repeated in her mind. Her head was spinny. She'd felt this before.

"Outside access, through there—she took the other stairway."

A police officer in navy blue barreled down the wood steps carrying a large red case. His badge read LAKE HAVEN PD. She was immediately thankful that Jordan had added local law enforcement to the sheriff's department's team.

Savanna sat down. The dirt floor was cool and dusty. She stared at the hair tie that was perpetually on her wrist. She snapped it, hard. And snapped it again and then again, sharp pain making her gasp and jolting her smack into the chaos around her. She scrambled to stand, an officer helping her and sweeping an arm out, guiding her behind him.

Light swung across the basement walls, shadowy figures scuffling, a grunt as someone landed on the ground. The clear, ratcheting sound of handcuffs snapping closed. Detective Jordan emerged from the low light with the big man who had to be Daniel in front of him, thrusting him forward toward the stairs.

Someone's radio crackled. "Got her."

Chapter Twenty-Nine

"THEY GOT WINNIE?" Savanna asked.

The radio emitted static again, then, "Need a medic. Suspect is injured, requesting assist at the bulkhead doors."

Jordan directed an officer at the top of the basement stairs. "Nelson, head outside. Grab a paramedic. The external cellar door is at the southeast corner." Turning back toward her, he nodded once at the deputy standing guard over her. "She needs to be checked out, too, along with Charlotte Shepherd."

An officer helped a disheveled Charlotte toward the stairway where Savanna stood. Her mom's blouse was torn at the shoulder, one sleeve hanging halfway down her arm. Dirt smudged her face and neck, and her hair was a tangled mess. She was perfect. She was alive and whole.

Savanna clung to her, hugging her tightly. "Are you okay?"

Her mom nodded, hanging on to her, not speaking.

"Charlotte! Savanna!" Harlan's voice boomed through the house. "Where are they?" He filled the doorway and was quickly down the steps, encircling them both in his arms.

Her mom burst into tears, sobs racking her slight frame.

They stayed that way, the three of them, until the deputy gently ordered them outside, where Finn and a fireman met them halfway across the lawn. Savanna recognized the fireman as Jake, another of Sydney's exes. The county was littered with them, apparently. Just Finn and Jake, hanging out on the job. A giggle burst quietly from her, and she stifled it.

"All right, sister," Finn said, sitting her down on the back of the ambulance ledge and wrapping a blood pressure cuff around her arm. "No passing out on us. Do you feel light-headed?"

"No."

"Were you hurt?"

"No. I'm fine. Really. Thank you." She glanced at her mom beside her. Jake shined a small flashlight into her mother's eyes and then set about cleaning and bandaging a large abrasion on her arm.

Winnie was wheeled by them, her left leg immobilized in a splint and left wrist handcuffed to the railing on the mobile gurney.

"Wait. Why?" Charlotte asked her. "Winnie, why would you do this?"

The officer pushing her halted, giving them a moment.

Winnie's expression reflected none of what Savanna expected—no remorse or apologetic tears.

She looked mad. "Don't you dare judge me. I waited so long. *So* long. Then, when he's finally ready to get back out there with his art, he decides to divorce me! How do you think that feels? What if Harlan did that to you?" she asked

Charlotte.

"You could've killed my dad," Savanna said. She was floored by Winnie's indignation. "You killed Kyle after you used him up. You killed your husband. He's never coming home."

"They told me. Half of what he had is mine. I deserve it," she spat.

Savanna shook her head, overwhelmed by the sadness of it all. Winnie hadn't come to terms yet with reality. A great artist was dead. Kyle Bishop was dead. His sister, Sara, would attend her brother's memorial Saturday after learning who the engagement ring was really for. "Did you know Kyle was going to propose? It was you, right? You pushed him. He would've done anything for you—and he did. For what? Some money you'll never see?"

Winnie glared back at her. "Don't feel sorry for him. Kyle was happy as long as I was happy." She stuck a hand out, gripping Charlotte's forearm until Finn pried her fingers away. "Charlotte, you have no idea. I wasted my life on him," she said. "Waiting for him to be the man I fell in love with. I'm taking half the estate. I earned it."

"That's enough. Let's go," the deputy said.

"Who's shot?" Savanna asked as he passed her. "Are they okay?"

"Deputy Miller, my partner," the young deputy told her. "We think it grazed his leg; it doesn't look deep. Hope that's the case, anyway."

IN THE DRIVEWAY, Detective Jordan assigned a deputy to drive Charlotte's SUV back to Carson, putting the family trio into Harlan's truck with him behind the wheel.

"Jordan, I'm so sorry," Savanna said.

He put a hand on the window frame. "We'll talk tomorrow. I'm going to need you both to come make a statement but not tonight. Get home. I'm glad you're all right, both of you," he said.

On the short drive home, Savanna's purse vibrated, her phone lit up with an incoming call.

She shook her head. "I can't. I don't want to talk to anyone. What time is it, like, past midnight?"

Harlan nodded at the dashboard clock. "It's 9:45."

She sighed. She dug around in her purse, fishing out her phone. Britt Nash was calling.

They rarely called her just to chat; she had to answer. "Hey, Britt. What's going on?"

"I'm sorry to bother you; you weren't in bed yet, were you? And to think I almost used video call," he said.

She laughed but it didn't sound like laughter to her ears. This had been the longest night ever. Again. "No, I wasn't in bed."

"Good. Something very odd just happened. I'm letting you know first, but we'll need to notify the police too. Those Sebastian Alexander pieces we transported earlier today? We finally got them all secured and checked in…"

"That's great."

"Sure. When the check-in process is complete for an incoming collection for exhibits, the museum's automated system triggers an e-document that's emailed to involved parties. The artist, the gallerist, the collector. You get the idea."

"Yes. Kenilworth had a similar system. We'd countersign once the artist or collector signed, and then file the e-doc."

"Right," Britt said. "Same procedure. Savanna, we just received the signed e-document back from Sebastian Alexander."

Chapter Thirty

AIDAN WAS WAITING for Savanna on her deck when her dad dropped her off. Fonzie launched himself at her as she climbed the steps; she hugged him through his wiggles, smiling but exhausted. Aidan raised a hand in a wave to Harlan and Charlotte as they pulled out of the driveway, and then wrapped her in his arms, burying his face in her neck. When he eventually loosened his hold, he cradled her face in his hands, searching her eyes. "Are you all right?"

"I am. I promise."

"I had no idea anything was going on. I'm so sorry. By the time I got out of surgery, I had a bunch of messages from Finn." Aidan scrubbed a hand through his hair, scowling. "He'd tried to get ahold of me to go with them on the run, to get to you. I hate that I was completely unaware until it was all over. It sounds awful. I should've been there for you."

She sank onto the bench seat, pulling him with her. "Don't be ridiculous. Seriously, Aidan. I understand it's not always possible for you to drop everything anytime I need you." She held his hand in her two, turning his over and studying it. "Your time often means the difference between life and death for people. I know you love me—I know how important I am to you. I do. But when you can't always be there for me, it's really okay. You have to stop saying sorry so much. Seriously."

He wrapped an arm around her shoulders, settling her against his side. "I appreciate your perspective. It's a little foreign to me, you know that. I'll work on it." He kissed the top of her head through her hair.

They'd discussed this in the past too. Aidan had dealt with a lot of guilt in his marriage to Mollie's mother, constantly feeling like he'd let her down when he had to miss things, especially once she got sick. Savanna suspected the push and pull of his career and their relationship might always be a point that required some extra compassion and grace, for both of them.

She changed the subject, filling him in on the revelation that Sebastian might be alive. "I'm not sure whether to say anything to my dad yet. I almost did as soon as I hung up with Britt, but what if it's not really him? What if someone else signed for Sebastian, making it look like he's alive?"

Aidan frowned. "Like who?"

"Anyone who had access to his email and a good motive for wanting everyone to think he's alive and well, I guess. I can't tell my dad... He's been so worried, but I can't give him false hope."

"You're right. It makes sense to wait, at least until you know for sure."

She tipped her head back, looking at the night sky. "Can you believe in two days your brother will marry my sister?"

"I wouldn't have believed it a year or two ago. Now, I can't imagine either of them with anyone else."

She nodded. "He really loves her. Like, a lot. I'm so happy for them."

"Savanna. How would you feel about New Year's Eve for our wedding? We'll have plenty of lead time, and it might be perfect for celebrating our anniversaries in a big way each year. What do you think?"

It was the word *anniversaries* that got to her. Anniversaries, plural, as if it was already a given that they'd be together years and years from now, old and gray and celebrating their New Year's Eve anniversary each year. "I think I love that. December 31," she said, a little choked up. "But there would have to be snow. A lot of snow."

"I'm sure that can be arranged. December 31. It's official. The *Farmer's Almanac* is calling for early snow, so we'll be all set there. Your uncle Max has some serious thoughts on poinsettia bouquets."

"You've really been thinking about this, huh?"

"A little. All the time. Every time I have to leave you. Every time I wish we were under the same roof. Each night, when I close my eyes and each morning when I wake up, and every minute in between."

Her cheeks flushed with warmth. She nuzzled his neck, wrapping her arms around his waist. "You say the most amazing things to me. You could stay here sometime, if you want. Next time Mollie's at her grandparents'."

She felt him tense, felt the slightest retreat within him.

"I probably shouldn't." He scrubbed a hand roughly through his hair. "I have to tell you something. Ugh—I don't want to. But I need to."

He was scaring her. "What is it?"

He sighed heavily, turning to face her. "Mollie's grand-parents are taking me to court for custody. Partial custody," he corrected. "I just—I can't believe they're doing this."

She covered her mouth, staring at him. She had no words. They'd seemed like nice people.

"They're using the grandparents' rights statute. They want a legal agreement that they're able to see Mollie a specified number of days or weeks per year, keep her over-night, take her on vacations with them... I wouldn't have fought them on that. She loves them and I know they love her. But the way they're going about it is just wrong."

She felt like she was missing something. "I don't get why they'd do this now. You've never stopped them from seeing Mollie." It dawned on her. Of course. "It's me."

"They're operating from a place of fear. Nothing good ever comes from that. They're not bad people. They're just afraid. They're assuming the worst of me, of us, as if once we're married we'll just cut them off. For God's sake, I stayed in Carson after Olivia died so Mollie could keep them in her life," he said angrily.

"I know," she said. "They know that too. What can I do? How can I make this better? I could talk to them."

He shook his head. "It won't help. In the subpoena I got for mediation, they reference the sleepover the kids had. They're trying to show that we're both bad examples for Mollie, since we spent the night together with my daughter present."

"What? How—we didn't—okay, so we spent the night

together, all of us, you on the couch, me on the love seat, Mollie and Nolan in separate sleeping bags! It doesn't get much more innocent than that. Aidan, I'm so sorry."

"My attorney is telling me not to worry. I can agree to an arrangement for grandparents' rights without giving up any actual custody. He says it will work out. I mean, it better." His brow was furrowed. "I didn't expect this kind of ugliness from them."

"You really don't think it'd help if we tried to clarify that sleepover? Or maybe I can write them a letter, and say I would never try to keep Mollie from them?"

"I've clarified the sleepover. It doesn't seem to matter to them. We'll deal with this. I have to trust the lawyer; I do trust him. I'm sorry too, Savanna. I was trying to avoid telling you any of this."

"Listen, Mollie is—and should be—your first priority. Promise you'll tell me if there's something I can do. Okay?"

"I will. I promise. It'll be okay," he said, more to himself than to her. "But between now and the mediation, or I guess between now and our wedding, we can't give them a single thing to latch on to. So, no overnights yet." He kissed her temple.

"Of course." She was reeling.

She loved his daughter. She fully believed Mollie's life was better with her grandparents in it. But this…they had to resolve this, and soon. Aidan didn't need this stress and neither did she.

"Are you tired, after everything that's happened? I can go and let you get some sleep," he said.

"Not yet. Stay a little longer, unless you don't think you should." She fought the sudden urge to cry. This would all work out. It had to.

He pulled her close again. "I'm not leaving. Not yet."

Chapter Thirty-One

IN SYDNEY'S KITCHEN Friday evening, Finn perched on a stool at the counter while Savanna waited by the back door for her sister. Sydney slid into the room in stocking feet, purse over a shoulder and cute black ankle boots in one hand.

"Where are we eating? I'm starving."

Savanna shrugged. "I don't know. Maybe Giuseppe's? What do you feel like?"

"I don't care. Let Mom pick," Syd said. "You're really sure she's okay? I can't believe you guys went through all that last night. So scary. Any of you could have been shot." She stepped into Finn's open arms, hugging him.

"But we weren't. All good," he said. "Your mom's tougher than she looks."

Syd laughed. "True statement."

"For real," Savanna agreed. "Ready?"

"Yep. Ready."

"Put your shoes on," Savanna said without thinking. Her little sister activated her teacher mode sometimes.

"I'll put 'em on when I'm ready, bossy. Let's go!" Sydney kissed Finn. "Lock up when you leave, okay? I'll see you tomorrow."

Finn pulled her back into him for one more kiss. "I can't wait."

Sydney climbed into Skylar's SUV, gasping. "Ellie! I didn't know you were coming. I'm so glad!" She dove into the back seat and wrapped their cousin in a quick hug.

"Yay! Me too!"

"You guys…" Syd said. "Tomorrow at this time, I'll be married to Finnegan Gallager. I will be the wife of ultra-fine, mega-hot, cinnamon-roll-of-a-man Finn Gallager." She beamed. "Can you believe it? And, okay, so what is this because now I'm suspicious. Are we actually only going to dinner?"

Charlotte turned around from the passenger seat, reaching back to squeeze Syd's hand. "Not only, but we are going to dinner. We have a few other stops."

"You'll have to be patient and go along for the ride," Skylar said.

Syd zipped her ankle boots on. "Awesome. As long as you have me home before tomorrow, I'm in for whatever. But Mom and Savvy just had a near-death experience, so whatever we're doing better be pretty tame."

"We're fine. Don't worry," Savanna said.

In Grand Rapids, after a delicious meal that was not had at Giuseppe's, Skylar parked in front of Starlight Tattoo Studio.

"We're doing what now?" Sydney looked up at the pink and black sign, the shop sandwiched in between a cute indie bookstore and a coffee shop.

"We're getting tattoos," Savanna said. "All five of us.

We'll show you your choices inside—our appointment is at seven and it's seven sharp now."

Charlotte volunteered to go first. The studio had a chic upscale salon vibe, done in pastels and gold fixtures. A sweet middle-aged woman with arms covered in ink and hair in Princess Leia buns greeted them. She settled Charlotte in the tattoo chair while Savanna laid out three designs for Sydney to choose from. Each one was a depiction of two hearts, but in different configurations—linked, side by side, and open. Sydney touched the open heart. Two hearts, one upside down and one right side up, drawn with one continual line and each left slightly open on one side. "This one. I cannot believe you remembered," she said, looking from Savanna to Skylar.

"How could we forget?" Skylar asked. "You gave a whole speech at my bachelorette party, about how powerful sisterhood is, how we'd always be connected, and no man would ever separate us, not due to marriage or babies or moving away—" Her gaze flitted to Savanna for a moment, and she faltered.

Savanna finished for her. "You almost made us get matching tattoos with you that night, remember? But you'd had too much to drink and the artist wouldn't do it. Skylar wasn't ready at that point yet anyway. Plus, now we get to rope Ellie and Mom into your plan too."

"My plan," Sydney said, rolling her eyes. "From over a decade ago. So, we're really doing it this time? Because I don't want to get faked out again. I'd like these hearts on my ankle, please, ma'am," she told the tattoo artist. "Right after my mom gets hers."

Charlotte raised an eyebrow at Sydney. "You think I won't do it?" She held out her left hand, palm up, and tapped her wrist. "I'd like mine right here, about the size of a quarter. Oh, this will be fun; your father's going to be shocked," she said, chuckling.

Even with the five of them and just one artist, they were back in the SUV in under two hours. They'd all kept their new tattoos small, nickel-sized to quarter-sized. Ruth, the artist, was quick and good. She instructed them to apply lotion in the first few days and then commemorated the occasion with photos—a close-up of their five open heart tattoos, and one of their family tangled huddle, laughing and displaying their new artwork.

On the way to their last stop, Skylar spoke, looking in the rearview mirror at Savanna. "What did Jordan say today when you guys went in to give your statement? Were Winnie and her brother arraigned yet? Did he have any new information about Sebastian?"

"I'm not sure about Winnie and Daniel. Winnie's leg was broken, she went to the hospital first, not jail," Savanna said. "As for Sebastian, Britt called and updated Jordan last night about the e-signature coming in. He told Britt they had no leads and it's unlikely Sebastian had survived. But today, when Mom and I were there, I asked whether they can trace where he sent the email from somehow. Like, an IP address location or something? I don't know how it works, but they were already doing that." She paused, not meaning to get off track. "He said they think Sebastian is in Chicago.

When Mom and I left him this afternoon, Jordan shared with us that law enforcement was checking in with Maeve Davis, looking for any sign of Sebastian. She's his only contact there; it makes sense he might have connected with her."

"That'd be wild if he somehow made it to her place," Skylar said. "I can't imagine how it'd be possible, though."

"He did have the dinghy for several days," Savanna said. "But that washed up empty onshore. Why didn't he starve or die of dehydration? Or from whatever wound he was bleeding from, with the blood on the yacht's bow?"

"And how would he have gotten from Door County, Wisconsin, all the way south to Chicago where Maeve is, with no one knowing he's alive?" Charlotte added.

Syd spoke. "Do you really believe it was him? What if someone else e-signed for him?"

"Yeah, that's possible," Savanna said. "I really hope Maeve has him. I hope he's alive. I've wondered if he knew Winnie was plotting to kill him, so he stayed out of sight all this time." As things turned out, she thought Sebastian's son might have been correct. Griffin had theorized Sebastian had faked his own death. It'd sounded insane when he said it, but that might not be far from the truth.

Chapter Thirty-Two

SATURDAY MORNING, SAVANNA groped around her nightstand, finding the ringing phone and answering, groggy from the late night spent dancing with her mom and sisters and Ellie. "Hello?" she murmured.

Maeve Davis spoke. "Savanna? Did I wake you? I hate when I do that." She didn't sound sorry. She had to be one of those people who enjoyed getting up at an ungodly hour before the sun.

Savanna rubbed her eyes, getting her alarm clock to come into focus. She sat up straight in bed. "It's nine thirty? Oh holy cats, I can't believe I slept this late. I'm glad you woke me up."

"Good! So, about our mutual friend. I wanted you to hear it from me, before your Detective Jordan or Admiral Moore share the news and blow it all out of proportion."

Savanna held her breath, waiting.

"Sebastian and I are about an hour away from Carson now. He's been staying with me since he got out of the hospital two days ago. Say hello, my friend," Maeve said.

"Savanna, hello. How are the authentications going?"

She burst out laughing. "Sebastian. I—Just—Wow. Are you okay? Really? And *how*?"

"Cold water, a kind fisherman, and luck, I suppose. And a couple pockets full of granola bars. Maeve's driving me straight to the sheriff's station to give my statement. I imagine that'll take a while, and you'll be busy with your family's happy occasion later on, yes?"

"Yes. I'm so glad you're okay! How amazing. How did you end up at Maeve's? And…Maeve, you knew? Did you know he was alive all this time?" She padded in bare feet to the window and opened the curtains to a gorgeous, sunny day.

"Oh no," Maeve said. "No, he called me Wednesday from the hospital up in Door County. The whole story is pretty amazing. We were hoping we might get together tomorrow and catch up? Sebastian is dying—well, actually, not dying—to see your dad. He was terrified Harlan didn't make it."

"I just hung up with your dad before we called you," Sebastian added. "I'm so relieved he's fine."

"He is. He's completely recovered. But—we heard you'd been badly injured. There was blood on the bow. You're healing all right?"

"There's a lot to catch up on," he said, the understatement of the year. "Let's talk tomorrow. Your dad invited us to dinner—Maeve's staying with me for a bit, until I'm…back on my feet."

Chapter Thirty-Three

O N PARADISE BEACH, beside the daisy-covered wedding arbor, Savanna watched through teary eyes as her father walked her sister down the aisle; if rose-petal-strewn sand could be called an aisle. A few feet away, Finn Gallager stood waiting. The adoration in his gaze, watching Sydney approach, was worth a thousand handwritten wedding vows.

When they reached the altar, Sydney turned and hugged her dad. As she let go, Harlan put his head down, saying something only his youngest daughter could hear. She smiled and nodded. She stood on tiptoe to kiss her dad's cheek. His eyes glistened as he shook Finn's hand. Finn leaned in, and Savanna heard his words to their dad.

"The rest of my life will be spent making her happy, sir."

Her father's response was inaudible. He took his seat beside her mother, and she placed a tissue in his hand, squeezing his knee.

Sydney and Finn faced each other as the wedding officiant directed them to. They'd written their own vows and read those to each other first. Skylar passed the note card with Syd's vows to her while Savanna held the bride's overflowing daisy and daffodil bouquet.

Finn followed with no notes; he'd either memorized exactly what he wanted to say, or his feelings for Sydney were so powerful in the moment, he had no trouble at all expressing himself.

The officiant led the ceremony after their vows were complete, speaking about lasting love, weathering changes as a cohesive pair, and the ways in which love sometimes took us by surprise with its all-encompassing power. Beyond the couple in front of Savanna, Aidan caught her eye. He held her gaze throughout the wedding sermon, the words a promise of things to come.

Before the officiant finished with the exchanging of their rings, she opened a small book for the wedding reading Syd and Finn had requested. Sydney looked out over the group of friends and family gathered in satin and tulle covered beach chairs, offering a wink as the officiant began.

"Excerpt from 'How Falling in Love is like Owning a Dog' by Taylor Mali.

'First of all, it's a big responsibility. So think long and hard before deciding on love.

'On the other hand, love gives you a sense of security: when you're walking down the street late at night and you have a leash on love ain't no one going to mess with you.

'Because crooks and muggers think love is unpredictable. Who knows what love could do in its own defense?

'On cold winter nights, love is warm. It lies between you and lives and breathes and makes funny noises. Love

wakes you up all hours of the night with its needs. It needs to be fed so it will grow and stay healthy.

'Love doesn't like being left alone for long. But come home and love is always happy to see you. It may break a few things accidentally in its passion for life, but you can never be mad at love for long.

'Is love good all the time? No! Love can be bad. Bad, love, bad!

'Love makes messes. Sometimes you want to roll up a piece of newspaper and swat love on the nose, not so much to cause pain, just to let love know don't you ever do that again!

'Sometimes love just wants to go for a nice long walk. Because love loves exercise. It runs you around the block and leaves you panting. It pulls you in several different directions at once, or winds around and around you until you're all wound up and can't move.

'Throw things away and love will bring them back, again, and again, and again.

'But most of all, love needs love, lots of it. And in return, love loves you and never stops."

With that, the officiant gave a simple nod to the couple while the wedding guests were alternately still smiling and dabbing at their eyes.

Finn turned to Aidan, who stood with two of Finn's med flight paramedic friends, each sharply dressed in their white tuxedos. Aidan pulled a small black box from his pocket and handed it to Finn.

Ellie passed a small box to Savanna, who passed it to

Skylar, who passed it to Sydney with a quick hug and a kiss on the cheek. The officiant walked the couple through exchanging their rings, finishing up with, "I now pronounce you husband and wife. Finn, you may kiss your bride!"

Finn pulled Sydney to him, wrapping her in his arms and planting a respectful wedding kiss on her as their photographer snapped photos...and then he swept her off her feet, turning in a circle while she cupped his face and kissed him for real.

Chapter Thirty-Four

S UNDAY DINNER WAS an eclectic collection of Shepherd family members and a few friends thrown in for good measure. Sydney and Finn were absent; they'd flown out that morning for their honeymoon backpacking in Alaska.

Nobody cooked. Across the entire kitchen island, Charlotte and Harlan had set up an array of food from last night's wedding dinner. Chef Joe Fratelli had prepared an abundance of pasta, potatoes, and chicken, salmon, and prime rib, three types of salads, and an enormous tray of tiny cupcakes, cheesecakes, and cookies that Nolan and Mollie were obsessed with, all of which made it back to the Shepherd household in varying amounts, the leftovers neatly packaged and ready to serve.

With Travis missing as well, out of town in Florida on another quick work trip, the dining room table was no more crowded than it normally was. Sebastian and Maeve arrived with a bottle of wine from a local Chicago winery. Savanna had taken the liberty of inviting Nick Jordan. Since the plan was to catch up on the last two weeks, she figured it'd help all parties involved if Jordan was part of the conversation.

Savanna tried to maintain polite dinner etiquette; she should give everyone a chance to enjoy their food before she peppered Sebastian with questions. But when he and Harlan dove into a debate over what type of spinnaker Sebastian should add to the *Serendipity* before their next sail, she couldn't take it anymore.

"I'm sorry but if no one is going to bring it up, I will." She held her fork in the air, a piece of salmon speared with a bit of asparagus. "Sebastian, the night you and my dad were attacked, what do you remember? Did you see Kyle or—"

Jordan cleared his throat. "Sebastian's already provided a detailed statement. He may not wish to go through it all again, and that's fine. Savanna, I know you've been instrumental in us gaining insights and answers in this case, I'm happy to bring you up to speed on everything tomorrow."

"You're right. Of course," she said. "I didn't mean to be insensitive. You and my dad went through a horrible ordeal; we don't have to dissect the details," she told Sebastian.

Harlan spoke. "You were on the bow, messing with the jib. That's the last thing I remember. I was hit and went down—I lost sight of you."

Sebastian put his fork down, dabbing at his mouth and red beard with his napkin. "I'm finding that the more I talk about it, the fewer nightmares I have. I don't mind," he said to Jordan. To Harlan and Savanna, he said, "I saw Kyle. I wish I hadn't. We'd been friends for twenty-some years...at least, I thought of us as friends until last year. I can't explain how he looked me in the eye and stabbed me. I might never be able to make sense of that."

"So that was the blood on the—" Savanna started, but Charlotte interrupted her.

"That sounds incredibly traumatic," her mom said. "Seeing a supposed friend come at you, prepared to do their worst. I'm sure your mind couldn't make sense of it in the moment."

Sebastian pointed at her. "That's exactly it. You're right. I think if it had been anyone else, I'd have reacted quickly enough to stop it from happening. Kyle rushed me, and before I could even fully stand, he'd knocked me on my back. We fought. I saw the knife, tried to get it from him. When I couldn't, I twisted away, got to my feet, tried running toward the stern. I hadn't seen you go down," he told Harlan.

"The sail was whipping around," Harlan said. "I wondered about that."

Sebastian shook his head. "No. And I had a good couple strides away from him, but he caught me by the ankle, pulled me back, and plunged that knife in right here." He winced at the memory, one hand hovering over his left thigh. "The surgeon at Door County Medical Center said if the knife had gone even a quarter inch deeper, my femoral artery would've been cut, and I'd have bled out right then and there. As it is, he sliced the ligament. He stabbed me a second time but good, right in the gut. I'll need the cane for a while, maybe always. And there's a lot of physical therapy in my future."

Savanna'd clapped a hand over her mouth, listening to him recount the attack. Now, careful to muster the tact she'd lacked earlier, she said, "I think it's amazing you've done so well, Sebastian." She waited, as she did with her students when one of them was trying to tell her something but struggling to get all the details out.

"Thank you. I wasn't kidding when I said I'm only still here because of cold water and luck—and a kind fisherman. I heard Kyle take off in some kind of runabout. Detective Jordan said you're the one who made the connection there, Kyle renting the speedboat from Gus at Sweetwater and coming after us. He must have tied on and come aboard, and then easily gotten back to Carson Marina before daylight. Anyway. I had to have passed out where he left me, at the front of the bow near the dinghy. When I came to, the jib sail had freed itself and the yacht was heeling something fierce. I tried to get to the cockpit, needed to get to you," he told Harlan. "I must've lost consciousness again. I don't know. When I woke up it was daylight. I don't know where we were. I didn't see you; I yelled and yelled for you. I thought—" He stopped abruptly and covered his eyes with one hand.

Beside him, Maeve put a hand on his back, leaving it there but saying nothing.

After a minute, the room silent, Aidan spoke. "What you went through might take a while to deal with, Sebastian. Sometimes people need to sort the pieces of an ordeal little by little, with help from a professional. It'd be very normal to need some time and space to process everything."

Sebastian nodded, dropping his hand. "Yeah. I can see that. I tried—I guess that's the point. I didn't want to leave you," he told Harlan. "I thought you were dead or in the water. The only thing I could reach, since I couldn't get up, couldn't stand, were the lines holding the dinghy. I rolled into her and loosed the ropes. She landed in the water with me, but I lost her at first, and then didn't have the strength to get back in. But being in the cold water for a while, hanging on to her, before I could climb inside and lie down, probably slowed my bleeding and saved my life. That's what the doc said, anyway. After that, I don't remember much but the sun and the night. I guess I was dying toward the end there, when the fishing boat found me. I'll have to track down the man who pulled me from the dinghy and got me to the hospital. Michigan Coast Guard and our good detective here would have been alerted right away if I'd had the luck to be rescued closer to the Michigan coast instead of Wisconsin. The admiral said the EMA was only issued to Michigan hospitals. They never expected I'd end up in Door County, Wisconsin. And I wasn't kidding," he said to Savanna. "My windbreaker pockets were full of granola bars, they always are. I think that kept me alive just long enough."

Maeve spoke for the first time. "He called me from the hospital a couple days ago and I drove up and got him. He made me promise not to tell a soul, after what Kyle had done. Love isn't always something one can just turn off, like water from a tap. The feelings you still held for your wife clouded your vision, Sebastian, and that's understandable. You were a loyal, loving partner to her for twenty years. You were afraid Winnie and Kyle had done this together, right?" she asked Sebastian.

"I was sure they had. They'd been carrying on with each other for a while. I found out a year ago. Winnie wasn't as discreet as she probably thought. I just...I wasn't ready to end things. It took me a while to figure out what I wanted to do about it. I can see now that I likely escalated the whole thing by serving her with divorce papers."

"From what she said at her brother's house, she'd hoped to gain what she thought was her share if you'd died," Charlotte said. "I don't know if this makes it worse or better to hear, but Winnie used Kyle, Sebastian. She didn't love him."

"But he'd gone way over the deep end for her," Savanna said. "Clearly. His sister found the engagement ring he planned to propose with."

"We've gleaned that Winnie took Kyle out of the equation," Jordan said, "to avoid having to share the wealth she thought she was coming into. Last night, as part of a plea offer, she confessed to pushing him off the catwalk. She denied premeditation. She says they were arguing, and it happened in the heat of the moment. That's a ploy to try for a reduced charge, according to the prosecutor. Ringo's noseprints matched with the prints on the patio, so that's now been entered into evidence, supporting the events surrounding Kyle's death. Even if her plea results in a reduced sentence, with her being an accessory in the attack on both of you on the yacht plus killing Kyle, she'll be behind bars for a very long time. Her younger brother, Daniel, really didn't get involved until that night, but he did brandish a gun, and he fired on law enforcement. He'll have his own hefty charges to deal with once he's arraigned."

"My kids are struggling with what's happened," Sebastian said. "Griffin and his stepmom were close. He truly looked up to her as if she was his mother. This has been devastating for him to learn about. Chelsea has never been as close with her, but it's still tough to deal with. The one silver lining in all this is that it seems to have brought Chelsea and her brother closer together, especially since I checked in with them a couple days ago."

"What's going to happen to Griffin?" Savanna asked. Maybe it was none of her business, but she didn't care. She was torn between hoping he'd have a consequence for his theft and prematurely declaring his father dead and hoping he and his father could find a way to reconcile.

"He's moving in with me," Sebastian said.

Savanna's eyes widened. That was the opposite of what she considered necessary for him to learn how to support himself and find his own path. She pressed her lips closed; not her family, not her son. She had no space to weigh in.

"He'll be paying me rent, handling the maintenance and grounds, and working full-time at the coffee shop because he apparently really loves his work," Sebastian said, unable to suppress a small eye roll. "I've agreed to tutor him. He's got something—not the technique or interests that I have in terms of Postimpressionism. He's more modern contemporary, anyone can see that. But he's been trying so hard to emulate me and rebel against me at the same time, he's dug himself into a deep hole of failure. We're going to give this a try. Maybe it'll help him find his own style."

Maeve smiled at him. "Not an easy decision, but I think it's a good one, for both of you."

As they said their goodbyes after a large portion of the

dessert platter had been devoured, Savanna hugged Skylar and Nolan and kissed Hannah's chubby little cheek. She helped Skylar get the kids buckled in and waved as she pulled out of the driveway, realizing her sister had probably purposely avoided sharing her and Travis's news with the family. As Skylar had said, it wasn't like they were moving right away. But she needed to find the courage to let the rest of the family in on what was happening; the secret was getting heavier by the day for Savanna.

Chapter Thirty-Five

THE SUN DIPPED low in the pink sky Sunday evening as Savanna and Aidan motored out of Carson Marina, leaving the sails down until they were out of the channel. Once they reached the open blue water of Lake Michigan, she cut the motor while Aidan hoisted their Catalina's mainsail and unfurled the jib. The sailboat's instantaneous push forward with the wind was as smooth and gratifying as always, the only sound the faint rustle where the lines met the corner of the jib sail.

Aidan joined her on the bench, the steering locked for the moment. "Good enough, boss?" He tipped his head back, looking up the mast at the white sail above them.

"Like a pro," she said, smiling. "Is it still as scary? As thrilling as when we first started?"

He slid his hand into hers, lacing their fingers together. "Of course. But isn't it supposed to be? Thrilling," he added.

She looked down at their hands. "I think so. If we're lucky, I think it'll always be."

"I'm positive it will."

She met his eyes, the intensity in Aidan's gaze overwhelming and exhilarating and everything she'd ever wanted. She was grateful for every big and little thing that had happened in her life so far to gift her this moment, in this place, with him.

The End

Acknowledgments

When I was eight, around Mollie's age, my dad became a sailor. He bought a used red sixteen-foot sailboat and named it *Tomato Sloop*. After building his captain skills and confidence, he slowly traded up until his final sailboat, a thirty-something-foot yacht named *Snowbird*. When he was sailing or racing in regattas on one of the Great Lakes, usually Lake Erie, he was home.

One day, when we were still sailing on little *Tomato Sloop*, we encountered a storm while out on the water. The sky suddenly went dark, wind kicking up and tossing us into growing waves while we were pelted with small hailstones mixed into the rain. My mom's words, *Don't worry, we're having an adventure*, almost convinced me and my sister that all would be okay. But in a flash of lightning and clap of thunder, the sidestay keeping the tall mast upright snapped, the metal cable smacking against the rigging. The boat listed to one side from the weight of the partially untethered mast. The mainsail flapped and cracked in the wind, heavy lines and metal grommets whipping about. My sister and I scrambled to the high side of the cockpit and watched water pour over the railing into the boat. The top of the mast kissed the choppy, churning water. One of us screamed.

Somehow, my dad got control of the mainsail, tightening

it and the boom and pulling the keeling boat back from the tipping point just long enough to sail aground onto a peninsula, bringing us to safety.

My mom's assurance was one I heard frequently as a kid. "Don't worry, we're having an adventure" was a pretty effective way to tamp down any anxiety or fear in unpredictable situations. It usually worked. But that day on the boat, amid the chaos making eight-year-old me imagine I might die of drowning in a shipwreck, it was my dad's calm that kept me from completely losing it. I'm sure he was scared. But he ordered us to the high side, checked our life jackets were tight and our white-knuckled fists grasped the deck railing and got us to safety. As a kid, I remember thinking the boat didn't capsize because he refused to let it. I didn't know the mast was still somewhat secured by the forestay and shrouds on the opposite side. My mother's sunny point of view gave me the option to see a catastrophe as a quest. My dad's quiet strength gave me the courage to embark on the journey.

I enjoyed writing this story so much, in part, because my dad is in it. The character of Harlan Shepherd was largely inspired by my late father. Harlan is strong without being tough. He's comfortable with silence. He'd do anything for his wife and daughters. Writing the sailing scenes was like slipping on an old, well-loved coat.

I still feel so lucky that I get to do this: to tell the stories in my head and connect with readers who might enjoy them. I'm thankful for my superhero literary agent, Frances Black of Literary Counsel, whose belief in me is phenomenal. I'm thankful to have found a wonderful home for the Shepherd Sisters Mysteries in Tule Publishing. Meeting multibestselling author and Tule founder, Jane Porter, last summer was a high point of my writing career. Her warm, inviting charm and intelligence make her a joy to talk with, her work ethic and creativity truly impressive. I am fortunate to have the amazing Tule team in my corner. Editor Kelly Hunter's sharp eye and notes are priceless; she's made these stories stronger and I'm so grateful. Likewise, editors Monti Shaloskey and Beth Atwood's astute observations and suggestions were spot on and much appreciated. Enormous thanks to Meghan Farrell and Julie Sturgeon for taking on and championing the series, and to Cyndi Parent, Lee Hyat, Mia Gleason, and Jaiden Colling for pulling so many details together to make sure these books do well and find their audience.

Taylor Mali's beautiful poem, "How Falling in Love is like Owning a Dog," became a true gift to the Sydney and Finn storyline. I feel so lucky to have discovered Mr. Mali's works (check out the rest of his work on his website, especially another favorite of mine, a stunning poem called "What Teachers Make"). I'm even luckier that, when I sent him a letter in the mail requesting permission to use his "How Falling in Love is like Owning a Dog" poem, he graciously gave me his blessing. Nothing would have made that scene quite so perfect as Mr. Mali's poem. I'm forever grateful!

Even though I'm creative with words, I am the worst artist imaginable. There isn't a shred of artistic ability in these hands, but it doesn't matter, since I'm fortunate to have a few excellent artists in my bookish corner. Thank you to ultra-talented author and artist Kalie Holford for graphics and book trailers, artist and magician Lau Blanco for graphics and reels, and brilliant London artist Charlotte Lonsdale of CL Designs Studio Art for creating the perfect map of Carson, MI.

When it comes to getting the word out about a newly published book, there is no greater force than the book lovers of Instagram (affectionately referred to as Bookstagram). I love and appreciate you all so much! I'd be lost without Kristyn Fortner of Delightfully Booked, an amazing book and author champion who makes this process rewarding and fun.

I owe my dad and mom, David and Joni, a world of thanks for raising a reader who became a writer. My husband, Joe, has a unique understanding of my need to write. He holds me accountable. Even when I doubt myself, he never doubts me. He's still my crush, my person, after all these years. I'm so grateful for my three amazing kids who constantly teach me more about the world and about myself.

I am blessed with devoted, lovely friends who make life and writing life easier and more enjoyable: my longtime friends Ann Sullivan and Rocsana Oana, my sister Julie Velentzas, a community of nurse friends who keep me sane during long workdays. Likewise, I'd be lost without my community of writing friends, including Holly Danvers, Victoria Gilbert, Lisa Peers, Darci Hannah, Jody Holford, Annie Catherine, Kalie Holford, Katherine Cowley, and

Janice Lynn. Special thanks to my friend and concert wife Ann for allowing me use of her beloved mom Dorothy Harden's delicious recipe for crepes Ensenada.

Much love and gratitude to you, wonderful reader. I hope you find something of yourself in the sisters and their world. Enjoy!

Harlan's Favorite Crepes Ensenada

Crepes:

12 flour tortillas

12 slices cheddar jack cheese

12 slices of ham

1 can green chilis

Sauce:

¼ cup butter

½ cup flour

1 quart milk

1 teaspoon prepared mustard

¾ lb cheddar cheese, grated

½ teaspoon salt

Preheat oven to 400 degrees F. Grease the bottom of a 13 x 9 inch casserole pan.

In the pan, assemble the crepes:
In the center of a tortilla, place one green chili (or green chilis cut into strips), followed by one slice of cheddar jack cheese on top, and then one slice of ham atop the cheese. Tuck each end in, then roll into a rough rectangle. Place in bottom of baking pan and repeat for remaining tortillas.

Prepare the sauce:

In a saucepan over low-medium heat, melt butter. Blend in flour, then add the milk. Gradually add remaining ingredients, stirring almost constantly. Continue heating and stirring until sauce has thickened.

Pour sauce over assembled tortillas in pan.

Bake at 400 degrees for 45 minutes or until bubbly.

Remove, cool five minutes, and enjoy.

*Crepes Ensenada Recipe courtesy of Dorothy Harden and Ann Sullivan

If you enjoyed *A Brush with Murder*,
check out the other books in the

The Shepherd Sisters Mysteries series

Book 1: *Death by Deception*

Book 2: *Murder on Display*

Book 3: *Still Life and Death*

Book 4: *A Brush with Murder*

Available now at your favorite online retailer!

About the Author

Tracy Gardner is an Edgar Award nominated author of two cozy mystery series, one recent novel earning a spot on New York Public Library's Best 100 Books list. Tracy also writes book club fiction with heart and grit under pen name Jess Sinclair. A Detroit native with one foot in the sand of Florida's Gulf Coast, Tracy is a mother of three, the daughter of two teachers, and works as a nurse when not writing. She lives with her husband and a menagerie of spoiled rescue dogs and cats who inspire every fictional pet she writes.

Thank you for reading

A Brush with Murder

If you enjoyed this book, you can find more from all our great authors at TulePublishing.com, or from your favorite online retailer.

TULE
PUBLISHING